W9-BDF-472

RAVES FOR

LOOKING FOR
MR. GOODBAR

"Bars have become the living rooms for today's counter-culture. They are places to go when it gets dark. Bars provide wine, laughter, and friends without the close emotional attachments that rule the outside world. This is the story of what happens to Theresa in the world of bars. She doesn't go there to be depraved. She doesn't always pick up men. She escapes. . . ."

—Rex Reed

"HARD, FAST, FRIGHTENING . . . *Looking for Mr. Goodbar* has gut excitement."

—*Newsweek*

More . . .

THE BOOK
EVERYONE IS READING . . .

"HAUNTING, COMPELLING . . . Theresa Dunn acts out a fantasy many women will identify with, but few will admit to."
—*Ms. Magazine*

"A BITTERSWEET CAVALCADE"
—*Cleveland Plain Dealer*

"It compels the reader by its sheer energy and force."
—*Houston Chronicle*

"It grips you with its power and chills you with its inevitability. From the first page, we have known how it will all end, but the story's relentless inevitability holds us fast . . . until that last dying scream we knew all along was coming."
—*John Barkham Reviews*

"AN EMOTIONAL HURRICANE"
—*Carol Hill, author of Let's Fall in Love*

... ABOUT A WOMAN
EVERYONE KNOWS

"PENETRATING, FRIGHTENING, AND UN-FORGETTABLE ... it would be hard to over-praise *Looking for Mr. Goodbar.* ... Perhaps today's reader has grown up and wants her emotions wrapped around a lovable but confused character, in this case, Terry Dunn, who resembles every woman you've ever known."
—Philadelphia Inquirer

"IT MAKES US CARE ... because we know there are Theresa Dunns in our lives, in our offices." *—The Wall Street Journal*

"DAZZLING ... I, for one, won't ever look at a young woman prowling a bar quite the same way again." *—Detroit Free Press*

Books by Judith Rossner

Any Minute I Can Split
Attachments
August
Emmeline
Looking for Mr. Goodbar
Nine Months in the Life of an Old Maid
To the Precipice

Published by POCKET BOOKS

Most Pocket Books are available at special quantity discounts for bulk purchases for sales promotions, premiums or fund raising. Special books or book excerpts can also be created to fit specific needs.

For details write the office of the Vice President of Special Markets, Pocket Books, 1230 Avenue of the Americas, New York, New York 10020.

LOOKING FOR MR. GOODBAR

Judith Rossner

POCKET BOOKS

New York   London   Toronto   Sydney   Tokyo   Singapore

Any resemblance between characters in this book and any persons living or dead is purely coincidental.

POCKET BOOKS, a division of Simon & Schuster
1230 Avenue of the Americas, New York, NY 10020

Copyright © 1975 by Judith Rossner

All rights reserved, including the right to reproduce
this book or portions thereof in any form whatsoever.
For information address Simon & Schuster,
1230 Avenue of the Americas, New York, NY 10020

ISBN: 0-671-73575-6

First Pocket Books printing April 1976

50 49 48 47 46 45 44 43 42 41

POCKET and colophon are registered trademarks of
Simon & Schuster.

Printed in the U.S.A.

For
Joseph Perelman

ABOUT
THE CONFESSION

Gary Cooper White was born in Jersey City, New Jersey. He moved to Georgia the year he began school, when his mother's husband, number three of five, got a job in a mill there. Some of the feeling you get from the resulting combination of accents is, inevitably, lost in the transcription from the police tapes. But I've tried to note questions, interruptions and clear changes in emotion that came through in his voice.

The police found him a particularly cooperative witness. He got somewhat violent and incoherent while being taken to New York on the plane, but he'd offered no resistance to those in Ohio who found him. At that point he was *eager* to unburden himself. Back in New York, he never denied the murder; he wanted the *circumstances* understood. He seemed to think that almost anyone in the same situation would have committed the same murder.

For me, as a matter of fact, this was the most notable quality of his confession—that Gary White, who had brutally assaulted and murdered

3

Theresa Dunn a few hours after meeting her in a Manhattan singles spot called Mr. Goodbar, had a very clear sense of himself as the victim of the woman he had murdered.

He had just come up from Florida, where he had a very young (sixteen) and pregnant wife. There was a warrant out for his arrest (armed robbery) and he couldn't work there. In South Carolina a careless driver gave him a hitch and left his jacket on the seat between them. From the pocket White extracted a wallet containing more than thirty dollars and enough identification to get him jobs in North Carolina and Virginia. Each of which he left after his first paycheck.

He was a handsome young man, from the photos that are available. Blond and square-jawed. Looking, in his faded denim jacket and jeans, like an extra in a cowboy movie. It wasn't difficult for him to get jobs or pick up girls.

He arrived in New York with the intention of staying with a buddy from his unit in Vietnam until he could find a job. But his friend was no longer at the Greenwich Village address he'd given White. He wandered around for a while and that night found himself in a place which he eventually recognized as a gay bar. It was there he met George Prince (or Prince George, as he sometimes called himself), who some days later would give the police the information they needed to find Gary in Cleveland. Gary told George how he'd come to New York for a job, counting on his war buddy for a bed until he could get work, only to find his buddy gone. George offered him a place for the night. One of the few contradictions within White's confession is that he at first claims not to have realized George was a homosexual who would want him, while at some later point he says he knew George was gay but he figured he could handle it.

The way he handled it was to have sex with George for a week or so without ever suggesting to George that all he really wanted was a place to stay while he found a job. Only when George brought another man onto the scene did Gary rebel and then he seems to have been more perturbed by the idea of the extra man as a *witness* than by the notion of a third sexual partner. Until then he had regarded what he was doing as a practical matter. He redoubled his efforts to get a job. But the holidays were already upon the city, most temporary winter jobs were filled, and he didn't score those automatic points that a drifter in the South gets for being white.

He became increasingly hostile to George, who retaliated by taunting him about his good looks, and finally, on New Year's Eve, by insisting that Gary dress in drag for a dance they were attending. In contrast to his readiness to relate much of what happened with Theresa, Gary *gagged* as he described, at the urging of the police, the wig, tiara, white satin gown and silver platform sandals George had provided for him.

As in his dealings with Theresa, Gary lacked any sense of having done something wrong or avoidable. He was bitter toward George for forcing him to have sex while admitting that no actual force was involved. He could not see any way in which he had exploited George. (His response at a later date, when he was being interviewed by a court-appointed psychiatrist who asked if he thought people would criticize the idea of taking money, food and lodging from someone you didn't like, was, "But he was just a dumb ugly queer!")

He seems to have lived always with the sense of fighting for his life with his back against the wall, a context in which otherwise insane acts seem quite reasonable. The supreme irony of his situation being provided by the fact that the police who searched his clothing after he was booked in New York found more than a hundred dollars in fives and tens tucked into the hem of his coat lining. He was startled when they asked him about the money.

He had saved it for his pregnant wife out of the pay he earned during his weeks on the road. He hadn't wanted to mail the cash or risk going into a Southern post office for a money order. So he had hidden it in his coat lining with the intention of mailing it with his friend's help when he got here.

When he arrived in New York he had six dollars in his jeans and never remembered the money in his coat until the cops found it on January 13th, not quite two weeks after the murder of Theresa Dunn.

THE
CONFESSION

. . . *It was like he was doing me a favor taking me to this place. Because it wasn't just for queers. It wasn't a bad place. I don't remember the name. There was some old movie on the TV, with no sound. George was talking to some guys he knows. I was just watching the TV. Thinking how I could get out of George's place. I figure I'll split New York altogether if I can't get work.*

She's sitting on the last stool, you know, against the wall. I wouldn't've even noticed her except she's reading a book. In a bar. Not looking at the TV. Once in a while she talks to the bartender. They laugh, talk, whatever. I'm too wasted, I don't care.

George says to me, "She's got her eye on you, sweetheart."

I say, "No shit."

George says, "You can have her if you want her."

"Oh, yeah?" I say. Just making conversation.

"She's in here plenty," he tells me. "She fucks anything in pants."

11

I tell him she don't particularly turn me on. Not that she's all that bad-looking, but . . . blondes turn me on. For a few minutes there was this other chick there talking to her, a real sharp-looking blonde. The kind you don't talk to so fast, you know she'll just cut you.

"Not like some of those beauties last night," George says. Meaning the queers at the dance. "They really turned you on, huh, Gary?"

I said to myself, Oh, shit, here we go again, he's gonna tell me he don't believe I got a pregnant wife. I had it up to here.

The bartender says something about her. I don't know. It was like he was asked to introduce us. We all started talking. The only thing she said in the bar bugged me, was, she started on my accent. "Where'd you-all get that accent?" Where the fuck did she think I got my accent? I got it from my mama and the rest of them. All week long I was getting that same crap from George's friends.

Anyhow, we're talking and after a while she pretends like she can't hear something I'm saying and she moves over next to me. Tells me she's a teacher. Boy, some of the people they got teaching kids, I'm keeping mine out of school. Especially if it's a girl. Anyhow, then she starts yawning, says she's tired. Do I feel like having a drink up at her place?

I figure what the hell, I was pretty wasted, like I said, and she didn't turn me on, but she wasn't all that bad and it's a flop for the night. I'll go home with this crazy chick, get some, you know. Get away from George.

So we go up to her place. One room plus the kitchen and bathroom. She makes a couple of drinks.

"How come you was reading in the bar?" I asked her.

"Why shouldn't I?" she says. "I like to read and I like to sit in bars." I don't say nothing. "I don't like four walls," she says. "I'd go nuts if I had to stay in my apartment."

That I can dig. "You should try jail," I tell her. "You'd really go for that."

"You been in jail?" she asks. Not scared, almost the opposite. Like it turned her on. She was a fucked-up chick. She asks what'd they get me for and I tell her petty larceny, assault, possession, robbery one, and she smiles. George used to do that, groove on my fuckin' record. It really bugged me. Where I come from no one thinks it's cute to have a record. Marilyn almost didn't marry me when she found out I had a record.

I just sat there, drinking. Looking at this broad. Thinking if I even feel like balling her. Wishing I was home. Of all the warrants that's the one . . . the one that keeps me outa Florida. That one I could've gotten out of with a good lawyer. The guys that got me into that one . . . I didn't even *know what we were doing to the last minute. I practically went along for the ride.*

"Who'd you assault?" she asks me.

"A cop," I tell her. "I was just trying to get away."

"I once hit a cop," she says. "In Washington. I was in a demonstration."

"You get busted?" I ask. I figure that's what she wants me to ask.

"We all got taken in but they didn't book all of us," she says.

"How come?"

She shrugged.

"Did you have the limp then?" I ask. I figure maybe that's why they didn't book her, she's got something, this funny walk, like a short leg or something.

"No," she says. "I have an ingrown toenail."

I don't say nothing. I'm thinking maybe George won't even go back to his place. I could go back there and get away from this crazy broad and maybe even get a night's sleep. I don't sleep since I been in Nam. Maybe two, three hours, the most. . . . I'll tell you something weird. The times I got into trouble it was never doing something I wanted to do. Always I was just sitting there and someone asks me do I wanna go along. (His voice begins to sound excited.) I swear to Christ, that's the truth, I didn't even wanna . . . (after a long pause) . . . Then she says to me, "You queer like your friend?"

14

"No, *cunt*," I say. "I'm not queer like my friend."

God is my witness, I never talked that way to a woman in my life. She just . . . anyhow, she sort of yawns. Stretches out. And she says, "I think you are. I think maybe if I feel like getting laid tonight I oughta go back downstairs and find someone straight."

Naturally that pisses me off. All I need is for this miserable cunt to go back down there and tell everyone I'm a queer. As soon as I get pissed off . . . I get a little turned on, right? So I say to her, "You're not going nowhere."

"Mmmm," she says. "Maybe you're right." She starts to get undressed. "Maybe you're right. I'm tired. I'm going to sleep." Getting undressed like I wasn't there. Then she says to me I should slam the door on my way out, so naturally the next thing you know I'm balling her, right? (A long silence.) We went a good long time, I don't know, or, fuck . . . what's the . . . yeah . . . so then we're finished and I'm feeling okay. You know, relaxed. The only thing in my head is now maybe I can get some sleep. Now I don't have to hear any more of that queer shit. And I close my eyes and . . . (His voice trembles and he has difficulty continuing. After a while another voice prods him gently. With great effort he forces himself to start talking again, although his voice cracks) And then . . . then . . . I'm half asleep and this voice says, "You can go now."

At first it didn't even hit me. The words. I didn't know what she was talking about. I'm out of it, y'know? Then she starts tapping my arm. I don't say nothing. Then she says, "Hey, don't fall asleep."

I'm beginning to think there's something wrong, but still it don't really hit me. I say something. I don't know, like, Why shouldn't I—I don't know. I figure maybe I'm taking too much space on the bed, I never think . . . (Voice trembles again.) Then she says, cool as anything, "Because you ain't sleeping here."

That really jolted me. It was like . . . like . . . all of a sudden I'm wide awake and spinning. My head. The rest of me is . . . I'm paralyzed. I'm so tired I can't move. I remember this picture went through my head of my buddy Ralph who got it in the spine in Nam, and I caught his face when they was lifting him up onto the stretcher to the copter, and his face, you know, he can't move anything, he knows, and his face . . . but he can't move. . . .

"Why?" I ask her.

"Because I don't want you to."

"Why don't you want me to?" I'm stalling. I mean I can't do it. I don't give a fuck why. My head is . . . the blood's pounding in my head.

" 'Cause I hardly know you," she says. (His laugh crosses with a sob. Then there is another long pause.)

"I just fucked you pretty good, didn't I?"

"Okay," she says. "Just okay."

That really . . . anyhow . . . I say to her, "Fuck you, I ain't going nowhere."

That blows her mind. "What're you talking about?" she screams at me. "Where the fuck do you think you are?"

She sounds scared, y'know? I remember I thought that was funny. Like, what was she scared of? I was the one getting kicked out.

"I'm right here, cunt," I say to her. "And I'm staying until I get some sleep." I don't know what the hell I said it for. I was wide awake by this time. I shoulda just . . . but the idea of this lousy broad shoving me out (voice cracks again) . . . like I was a piece of shit. Shoveling me out like a piece of shit, that's what she was doing.

Then she says, "If you're not up in one minute I call the cops." And she reaches for the phone near the bed like she's gonna really do it and I grab the phone and pull it so hard the fucking thing comes right outa the wall, I had no idea, and I threw it across the room. Then I think I went out for a minute . . . no, I mean blank . . . I don't remember . . . everything was red or something . . . and the next thing I know she's half across the room and I'm going after her and she starts screaming and I gotta cover her mouth so the neighbors don't hear. By this time all I want is out. For her to shut up so I can let her go and get the fuck outa there. I swear to you, that's the truth, all I wanted was out and she

17

*wouldn't let me out. If she would've just stopped
struggling I woulda got outa there. But she
wouldn't stop. She was trying to bite my hand
that's over her mouth. (Long silence. The other
voice asks a question.) Mmm . . . Yeah . . . that's
when I decide I better tie her up. Just tie her
and gag her good enough to get outa there before
she gets loose. I get her back to the bed so I can
do it. (Long pause. When he resumes, his voice
has gone completely dead. As though he's re-
porting something seen at a distance and not of
any particular interest.) I get her back with my
arm around her face. I get her down. I don't
know how to tie her, to tie her first or gag her
first. Gag her. I figure I can use the phone cord
to tie her hands . . . and then . . . I don't know
what happened next. . . . (The other voice says
something, and for the first time he sounds angry
at the intervention.) What difference does it
make? I killed her, I said I killed her, I don't
know, I . . . (subsiding) Yeah . . . I know, I know.
All right.*

*When I first put the pillow down over her face
it was just to shut her up. I tried one hand but
she kept biting. I put the pillow over her . . . it
was, like, her mouth. I mean, I thought in my
mind I was covering her mouth. Then, I don't
know, we was both naked. I got turned on. (Other
voice.) Yeah. That's what I mean . . . mmmm . . .
So I (voice) No. I tried but while I'm trying to . . .
get in . . . (he chokes on the words) . . . all of a*

sudden she makes a big kind of . . . I don't know, I'm not thinkin' about the pillow and she gets it off and starts screaming and I'm scared shitless because of the neighbors and before I know it I pulled the lamp off the table and smashed it down on her head. It was like I wasn't thinking. I swear to God. It was like someone else was doing it. I remember I'm looking down at her just before I bring it down and I'm looking at her face . . . she's so scared . . . but it's like I had nothing to do with it. It's like I'm a million miles away. Then, when I saw the blood . . . I saw she was out . . . I got scared more. The phone was ringing, maybe it was the doorbell, I don't know, something was ringing and it didn't stop. I got crazy. I was afraid to leave. I started, I don't know, running around the place, then I wanted to . . . (breaks) . . . make sure. . . . I knew how bad it was and I . . . I better make sure. I got out my knife and I stabbed her. (He is crying as he talks.) I stabbed her all over. I don't know why I stabbed her. I stabbed her in the . . . all over. I don't know why, I don't know if I knew she was dead. There was no life in her. I think I went to sleep.

(Here there is a lengthy silence. The other voice says something.) When I woke up . . . (He breaks off, again a silence and then the other voice.) I still don't see what difference it . . . all right, all right. (But now there is a huge effort involved in his speaking, and his voice breaks frequently.) I was freezing. When I woke up I *was freezing . . . I was . . . (voice) . . . I was in her . . . I was coming . . . I don't know how . . . (voice) . . . Yeah. I knew. I was crying . . . I was . . . I think I was trying to warm her up. It was weird 'cause it was like . . . she was my friend. Then I, it hit me what a spot I was in. I had to get out fast. I got dressed and I went downstairs. The doorman wasn't there. I walked. I had a couple of bucks George gave me but I was scared to get on a bus or anything where there was people. I figured something might show. So I walked but it was rough because my leg was killing me. I don't know, I must've strained something. I couldn't walk straight. I was limping. I still am. I don't know what she did to me. When I got to George's he let me in. There was no one else there. I told him. He gave me all the money he had in the house. He said if they tracked him down he'd tell them I was just some guy he met that day.*

I don't know how I ended up in Cleveland. I meant to go to Miami.

Theresa

THEY DIDN'T LOOK at her for almost two years and then it was too late. Besides, once they understood what had happened there was nothing but guilt in their eyes so that when she saw them looking at her she had to turn away in shame and confusion. If it hadn't been for her brother's death they might have realized sooner that she needed help. She was willing to forgive them but they couldn't forgive themselves.

When she was four her limbs had been briefly paralyzed by polio. She remembered none of it. Not the hospital, not the sisters who took care of her, not the respirator she'd needed to breathe. The illness was said to have altered her personality, and maybe that was why she couldn't remember; she'd become another person. A quiet, withdrawn little girl with kinky red hair and pale green eyes and pale, pale skin beneath her freckles. Not the same child as the little girl who'd babbled incessantly in a near-language for months before she could slow herself down enough to attempt English. And let the water run over the rim of the tub into the hallway because she wanted to "make a ocean." And showed up in the living room one night naked and covered with flour, saying, "I'm a cookie, eat me."

She began school two months late catching up quickly with the other children. She was one of the first to learn to read and preferred reading and solitary make-believe to playing with others. (Later, her first vivid memory, aside from one bright flash of being at the beach when she was little, would be of telling the priest at her first confession how she read with her father's flashlight under the covers when she was supposed to be asleep. She could see herself at confession long after she'd lost the image of herself reading.)

She grew overweight from inactivity so that her parents began urging her to go out and play with the other children (she was the only one who was urged; the others got orders) but she didn't like the games they played, although she couldn't tell this to her parents. Hide-and-seek frightened her—the part where you were It and everyone else went away. Games that demanded that you move fast were difficult too, because of her weight and because she got out of breath very easily. When that happened she got upset and then angry and had to run into the house before anyone could call her a bad sport.

Brigid, who was only a year younger than Theresa, was exactly the opposite. Restless, athletic, totally uninterested in reading any more than she had to to escape punishment by the sisters, she spent almost as much time out of the house in the winter as she did when it was warm. She got along with everyone. There wasn't a child in the neighborhood who wasn't her friend or an adult who didn't consider himself some sort of godparent of Brigid, who from the time of Theresa's first illness, when she herself was three, seemed always ready to leave home and find herself a healthier family.

Theresa didn't like Brigid too much, not because of any one thing Brigid did but because she felt reproached in some way by Brigid's existence. Her parents never asked her why she wasn't like Brigid but the question somehow hovered in the air every time Brigid hit another home run or was invited someplace. Not that Theresa minded her sister's popularity; if anything she minded those rare periods when Brigid spent a lot of time at home.

Thomas and Katherine were something else. They were like a second set of parents to her and she adored them both, particularly Thomas, who never bossed her around. Thomas had been eleven and Katherine six when Theresa was born. (The Missus' Second Thoughts, Mr. Dunn had once called Brigid and Theresa, and their mother had gotten very angry. Later, when the company was gone, she'd accused him of making it sound as though it happened that way on purpose. And then her father had said, "Indeed," which no one understood except maybe their mother, who was the only one supposed to hear it, anyway.)

Thomas was her mother's favorite of them all and his death in a training-camp gun accident when he was eighteen dealt her the most staggering blow of her life. She turned gray almost overnight, a woman thirty-seven years old. She lost her famous temper but she lost her liveliness, too. At first she cried all the time. Then she stopped crying and there was a period when she just sat on a hard chair in the living room, staring at the rug. Which had no pattern.

Her father grieved too but couldn't match the length or depth of her mother's mourning and became for a while like a ghost around the house. Hovering gray in the black shadow of her mother's grief.

Katherine doing the ironing and watching TV. Her mother sitting looking at the rug.

Theresa on the floor in one corner of the room, curled up with Nancy Drew, *looking up occasionally to catch the thread of the movie on the TV.*

Brigid out somewhere in the neighborhood.

Her father comes in from work.

Katherine puts down the iron and runs to kiss him. He hugs Katherine, fondles her long silky auburn hair. Her hair which is the way red hair is supposed to be when it doesn't go wrong, like Theresa's, and become fly-away kinky and orange.

26

In this period Katherine is the only one who dares demand affection from their father. And she gets it. She's his favorite, anyway. She knows it and Theresa knows it. If Brigid knows it she doesn't care. Katherine goes back to her ironing. For a moment her father just stands there, uncertain whether he must come further into the room. Penetrate the shroud of its atmosphere.

"Look at her," Mrs. Dunn says. "Reading. Do you remember the way Thomas read to her all the time when she was sick?"

Thomas spent more time in the hospital with her than anyone except her mother. Thomas read to her for hours at a time, holding up the books for her to see the pictures. Thomas brought her flowers from the lot on the corner. Thomas was a saint. Thomas had thought he might be a priest when he got out of the army but didn't mention this to the recruiting officer. Theresa had loved Thomas very much but when her mother recited the Thomas litany Theresa wished that he had never lived so that this could never have happened.

After the first year her father began keeping longer hours at work. Or wherever. Sometimes she heard her mother accuse him of being delayed by drink, not work. The accusations were dull and toneless, not as they'd been in the days before Thomas's death. If they were made in

Katherine's presence Katherine would take her father's side or try to mediate between them.

Sometimes Theresa's back hurt, particularly if she tried to sit straight and still for a long time. It wasn't the kind of thing you bothered your parents with, even in normal times. It wasn't bad enough. Besides, it might be something you were doing that was causing you the pain, and then to tell them would just bring anger and recriminations down on your head. At home she lay curled on her side whenever she could to accommodate the discomfort, but in class Sister Vera was always telling her to sit up straight. She began sitting on one foot or wedging a book under her left buttock so that she would appear to be straight. Then one day she forgot to remove the book when Sister Vera came around checking homework, and Sister Vera saw it and sent her to the office. There, so frightened that she had to cross her legs for fear of wetting her pants, she haltingly explained to the Mother Superior, who, unlike Sister Vera, had known her since she began school, that she couldn't actually sit the way Sister Vera wanted her to without doing that thing with the book.

Her spine had curved.

Years earlier the polio had weakened the muscles on the left side of her back more than those on the right so that they exerted less pull on the spine. Slowly since then the stronger muscles had pulled the lower part of her spine out of shape. The gray-haired specialist shook his head. If only they'd caught it earlier. Any time during the first year or two a plaster cast might have done the job but now . . .

There were innumerable examinations and tests before she could enter the hospital for surgery. The first so bad that after that it almost didn't matter—she felt little. Or she felt a great deal but dimly, as though it were happening to someone else. The doctor asking her *in front of her father* if she got her period yet. The doctor asking her father if anyone in the family had ever had a hunched back. (It was the only time her father got angry.) The doctor making her bend forward and try to touch the floor while he sat in back of her and put his hands on her waist and all over her, squeezing and poking and feeling. For years she had drifted into fantasy as she lay in bed at night or sat quietly looking at a book without reading it. Now her fantasies began to serve a more urgent purpose. It was much more bearable to be a princess getting tortured in a dungeon than a crooked little girl being tortured by doctors; after all, if you were a princess being tortured by bad guys, the good guys might rescue you at any moment.

She was in the hospital for a year, her torso encased in a plaster cast both before and after the operation, which was in the third month. She never cried until the day they told her she was going home.

Brigid was too young to be allowed in the hospital so they hadn't seen each other for a year. That didn't matter; they'd been strangers before and they were strangers now.

"Hi," Brigid said, "it's nice you're home," and went off to play baseball. People were beginning to tease her about being a tomboy, now that she was eleven years old and still wrapped up in sports.

Katherine, in the early months, had been to the hospital a great deal. Then something happened which at first no one would tell Theresa about. After a few weeks they told her Katherine was upset because she'd broken off her engagement with Young John. Young John, so called because he had the same name as her father, with whom he worked at the firehouse, had become very close to her father in the year following Thomas's death. He'd spent a lot of time at their house and it had eventually become apparent to everyone that he was madly in love with Katherine. Katherine had finally agreed that she would marry him when she graduated from high school and now she'd changed her mind. At first that was all her mother would say.

Not that Theresa cared all that much. The truth was that although Katherine was very nice to her most of the time, it was still sort of a relief not to have her around. There was something about Katherine that filled up a whole room. Not just that she was beautiful and everyone kept talking about how beautiful she was, it was the way Katherine *was*. She always sort of expected you to be looking at her and admiring her like all those dumb teenage boys who hung around the house and wanted to take her to the movies. Like her *father*. Theresa didn't mind so much when it was going on, she'd gotten used to it, but there had been a feeling of not being in a hurry to get back to it, either.

Except it turned out that Katherine wasn't living at home, after all. It turned out that the way Katherine had broken her engagement to Young John was by running away with and marrying a cousin of Young John's whom she met at a wedding she'd gone to with Young John. Katherine's husband, Ronald, was a stockbroker, one of those terribly handsome superclean young businessmen who seemed almost as eager to please the rest of the family as to please his beautiful wife. Katherine seemed to run to the other end of the room whenever he came near her, but Theresa thought that might be her imagination.

Six months later her mother told Theresa that Katherine was getting an annulment, which was not like a divorce. It meant the marriage had never existed. Theresa asked how that could be and her mother just said that it was the law. Meanwhile Katherine had gone to live with their

Brooklyn cousins and was finishing high school there. Her mother said Katherine realized what a terrible mistake it had been to drop out of high school and she hoped Theresa would never do the same thing. Theresa said that she didn't mean to, that, as a matter of fact, she was going to go to college and be a teacher. She'd become very fond of the young sister who'd come three times a week the whole year she was in the hospital and left her homework so she could keep up with her class. One of the essays she'd written had been about her determination to be like Sister Rosalie when she grew up, and Sister Rosalie had laughed and given her a kiss. Now her mother laughed because finishing high school was one thing and going to college another.

Katherine finished high school and moved to Manhattan, where she lived with two other girls and was training to become a stewardess.

Her mother and the doctor worried about Theresa's weight; she was supposed to weigh fifteen pounds less than she did. She loved the diet the doctor put her on because it provided her with such a wealth of material for those times when her mother finally badgered her into going to confession.

Bless me Father for I have sinned. It is four weeks since my last confession. I went off my diet for three weeks; I ate seven chocolate bars

*and drank Cokes. I yelled at my mother and I
cursed twice.*

What difference did her weight make anyway?
It was true that clothes were a problem, or would
have been if she hadn't worn a uniform to high
school every day. Or if she'd cared. But she didn't
care. *What difference did it make?* What difference did it make if her red hair, pulled tightly
into a rubber band before she left for school,
was out of the band and flying all over by the
end of the day? What difference did it make if
the general effect was of sloppiness or, at best,
of disorder controlled at great cost? In her fantasies she was beautiful, more perfect than
Katherine, and in real life there was no Prince
Charming who, if she lost fifteen pounds and
turned beautiful, would swoop down and carry
her off to his kingdom. Her best friend, Gail, was
very small and skinny. People called them Mutt
and Jeff and they both sort of got a kick out of
that, the idea of making up a set that way. Gail
didn't care if she lost weight or not; Gail liked
her the way she was. When she thought about
graduating from high school and going off to
college, the only thing that bothered her was that
Gail wouldn't be going with her. She tried to talk
Gail into it but Gail just laughed, and it was true
that she wasn't nearly as good in school as Theresa
was.

The worst times were when Katherine came

home to visit once a month, and an hour later the house was magically full of her discarded boyfriends, and the phone was ringing all the time, if not for Katherine, then for Brigid. Brigid stared at Katherine over the dinner table as though she were a movie star. Their mother said little but fairly reeked of contentment at having Katherine home. And their father, usually so silent (except in the stillness of his bedroom at night, when occasionally Theresa, passing the door on her way to the bathroom, would hear his low voice in a steady outpour of words), her father, discussing Katherine's travels with her as though it were what she'd left home to do. Asking about the various cities as though he'd never expressed the opinion that people were best off taking the railroad if they really had to travel. Telling Katherine with a smile that yes, maybe he would take advantage of Eastern's reduced fares for the families of their employees. Maybe he'd go to Washington, if John Kennedy were to get in next year. Or California. A couple of the men at the firehouse had been to California and said it was worth the trip. Especially Disneyland. They weren't to laugh, he said, his friends told him it was just as good for grownups as for kids.

"For your thirtieth anniversary, Daddy," Katherine said, "I'm going to give you and Mom a trip to California."

"Don't be ridiculous, now, Katherine," her

father said. But he was obviously pleased that she wanted to do it.

Theresa went up to her room. A few minutes later there was a knock at the door and Katherine came in.

"Tessie," Katherine said, "is anything wrong?"

Katherine didn't know that she hated Tessie now, that she wanted to be called Terry. Tessie had been her name when she was a tiny child with reddish-blond curls.

"No."

"You sure? Lately when I come home you hardly ever talk to me."

"Everyone else talks plenty," Theresa pointed out.

"You *are* mad at me."

Theresa was astounded to realize that Katherine was close to tears. In all the years that she could remember she'd never seen her sister cry. What was she supposed to say now? Maybe it wasn't Katherine's fault that she was a movie star and this house was her fan club.

"I'm not mad at you," she said. "I just—sometimes I get—everything is so easy for you!"

Katherine stared at her. "Tessie, what are you talking about? Please sit up and talk to me."

Reluctantly she sat up.

"What's easy for me?"

"Everything! You run off and get married and then you change your mind and all of a sudden—poof! you're not married any more. Then you decide to be a stewardess, flying around, and just like that you're a stewardess, having a ball, not even caring what's going on here or if anyone misses you—" It was pouring out now, but what was she talking about? She *never* missed Katherine.

"But it's just the opposite," Katherine cried out. "This is the only place I really care about!"

"And then once in a while you just breeze in," Theresa went on, ignoring her, "as if—" As if what? As if she owned the place. As if no one else mattered at all. "As if nothing that happens here matters."

"Yes it does."

"No, it doesn't, and I know it really doesn't, I just . . ." Frustrated she lapsed into silence.

Katherine said, "I've been miserable since the day I left here."

Theresa stared at her.

"My marriage was miserable. A nightmare. The annulment was ghastly, worse than you can imagine. I had to sit there and lie and lie and know that no one believed me. The truth of what it was like was worse than anything I said, but that wouldn't have got me an annulment. So I had to say I was married for a year and the marriage was, you know, never consummated. I had to pretend to be, you know . . ."

Theresa nodded. A little of her anger had vanished at Katherine's admission.

36

"A virgin. I'm almost seventeen, for God's sake, you can—"

Katherine smiled. "That's true. I guess I always think of you as younger. Sometimes I've wanted to talk to you so much, Tessie. You don't know. There's no one I can really talk to."

"What about the girls you live with?"

"I don't live with girls," Katherine said after a moment. "I live with a man. Two men. One in New York and one in Los Angeles. Or I did until a couple of weeks ago."

"What happened?"

"I got pregnant."

"Mother of God," murmured Theresa, who immediately grasped the situation. "You don't know which one is the father!"

Katherine burst into tears.

"There's no use crying," Theresa said. She liked this new suffering Katherine a little better but was also less comfortable with her.

"I can't help it." Katherine was sobbing uncontrollably now. "I didn't cry the whole time. I had an abortion and I didn't cry!"

"You had an abortion?" Theresa whispered. She'd never even heard the word abortion said out loud.

Katherine nodded, looking at Theresa as though she expected to be yelled at.

"Did it hurt?"

Katherine shook her head. "But I've been miserable ever since I came back. From Puerto Rico, that's were I had it, it was like a vacation. It's almost like—it's not supposed to be that easy. It's too big a sin to get off that lightly."

Theresa nodded.

"You understand that, don't you?" Katherine said. She was calm again. "You're the only one. When I came back I was so depressed, I tried explaining to . . . everyone thought I was carrying on over nothing. All the girls I knew had had abortions. I didn't think I could— Oh, Tessie, tell me the truth! Do you think I'm really a bad person?"

Theresa smiled uncomfortably, shaking her head. The fact was she thought Katherine might really way down be a very bad person, but she didn't know exactly why except it had nothing to do with abortions.

Katherine sighed. "I used to feel you thought I was such an evil person. No, what it really was, I knew I did things that were wrong, or I thought were wrong in those days. You know, anything to do with boys, and so on. And I knew Mother and Daddy didn't see me that way. But I always felt as if you knew better, you were the only one who knew how bad I really was."

This was fascinating to Theresa, that Katherine should have the same view of Katherine that she herself had of Katherine. It made her sister a little more interesting than she'd ever seemed before. She smiled at Katherine with something resembling friendliness.

"I wanted you to like me," Katherine said. "I know that sounds silly, considering you were so much younger than me, but I always had a thing . . . from the time you were little and you came home from the hospital."

Theresa was startled. They had *never* talked of that time.

"I wasn't allowed in the hospital," Katherine said, "because I was only ten. I was very scared, even though they promised me you'd be okay if we all prayed. I went to church every day to pray for you. Before—you know, I didn't think about you that much before. I mean, you were so much younger, it was almost like two separate families. I was more like a mother to you than a sister."

Theresa had heard that said of Katherine before and she'd always resented it, though she was never sure why.

"I was terrified when you got sick. I knew people could die from polio. I remember when I prayed I kept telling God to save you because I didn't even know you yet. I didn't sleep before they brought you home. I mean *at all*. I was very happy but I was scared to death—I think maybe that you'd look different. Be a different person. Maybe that sounds silly, too, but the fact is . . . you were. You really were."

Theresa saw the tears return to her sister's eyes before she felt them in her own.

"Not just that you were thinner . . . you were so skinny . . . poor baby . . . it was more than that.

39

Your face. You looked a hundred years old. So old and wise. I remember thinking, Holy Mother, I only asked you to keep her alive, not to make her old!" Katherine burst into tears for the second time that night. Theresa wanted to tell her to stop but she was too choked up, and besides, she wasn't sure which she wanted Katherine to stop—talking or crying. "I'll never forget it," Katherine said, sobbing. "You looked as though you'd died and come back, Tessie, that's the truth!"

And finally Theresa could hold it in no longer. She sat, her back against the headboard, not moving, crying silently. Katherine leaned over, resting her head in Theresa's lap, sobbing loudly.

"From then on I always had the feeling," Katherine said after a long time, her voice muffled, "that whatever I said, you knew the real truth. But I wasn't scared. I knew you wouldn't tell. I always felt there was this good thing between us, even if we hardly ever talked to each other."

Theresa stroked Katherine's hair. She was feeling a mixture of emotions so strong that she was trembling—a nearly overwhelming love for her sister, a desire to hold her, soothe her, at the same time as she felt guilty over her dislike and mistrust of Katherine. But then beyond those feelings was the fact that she hadn't really lost that mistrust. Of her sister. Of this situation. What was Katherine trying to do to her, anyway? It was like someone you knew was an escaped murderer or something showed up at your door and got you to

40

feel all sympathetic and concerned for them to escape. Except Katherine hadn't really done anything like that. Or had she? She kept reminding herself she didn't trust her sister while remembering the feeling of the sobs that had racked Katherine's body.

"Stop," she said.

Katherine looked up. "What?"

"Nothing," Theresa said. "I don't know. I have a headache."

"Do you want some aspirin?" Katherine's mascara had streaked all over her face.

"No."

"I want a cigarette. Do you ever smoke, Theresa?"

"Once in a while." Now why did she have to tell a lie like that? Actually, she'd meant to try it.

"I'll go down and get them. I'll be right back." But she hesitated, as though afraid to break the bond of feeling between them by leaving the room.

"You better wash your face," Theresa said. "It's all streaked."

Two months later Katherine married a forty-year-old divorced Jewish lawyer from Boston named Brooks Hendell. Her parents were tight-lipped and upset but felt much better when they'd met Brooks, who was rich, handsome and likable and who when you looked at him, as Mrs. Dunn pointed out more than once, could easily have been a northern Italian. Theresa adored him, as did Brigid.

Brigid was going steady with a wiry, freckle-faced Irish punk named Patrick Kelly of whom her father remarked, upon being told he was Brigid's steady, that with Patrick in their house and the Kennedys in Washington, the Irish were finally in their ascendancy. Theresa thought Patrick was a moron but Brigid devoted to going steady with him, to baking Toll House cookies and knitting a sweater for him, that single-minded energy and consuming love which she'd once had for baseball and other games.

It was Katherine who persuaded them to let her go to City College. The men in the firehouse were telling her father he'd be crazy to let his daughter take a subway into Harlem but Katherine pointed out that thousands of white kids went to City College every day without getting raped or murdered. Katherine said they should be glad to have a daughter smart enough to get into college, and ambitious enough to want to be a teacher. She herself, she said, often wished she had the gumption to go back to school and get a degree. As a matter of fact, she was seriously considering it—and Brooks loved the idea.

On the night before she was to begin college Theresa took a bath, went back to her room, locked the door, took off her robe, and looked at herself in the mirror. In this light her skin was fair but not deadly; her breasts were round and full; her ten or fifteen pounds of extra weight were concentrated on her hips and thighs and looked quite all right without clothes straining to cover them. When she was naked she generally found her body rather beautiful, although she could never in a million years have admitted this to anyone. In clothes, in front of other people, she felt ashamed of her weight, her sloppiness, always *something,* but it was more because of what she felt *they* saw when they looked at her.

Now she took from the wall a small oval mirror and walked with it to the full-length mirror on her closet door. With her back to the large mirror she held the small one so that she could see her naked back. A shiny, pale-pink seam ran down the lower part of her spine; near the top curve of her left buttock, the crescent scar where they'd taken the bone for the spinal fusion matched the large seam in color. She shivered. In the six years since the operation she had never looked at her naked back. She returned the small mirror to its place.

It seemed to her that if you didn't know about her back, if you only saw her naked from the front, you would think she was perfectly all right. The curve of her hip to right was so minute as to be invisible; certainly no one else ever noticed it. She'd never thought about the scar since it had finished healing and the itching had stopped, but now she remembered how for a long time she'd had a sense of it not as a seam in her skin but as a basic part of her. As though the scar itself were her spine, the thing that held her together. During that period she'd sometimes dreamed that she was lying on the ground . . . or, rather, the spine, the scar was lying on the ground and the rest of her was floating off into the air like chiffon veils. But every time the veils were about to float away entirely into the sky to be free, the scar would pull them back to the ground. This night she dreamed a similar dream, except that it was happening in front of the stone building where she'd gone to register for her first courses at City College, and there was a statue looking at her, and people passing by started staring at her because they saw the statue staring. They didn't understand that it was a person they were looking at. It began to rain so heavily that people screamed and ran for shelter.

She woke up.

⌒⋚⋛⌒

Professor Martin Engle was tall and reed-thin, with curly gray-black hair, a gently sarcastic manner, and beautiful sad eyes, which you didn't really notice until he took off his glasses and ran a hand wearily across his face. He was a poet and had had a volume of poetry privately published, as she found out later from two girls in the class, Carol and Rhoda, who were also in love with him.

He began on the first day by reading them a poem by Rainer Maria Rilke:

What will you do, God, when I die?
When I, your pitcher, broken lie:
When I, your drink, go stale or dry?
I am your garb, the trade you ply,
You lose your meaning, losing me. . . .

He asked if anyone in the class hoped to be a writer. Both Carol and Rhoda raised their hands. Professor Engle said there was no reason for anyone to bother to write who didn't hope to create lines that were perfect, like these. Few would ever succeed, but those not ready to try should give up before they began. Carol and Rhoda looked solemn.

"Having said this," Professor Engle went on in his rather mournful manner, "I will tell you that it is my aim in this class to teach those of you who are wise enough to know you are untalented—" he paused "—but who say to me, in effect: 'Professor Engle, I know I'm no writer and never shall be, but I come to you from the public high schools of New York City, illiterate. Teach me to write a simple declarative sentence without risking humiliation . . .' to teach those of you wise enough to know this is what you require to do exactly that. Are there any questions?"

Most of them sat in their seats, feeling vaguely put in their places without knowing precisely where those places were. Carol and Rhoda looked crushed.

They were to write, in the first person, a brief description of an unpleasant experience. They were not to garnish it with a lot of silly trifles, like Cellophane panties on a lamb chop. Adjectives, where required for clarity, were to be simple and direct: pretty, ugly, green, purple, etc. Doors were to be open or closed, not ajar. There was to be no sunlight spilling through venetian blinds; if anything spilled, it must be liquid. Did he make himself clear? He stood at the window, looking down into the courtyard. The sunlight spilled through the open window and glinted on his broad gold wedding band.

She wrote a description of going to confession with a new priest who was a drunk. There was something she'd really had to confess, something that had happened that week with a boy she knew, but she could hear the priest's heavy breathing—almost *smell* him—on the other side of the screen, and when he talked to her his speech was thick from liquor. The booth reeked of cigar smoke. Without seeing him she pictured the way he'd looked at his first mass the week before; he was fat and red and she could see the veins in his nose.

"Bless me Father for I have sinned. I yelled at my mother three times and I ate a big bag of peanuts that was supposed to be for my sisters and everyone."

He gave her twenty Hail Marys and thirty Our Fathers. She left with the burden she'd carried into the booth.

They were allowed to look at their papers and then they had to give them back to him.

Good. This is exactly what I asked for.

"Not only is the content excellent, Miss Dunn," he said as she stood looking at the paper, a pleasurable flush on her cheeks, "but I hereby award you the 1961 Martin Engle Award for Best Penmanship by a Parochial School Student. Public school graduates aren't even allowed to enter; it would be a waste of their time and mine."

She felt pleased but also confused, a condition in which he would often leave her, because she'd been praised but somehow mocked at the same time. It wasn't really *important,* that was the thing. He was doling out great praise for what everyone knew was really a silly insignificant part of the paper. She was annoyed. She was his slave.

He asked her to read the paper to the class; she shook her head. He asked very gently if she would mind his reading it. She consented. When each student had seen his own paper and returned it, he read Theresa's aloud and asked for comments. There were none. Then he read another whose author he didn't identify.

"It is 1895," the paper began. "I have been forced to flee Russia with my family. We are starving. For days now, melting into weeks, we have had almost nothing to eat. We have slept in the hold of this filthy ship, sometimes with bodies that They neglect to remove. Huddled together for warmth, the smell sometimes so bad that I want to vomit."

Theresa was quite impressed with this dramatic paper and was prepared to hear Professor Engle say that the difference between the two papers was the difference between competence and talent. Then she became aware that, almost imperceptibly at first, then more and more openly, Professor Engle was making fun of the piece. By making it just a little more dramatic than it was meant to be, he was telling the class what he thought of it.

Theresa looked around her surreptitiously. Some of the class looked amused by the performance; others were uncertain or unaware. But Rhoda sat frozen in her seat, fighting tears.

Thank God it isn't me.

"We are standing on the soil of America at last. I can only pray that this ghastly ordeal will have been worthwhile."

He put down the paper and looked around the class—avoiding Rhoda, or so it seemed to Theresa.

"Any comments?"

Thank God it isn't me.

"It's pretentious," said a thin-lipped, pretentious-looking boy.

"Mmm. What's pretentious about it?"

"I don't know," the boy said uneasily. "There's a tone to it . . ."

That wasn't fair; the tone had been given it by the reading.

". . . and she pretends to be someone she's not."

"Are you trying to say," Engle asked incredulously, "that a writer who writes about other people is pretentious? Dickens? Tolstoy? Balzac?" His arms were folded and his manner stern.

"N-no," the boy floundered lamely, "but—"

"Is there anyone in the class who has something sensible to say?"

But of course everyone was afraid to speak now; the critic had come off somewhere worse than the author.

"Pretentious isn't the word for this paper, pretendy-ish is more like it." No one knew exactly what he was talking about. "The problem here is not that the author fails to be true to her own life but that she fails to be true to anyone's—to life itself." He quoted again the part about her getting nauseated. "Now for the information of the author, the furthest thing from the mind of someone who hasn't eaten in several weeks is vomiting. This is not something it takes either brilliance or talent to perceive. It takes only the willingness to get in direct touch with life instead of holding seances with the muse." His face mostly kept its gentle dreamy look but his lip was curled.

"All this other girl has done is to go directly into life—her own, because she has no grandiose ambitions to be an *artiste* and because that is the easiest and most obvious place to go—and simply record a painful experience."

Let him never know, God, that it didn't happen. That we've had the same priest for as long as I can remember, pale, thin, dreamy Father Francis, whose sister or mother always wins the washing machine or the TV set at the raffle.

After class she ran out without talking to anybody. Ashamed to face Rhoda. Afraid that if she had any conversation at all with Professor Engle, he would guess at the truth and she would be forever humiliated. She was astounded to see Rhoda there for the next class.

They got another assignment; this time it was a pleasant experience, with the other conditions being the same. They were to try to keep the essay down to under a page; brevity was not only the soul of wit but the foundation of many other qualities as well.

A PLEASANT EXPERIENCE

by Theresa Dunn

I was at the beach. There were many of us. There had been a clambake. All the others were still sitting around the fire, toasting marshmallows and singing. I wandered off by myself, digging my toes into the warm sand as I walked. Once in a while I stopped to pick up a pretty shell or a smooth pebble.

The fire seemed to have died down in the sun so that it was just a glowing red ball in the sky. I walked to the edge of the water. The waves lapped at my toes. The sun was very low. I had never seen it seem so close to the earth. The whole sky seemed very close. The wet sand moved beneath my feet. I didn't feel as though I was standing on the earth looking up at the sky. I felt that I was in a pocket whose sides were made of sky and sand.

Suddenly the sand shifted too fast and I was frightened out of my revery. I heard my name being called.

My companion had come looking for me.

Dear Theresa—

I doubt that you are an artist for you follow instructions too well. But this is a perfect piece—brief and beautiful. The Sacred Gizzard of Xavier—or whichever grove of academe had the privilege of spawning you —obviously did you—or your sense of language, at any rate—no lasting harm.

We must talk some time about your plans

for the future. If you are an education major I don't want to hear about it. Make up something else before we speak.

M.E.

He had definitely singled her out for some reason. She checked around surreptitiously, looking at the comments on other people's papers when she could, listening to him, and there was no one else, even of the kids he treated nicely, to whom he displayed such kindness and interest. This made her happy in a tense way; since she wasn't sure how she had earned this sole warm spot in the sunshine of Martin Engle's approval, she was terrified that she would just as ignorantly one day step out of it. Carol and Rhoda (his scorn for them had convinced them that he was even more brilliant than they'd first realized) tried to befriend her, as though some of that magic she possessed would rub off on them. She avoided them for the same reason. They waited for her after class because if she were with the small group flanking him as he left the building and headed toward the North Campus, there was a better chance that he would allow them all to remain around him. While if it were just Carol and Rhoda, for example, he was likely to suggest that they find some other shrine to worship at that day, he was too weary for adoration.

Finally a day came when not only Carol and

Rhoda but also Jules Feingold, the skinny, dark-haired boy who was the other regular kicked-around hanger-on, were all out of class and she got to walk the whole way alone with him. It was like being on a roller coaster, up and down, up and down, with no way to know which was coming next until you reached it.

"So, Theresa," he said as they passed through the gates to the outside walk, "Theresita . . . little Theresa . . . we are alone at last." Her heart began thumping wildly. "The moment you've been waiting for." The plunge down. Mortification. "And I have been looking forward to, I confess." Up, up, up. "Now you can tell me what it is that has put that haunted look in your beautiful green eyes." Up, up, up, but holding her breath. Haunted? "The fear of Engle? I think not, you had it the first time I saw you, before you could possibly have known what a ferocious, erratic creature I was. It drew me to you. Let's see . . . the fear of God? Doubtful. More likely of one of his messengers. Stern parents? Whiskey priest? Butch nun?"

Theresa sucked in her breath. She'd never heard anyone say anything like this out loud and straight, although the girls in school would occasionally giggle about some faggot priest, and of course she'd come across all kinds of characters in books.

"Do you know that you don't giggle when you're

nervous?" he asked. "And that this is an unusual quality in a young girl?"

She was silent.

"Ah." He pretended to be sad. "I see that I shall not hear the life story of Theresa Dunn before I reach North Campus. I shall have to have a conference with her in my office some time. As though she were one of my elective students. Would you like to do that, Theresa?"

"I guess." Her mouth was dry.

"Good." He took out his appointment book and made a great to-do about finding a time when he had a solid free hour. Then he wrote in "Phantom Guest" and showed it to her, explaining that he didn't normally reserve time for required-course students and he wouldn't want to be caught red-handed with proof to the contrary. His exaggeratedly furtive manner told her that he was making fun of her again, that none of it really mattered at all. Her head was swimming.

He was in a bad mood. He had lost—or misplaced—a set of papers. Not that he would give a damn except he'd marked half of them already. His tiny office was jammed with books and papers. He beckoned her to sit but then ignored her as he continued to search for the papers.

"Can I help?" she asked timidly.

"Feel free." He sounded sarcastic.

She wanted desperately to be the one to find them but she didn't, nor did he, and eventually he said, "Halt! That's it. I refuse to spend another minute on this nonsense. I'll tell them that the whole set was such drivel that I threw them away without marking them." He laughed but his crossness wasn't really gone and she held her breath.

"All right," he said abruptly, "what do you want to talk to me about?"

She stared at him. What had *she*—*he* was the one who'd scheduled the conference because *he* wanted to—in one swift motion she stood up in the tiny cubicle, opened the door and fled. He called her name once but she didn't stop. By the time she got halfway to the subway she was badly out of breath and she ached all over. It wasn't until she was on the train that she realized she had two more classes that day, including his.

She started every time the phone rang, then got angry at herself, reminding herself that she hadn't expected him to call; it would be *ridiculous* to expect him to call. Two days later, when she went to his class again, she walked into the room, sat in her seat with her eyes on her hands, and refused to look at him or anyone else.

"Theresa," he said as the class filed out, "will you stay for a moment? I'd like to speak with you."

She returned to her seat, eyes cast down. When the others had left, he came and sat in the chair next to hers, moving it to face her.

"This isn't an act, is it, Theresa? Because I will not be diddled by a—"

55

She felt a wave of helpless hatred so strong that it was like a massive electric shock going through her; he saw it and stopped.

"You're really this upset," he began again, slowly, "by the fact that I was cross with you? Not even you—I was just angry at something and you happened to be there."

And you happened to suggest that it was my own idea to be there! Not that she hadn't liked the idea, but it was *his*. That seemed very important for some reason.

"You're much too sensitive, Theresa." But his voice was caressing her now and her body felt like liquid and she couldn't be angry with him any more. "We'll have to work on raising your threshold of pain. Let's see. A small dose of nastiness every day, like a shot, until you build up an immunity? What do you think?"

He was smiling but she wasn't sure he was really kidding. She waited helplessly. Everything was churning inside her. She had to go to the bathroom very badly and she both wanted him to touch her and was terrified that if he did she would lose control and wet her pants and never be able to come back to this room again.

"Theresa," he reproached her, so softly that it was almost a whisper, "you have absolutely no sense of humor." But it was said like en endearment, not a criticism, and as he said it he very lightly touched his index finger to the middle of her chin, as though to make a dimple. She was in an agony of expectation.

"Well," he said—it was sudden but still gentle —"time to get up to North Campus. Coming?"

She shook her head.

"Why not?"

"I have some things I have to do here."

"Really?"

She nodded.

"All right. I'll see you on Friday. You are not to cut my class again, that would be taking advantage of my preference for you and I don't like being played with that way. Understood?"

She nodded again. Licking her dry lips.

"All right," he said. "Then we understand each other. You may write me a special essay for Friday—How I Lost My Virginity. Work from your imagination, if necessary."

And he disappeared before he could see the blood drain from her face.

He had to have been kidding.

But he was so *crazy*. Maybe he was serious.

No, he had to have been kidding.

She couldn't do it, anyway, so he'd better have been.

She sat for another ten minutes or so in the empty classroom before she could make herself get up, go to the bathroom and then walk over to the cafeteria for lunch. Jules was there, along with a couple of other boys; he tried to draw her into conversation, but she couldn't be bothered.

In her head she was going over and over the scene in the classroom and she was afraid she would lose pieces of it if she let herself talk with Jules or anyone else.

In her fantasies his wife had always just died in an automobile accident and he had sent for her. He made love to her passionately after explaining that all love had been gone from his marriage for years. Sometimes they played a game called Threshold of Pain, in which he and many assistants tested her to see where pleasure ended and pain began. Or vice versa. Afterwards they would bring her to a warm, healing bath.

He never asked her for the essay, and things went back more or less to where they'd been before. Several times it seemed that he was about to make some effort to be alone with her, but then he never actually did anything. She found out where he gave the class before hers and made it a point to be in that area when the class ended. But he came out with a girl with bouffant teased hair like Katherine's. (People on airplanes these days were always telling Katherine she looked like Jackie Kennedy. Katherine claimed to be irritated by this but she didn't change her hair style, either. It was ridiculous, anyway; Katherine's hair was dark red, not black. This girl's was black.)

Theresa felt toward this girl a hatred so consuming that had He—or anyone—spoken to her at that moment she could only have choked in response. This girl was talking and smiling and looking as though she *owned* him.

She was late to class and for several sessions afterwards refused to join the group around him as he left for North Campus at the end of the hour. She continued to get approving comments on her papers but grew desperate because he didn't seem to notice that she was boycotting him.

The end of the term was approaching. What if she couldn't get him for Comp II? Their last assignment was a free choice. It came into her head that she would write on the subject he'd suggested but then she was afraid she would give herself away. What she needed was to prove to him that she had a sense of humor. Sometimes she thought this must be why he had made no further move in her direction. *You have no sense of humor, Theresa. We must raise your threshold of humor.* Other times she thought it was her failure to take up his dare that had kept him from . . . from what? From whatever had been about to happen.

She wrote a piece called "The Fan Club" about a rock star named Elvis Angle and the silly teen-agers who waited for him after every performance. The would-be Jackie Kennedy, the two folksy Jewish girls in leather sandals (except she didn't say Jewish because she thought Professor Engle might be). In the first draft there was a freckled-faced redhead whom she later deleted, not wanting him to think of her as one of that bunch of starstruck idiots, even if she was.

"You gave me pleasure," he said when he returned the paper. "Very few students ever do that."

Her body was invaded by warmth. She had a brief image of herself in a beautiful blue tutu whirling across a tiny stage for an audience of one, Martin Engle, who clapped so wildly that he sounded like a hall full of people.

He told her that he was going down to a Cuban luncheonette on Broadway which had excellent coffee and no CCNY students and asked if she would like to come along. She nodded. (She never drank coffee. She hated the taste.)

She drank and loved the thick, sweet, milky coffee. He asked her about her plans, now that the term was ending, and she said she was going to take his Comp II class next term. He laughed and asked if she had any plans for the future beyond that. She blushed because the truth was that she did not. Where once she'd thought about being a teacher, and later about going into the Peace Corps, her planning energies were now entirely devoted to figuring out how she could stay with him—in any capacity, from student to whatever. Sometimes she thought maybe she could work for him. Grading papers and such. Her knowledge of grammar was excellent, as was her spelling.

"I always wanted to be a teacher," she said. "But I don't want to be an Ed major." They were the object of general derision, she'd discovered, and not just of his scorn. They were the ones who, when a teacher veered off on one of those interesting sidetracks that brought your attention back to class, interrupted to ask if this would be on the exam. "Sometimes I think I'd like to go into the Peace Corps for a few years, and . . ."

"And then get married and have six children."

"Oh, no!" She was genuinely aghast.

He watched her thoughtfully. "Usually when young girls say that to me their voices are thick with hyprocrisy."

She was silent.

"You're not going to have children and give them TV dinners and rush off to chair the PTA meeting?"

She shook her head.

"You just passed the acid test," he said. "Usually when I say that the response is, 'But if I ever did have children against my will I wouldn't *ever* serve them TV dinners.'"

She smiled. "Do you have the same conversations over and over?"

"Absolutely."

She was silent, upset not only by his admission but by his casual manner in making it.

Finally he said, "You want to be a teacher because you love children although you don't wish to bear them."

She nodded. Embarrassed because it was corny but true. She was earning a great deal of money these days baby-sitting. All the children adored her because she didn't care if they never went to bed.

"And you want to go into the Peace Corps because you want to teach small African children a language they have no desire to learn. Or build grass huts."

As usual when she was with him she felt dumb. He always said she was smart, but their conversations were a mined field in which at any moment she might make the wrong verbal move and find her ignorance exploding in her face.

"Or because you have some special affinity for Negroes."

She glanced at him, trying to tell if he was serious or still making fun of her, because this was a subject she had wanted to talk on with someone. The truth was that she was afraid of colored people. Men, particularly, but women, too. When she saw colored men on the subway looking at her she was afraid they wanted to rape her or murder her, and she was terrified if she was alone with one of them at an underground station. With the women it was different—there was no question of rape, of course, and yet she always felt they would like to do her violence, that they hated her because she was white. Perhaps they would steal from her. When they were talking and laughing she often felt she might be the object of their laughter, but worse, when their big white teeth flashed in the middle of their dark-brown faces (her fear was in almost direct proportion to their darkness; the pales ones were not nearly so bad), when they laughed and she saw their teeth, she sometimes had a *physical* memory of an old half-remembered dream in which a huge monster was about to devour her, and then a tremor would pass through her whole body, and when it had passed they were people again but still people to be wary of.

What would he think of her if she told him the truth?

"No," she said. "Not really. I . . . my parents are very prejudiced. You know, typical lower-middle-class Roman Catholics." She thought she sounded quite sophisticated. "I grew up with all that stuff, you know, the niggers are coming. They don't even like *Martin Luther King!*"

He laughed with her.

"I know they're—ignorant," she said carefully. "I mean, they're provincial—where I'm from in the Bronx it could be *Kansas*—and narrow-minded, and so on, and I want the Negroes to have equality . . . I know they're equal . . . but I feel as if they're different from me." There. It was out. She waited for an expression of disgust.

"Which explains why you want to join the Peace Corps and go to Africa. Or South America."

She flushed. Became aware for the first time that they were surrounded by small Spanish men

63

of various colors. Said, in a low voice, "I want to learn."

"How do you expect to learn why Negroes in America hate whites by building huts in a small village in Africa where no one's ever heard of America?"

She was silent. If he hadn't thought before that she was stupid he surely did now.

"I know it sounds dumb," she said. "It's not something I've really thought out at all, I just . . ."

He said she wasn't dumb but innocent, and that amazed her, for the one quality in the world that she cherished and knew she did not possess was innocence. She wasn't sure when she had lost hers, except that it had to be before the Church said she had. It had to do with things you saw that you weren't supposed to see.

"You once told me I looked haunted," she said.

"Mmmm."

"How can you be haunted and innocent at the same time?"

"Why don't *you* explain it to *me* since you're the one who's managed it."

"Ohhhhhhhh."

He laughed.

They fell into the habit of going to that little luncheonette every Wednesday, at first just for coffee, then after a while for lunch. In January he told her which one of his Comp II classes she should register for. It was held at four o'clock in the afternoon, and she was upset not just because it meant going home in the dark those days during winter but much more because it meant the end of their Wednesday lunches. Then it turned out he meant her to schedule her classes later in the day in general, rather than earlier, since his own classes were almost entirely in the afternoon and he thought she might like to work for him sometimes in the mornings. Did she type? No, it was a shame. She might learn over the summer while he was away. That would be a great help to him next year, when a book he was drafting now would be ready for typing. In the meantime, there were other jobs she could be helping him with, most particularly reading papers for his required classes and marking them for grammar and spelling in detail, since, as they both knew, the greater part of the student body of the college was not literate in English.

She had to hold her breath for fear of screaming, so intense were the two feelings that this little speech aroused in her—the pleasure that he had chosen her and the anxiety aroused by the very mention of the fact that at some point he would go away. This wasn't a reality she was prepared to face—that there would be a time when she could not see him for two solid months.

He lived across the street from the Museum of Natural History so she would have no trouble finding it. She didn't tell him she'd never been there. That she'd never been on Central Park West. That in point of fact she'd seldom in her entire life been out of the Bronx before she began attending City, except to go to doctors and hospitals, and then her father drove her. It wasn't until he gave her the apartment number—12B— that she ceased to picture the room where her richest fantasies occurred as being on the second floor of the mansion in *Gone With the Wind*.

Where would his wife be while they were working?

She couldn't tell how old he was but she thought if he had children they would be young.

They would have to be someplace quiet, the two of them, if they were going to get any work done. That was for sure.

She woke up at four in the morning on the first day that she was to go, having dreamed that she was locked with him in a tiny closet while outside there were thunder and lightning. Other children were banging at the door, screaming to get in, and she said maybe they should open the door but he said that there just wasn't room in that tiny space, even though the two of them were huddled close together under a blanket.

The dream was so delicious that she tried to get back into it but she was tense and excited and couldn't fall asleep at all.

When she told the elevator operator she wanted 12B he nodded and said, "Dr. Engle," which didn't strike her really until he let her off and the door facing her read "Helen Engle, M.D." She turned to the elevator operator and stammered, "I—I—"

"Is it the professor you wanted?" he asked.

She nodded. Her lips were dry.

He took her back down and directed her to an elevator in the back explaining that this was the entrance the professor's people used during the doctor's office hours.

The professor's people.

She was taken back up in a somewhat larger but less elegant elevator. She was nearly suffocating with tension.

He opened the door, yawning, looking barely awake. She wondered what the elevator operator thought. She mumbled "Thank you" to the operator without looking at him. Martin Engle was wearing a bathrobe.

"Come in," he said, "but don't talk to me until I've had my coffee."

She walked into a large foyer, ahead of which was a living room—not elegant, as the lobby had been, but comfortable looking. Full of big overstuffed furniture and bookcases. He walked off into another hallway; she stood indecisively until he called, "Come, come, come," at which she followed him into a messy kitchen. He began pouring water into a strange glass contraption on the stove.

"My wife is an otherwise perfect human being who cannot make a decent cup of coffee."

She laughed nervously. The water that he was

pouring into the top of the glass thing was dripping down to the bottom as coffee.

His wife was a doctor. An otherwise perfect woman.

"You may sit down. You may even take off your coat and put down your books."

She never took her eyes off him as he poured the coffee, fussed over it, brought cream and sugar, cups and spoons to the table, then did something with the glass coffeepot and brought that, too.

They drank their first cup in silence. (She had come to love coffee! When she drank it she was with him.) She began to relax, to feel at home, but then as that phrase, *at home,* entered her mind she felt uneasy again because it wasn't her own home, although she had been feeling as though it were. Somewhere within a few hundred yards of her, separated by maybe two or three walls, was a lady named Mrs. Engle who was a perfect human being except that she couldn't make a decent cup of coffee. What did that mean, anyway? She couldn't really be perfect, and when you thought about it it was the kind of thing you could say about someone without actually liking her. It made her sound formidable. And she was a doctor. That helped considerably, remembering that it wasn't Mrs. Engle but Doctor Engle.

"What kind of doctor is your wife?" she asked without thinking.

He looked up and smiled. "A pediatrician."

The words swam around in her head for a minute with a lot of other doctors' labels until she could identify it, fairly certainly, as a baby doctor.

"How's that?" he asked.

She shrugged. "I don't like doctors." She blushed. It had just popped out, like her question, and it didn't sound right. She never even *thought* about doctors, except once or twice a year when she had to see one, and of course that was never an experience you would look forward to, but now here she was . . . Sometimes she felt she could never just simply and easily say the right thing with him. Not that she could with other people, but with other people she didn't *care*. When she wrote an essay for him she scribbled it over five or ten times before it was good enough. Then he read it and thought it was natural to her. She was a fraud. Not even really intelligent, particularly. Certainly she would never have been a doctor. You had to be very smart to even get into medical school.

"Why?" he asked. "A lot of people would die without them."

"A lot of people die with them."

"Did you have a bad experience with a doctor?"

"No, not particularly."

"Why do you limp?"

She gasped. The sudden movement of her body made her coffee spill over the side of the cup as she held it. One hand got wet from it but she barely noticed; she was overwhelmed by a sense of unreality. He wasn't real; she wasn't real; they weren't here; he hadn't asked that question. He couldn't have. She didn't limp.

"I don't limp," she finally said, except that her voice came out in a whisper.

"I'm sorry," he said after a moment. "That may have been too extreme a word to use. You have a slight sway, imbalance, whatever you want to call it, to your walk. It's not unattractive. If I weren't aware of such things I might never have noticed."

No one, not her parents, not relatives, not anyone she ever knew had ever said anything about a limp. For a long time she'd had to wear one shoe with a platform in it, and then she'd started wearing regular shoes as though she'd always worn them. No one had ever said anything about the way she walked!

She had a wild desire to escape and stood up, about to walk away from him, from this place, when suddenly it occurred to her that as she went, he would see her limping. She sat down again. Staring at him. Frozen in the moment. Unable to make it pass.

"Theresa." He put his hands over hers. "I'm sorry I've upset you."

"You haven't upset me."

"Yes I have."

Silence.

"Come," he said. "Let's go someplace where we can talk. It's not very comfortable in here." He waited. She said nothing. "We'll go into my study.

We'll have our coffee there, it's much pleasanter."
He put the coffee things on a small tray and held
out his free hand to her. She stood up but she
didn't take his hand. The frozen moment was
passing and now she had to fight tears. He put
his arm around her and they passed gingerly
through the kitchen, down the hallway, into a
room behind a closed door. His study. It was
strange. Totally unlike the rest of the house, with
nothing out of place, and maybe quite beautiful,
although she couldn't tell yet, she wasn't familiar
with this kind of room. In front of one window
was a huge table with many plants and a couple
of piles of papers. At an angle to it stood a typewriter on a stand. In front of another window was
a big soft chair. Then there was a studio bed covered with an elegant embroidered spread and
dozens of pillows. One the floor was an Oriental
rug. The walls were covered with Chinese prints
and wooden carvings, most of which also looked
Oriental to her.

He put the tray down on the big table-desk.

"Sit where you'll be most comfortable, Theresa."

She sat down on the edge of the studio bed
because she was closest to that and now she was
self-conscious about his seeing her walk. He sat
down and put his arm around her; she grew rigid.

"I am not attempting to seduce you," he said.
"I am attempting to comfort you because I see
that I've hurt you."

But of course that was why she'd gone rigid.

With an enormous effort of will she turned to him and with a voice as steady as possible said, "But I'd rather be seduced than comforted."

He laughed and stood up. "That's marvelous," he said. "I think I'll have it embroidered and made into a wall hanging—no, a pillow cover."

She watched him steadily. She felt in some way that she'd gotten her own back. He gave her coffee, settled with his own in the swivel desk chair, facing her. One of the reasons she loved him was that she'd understood since she first heard him talk that all those sly or hostile or outrageous thoughts that had cropped up in her mind for years and remained unsaid because they would shock or upset or alienate the people she knew would be perfectly all right with him. If she could ever get herself to say them. He finished his coffee and poured another cup without offering her more. She wanted to get more but she wasn't yet sure that was all right.

"This is where we'll work," he said. "You may sit wherever you like, at the desk, wherever. I'm going to give you the papers before I look at them myself. You will scan them carefully and red-ink every grammatical or spelling error. Hopefully I will then be less distracted by their illiteracy and will be able to simply read them quickly and make some appropriate comment. Very quickly, I should say." He smiled. "At a glance. I have too much work of my own this year to be bothered with this nonsense."

72

"Poetry?" she asked, shy again.

"And a scholarly work that I'm doing, not out of any interest at all in my subject but in the interest of getting a promotion."

She smiled.

"You are amused."

"It sounds funny. Like going from seventh grade to eighth grade."

"Quite so."

He was friendly but businesslike. There would be four sets of papers a week because he had four required courses. Later on, if he were feeling really self-indulgent, he might get her to do the same for his elective papers, which shouldn't need that sort of thing but usually did. It would probably be best if no one in her class understood that it was she making the red marks; God's words always carried more weight than those of the apostles, even if they were the same words. She nodded; she never would have dreamed of telling anyone.

"What would you consider a reasonable rate of pay for this work?" he asked.

She stared at him. It had never entered her mind that he would pay her; she was working for the privilege of working for him.

She shrugged.

"You must have thought about it."

She shook her head. She didn't want him to pay her because it made the work seem less personal.

"Have you ever worked?"

"Just baby-sitting."

"And how much do you make as a baby-sitter?"

"A dollar an hour."

"All right," he said. "We'll start you at a dollar an hour. Slave wages. And if you are really good and fast we'll raise it from there. Unless you prefer to remain my slave."

I prefer to remain your slave. I prefer you not to pay me but to love me.

She was arrested by the sound of a baby crying someplace.

He smiled. "My wife's office is on the other side of that wall."

The wall the studio bed was against. His wife.

She stood up.

"Do you want me to begin today?"

"I don't see why not," he said. "You're here and I have some papers."

She went twice a week for the rest of the term, marking two sets of papers each morning. After a month or so he began to rely on her more completely. He told her to start making a lightly penciled estimate of the quality of each paper on the top. Before long he was just erasing the penciled words and writing a brief version of the same thing in his own hand. "I liked this," or "Dull," or "The opinions don't seem honest, though I'm not sure why." He was pleased to find that she, too, reacted when someone was trying to please rather than to express; to adopt an opinion not his own; to omit some essential part of an experience in the interest of self-protection. He always worked in the room while she was there, sometimes on his poetry (by hand on legal pads), sometimes on his scholarly manuscript (on the typewriter), sometimes, it seemed, just fussing with the papers she'd done or some other odds and ends. She would work in the big chair, watching him surreptitiously when she was supposed to be concentrating on the papers. Sometimes he just pulled dry leaves off his plants or stared out the window. He told her he didn't know how he had ever managed without her. Occasionally she asked him a question about some paper and then he might lean over to her to see what she was talking about. Once in the spring she looked up as he was doing that and he kissed her mouth. Then he walked away. The next time she asked him a question he stayed in his chair and told her to read it aloud to him.

"You know that I love you, don't you, Theresa?"

"Ssshhh. She's going to hear us."

"The hell with her, let her hear us. Let her divorce me."

"She's the mother of four of your children, Martin."

"As a matter of fact, they're not my children at all. They happen to be her children by a previous marriage."

She dreaded the summer, when they would go to their home in Connecticut. (His wife would commute in July but stay there in August.)

She was going to take both typing and steno in the adult education program at Columbus High School in the evenings and work full time baby-sitting during the day. She talked about baby-sitting and kept hoping he would tell her to forget about the typing and come be their sitter for the summer, but when she told him her plans, he simply nodded in approval.

In the middle of May she started getting head-aches. She would be sitting in the big chair, marking papers, and the words would blur in front of her eyes. When she forced herself to focus on them, the headaches would begin. She didn't tell him, but then a short while later the back-aches began. Not backaches, exactly. As she sat working, the lower part of her neck would feel cramped and uncomfortable; when she moved from her original position, she would feel a sharp pain, as though she'd been locked in and had forced the lock. Then she would have to get up and stretch. Or go to the bathroom. He'd never again asked her about her walk. Until now that first morning had been pushed to the back of her consciousness, but now it forced its way back every time she stood up and feared that he would see how hard it was for her to stand straight. It became a game to see if she could bear to wait until a moment when she knew for sure he couldn't see her. At the end of the second week of this she waited so long one morning that by the time she got up, the lock was too strong to break and she staggered. She almost fell to the floor but just in time reached out to the studio bed, leaned on it, then sat.

He swiveled in his chair and faced her.

"I don't dare ask what's been bothering you for the last few weeks," he said coldly, "for fear that you'll jump out of the window. Or turn into a block of ice again, then melt away until there's no Theresa left to do my papers next year."

Tears welled in her eyes. Her whole body wanted to cry. She was an idiot. She didn't blame him for being angry with her. For hating her. She hated herself. Her back ached; she wanted very badly to lie down.

"But I hope that if you can't trust me enough to tell me what's going on, at least you're seeing a doctor."

"It's my back," she said weakly. "Can I lie down?"

"Of course you can lie down. What do you take me for?"

Ashamed but relieved, she stretched out on the studio bed, looking up at the ceiling, still badly wanting to cry. He probably wouldn't want her to come back after this. He'd find someone else who could do the same work and wasn't sick-crazy.

He came over to her and sat down on the edge of the bed.

"What about your back?" he asked, more softly, now.

"There's nothing wrong with it, really," she began, but then he seemed about to get up and walk away so she said quickly, "I'm not lying to you, I had—when I was a kid I had trouble with it, but it hasn't hurt me in years."

He relaxed. "What trouble did you have with it when you were a child?"

"It's called scoliosis. Do you know what that is?"

"No."

"It's something wrong with the spine. I had an operation for it and it was all taken care of. I see the doctor a couple of times a year just to make sure, and it's perfectly okay now."

"Except that you've been in pain for a couple of weeks."

"Only here." It came out without thinking. "I mean," she said quickly, "only when I sit in the same position for a long time. I think I strained it a couple of weeks ago." She cast around in her mind frantically. "I was moving some heavy furniture. In my room. I think I just strained it."

"I think you should see a doctor."

"I just went a couple of months ago." But he was tender now, and her fear was going away. "You don't know how my parents are about . . . if I just tell them something's hurting me they'll have a . . ."

"Then perhaps," he said after a moment, "my wife should have a look at you."

"Oh, no!" She bolted up. "I'll go to the family doctor. I promise." He gently pushed her back on the bed.

"How old were you when all this happened?"

"Eleven, twelve," she said.

"Which?"

"I was eleven when I had the operation."

"How long were you in the hospital?"

She looked at him tearfully. Wanting to lie but afraid to. His wife was a doctor, anyway. He could find out. There was no point to lying.

"A year."

He stared at her. He was obviously shocked. His shock stirred up something buried way down inside her, that sense of her illness as a badge of shame. In knowing that she had been in the hospital for a year, he knew something about her against which little could be balanced. She closed her eyes. A moment later she felt his cool hand on her forehead, stroking it softly, brushing back the wispy hairs. She wanted to open her eyes and look at him but she was afraid if she did he would take away his hand so she kept them closed. She held her breath as he bent over her, kissed her forehead, her eyes, her nose, her mouth. She couldn't believe how tender he was being with her. Not at all as though he'd been repelled by her confession—almost the opposite.

"Move over," he whispered.

Her eyes still closed she made room for him

on the bed and he lay down beside her, on his side, stroking her hair, kissing her cheek.

"Poor little fishie," he murmured softly.

She opened her eyes and turned on her side to face him.

"Why did you call me that?"

"I don't know. Do you mind it?"

"No." Because he had sounded as though he loved her when he said it.

"Then it doesn't matter."

She smiled.

"Such a sad smile you have, Theresa."

She stopped smiling.

"And such beautiful green eyes. Or are they beautiful gray eyes?"

She shrugged. Their faces were so close—if only he would really kiss her. She moved toward him just a tiny bit. The room was very quiet; there were sounds from the other side of the wall but no crying. Maybe a radio was on.

"Were you in a great deal of pain?" he asked.

It took her a moment to realize that he was asking her about the operation.

"I don't remember," she said. "The only thing I remember is the scar itching afterward. The whole thing, itching." The plaster cast. She'd gotten some kind of rash from it.

"Do you still have the scar?"

"A little, I guess."

"Let me see it."

She was dumbfounded. At first she thought he

must be joking, but then she saw that he was perfectly serious. She didn't know what to do.

"It's just down my back."

He nodded. He was waiting.

She was wearing a navy cotton shirtdress. (Katherine was trying to get her to wear brighter colors; Katherine said she dressed as though she were still going to Catholic school.) She could turn over and just pull it up from the bottom but somehow that image . . . of herself, with her back to him, pulling up her dress over her cotton pants and . . . she couldn't do it that way. She would have to take off the dress. Or at least open it and partly take it off. She began undoing the buttons that ran the length of the front. Her cheeks were burning. She was excited. And ashamed. She looked down at the buttons as she undid them, squeezing them tightly to control the trembling of her hands. She ended up undoing all the buttons because she didn't know what to do when she was finished. Finally she sat up and got her arms out of the sleeves, letting the dress fall in back of her, looking down to see what he saw. Pale, freckled skin. A plain white nylon bra. Katherine wore flowered bikini sets of lingerie. At that moment she wished—ached—to have had lingerie like Katherine's. Without meaning to she looked up at him. And met his eyes, because he was watching her face, not her body. Quickly she turned over and lay face down on the bed, her face buried in her arms. In this position she felt her back again for the first time since she'd stretched out on the bed, but it wasn't unbearable, just a dull ache. She was holding her breath; she forced herself to exhale slowly.

He undid her brassiere although it wasn't necessary to see the scar, which began some inches below it. With one finger he began at the top of the scar and traced a line down it; when he got to her underpants he slowly pulled them down over her buttocks, reaching around her front when necessary to get them down. Then he went back to the beginning of the scar and traced slowly down again all the way. Then he touched the half-moon.

"What's this?"

"It's from the same operation."

He leaned over her and kissed the half-moon, then the long scar, from the bottom to the top. Fondling her buttocks, her back, her shoulders. She wanted desperately to turn over and embrace him but she knew he didn't want her to do this. Now he was doing something else—getting undressed?—she dared not turn to look for fear of displeasing him, and now he was climbing over her, straddling her, half-sitting on her, but without pressure. He wasn't wearing his pants. He was leaning over her, kissing her—Oh, God, Martin, let me turn over, it's hurting me! He was holding her buttocks now, raising them; if she arched her back it didn't hurt as much but that was difficult. Now he was rubbing his penis between her legs, feeling for her opening, and then he was pushing into her, hurting her because she was dry and tight, slowly pushing in anyway until he was all the way in. Hurting. Feeling as though he were piercing some solid wall deep inside—maybe he would come right through her! Just when she thought she would scream out because the pain was unbearable, it lessened, and pleasure began to mingle with it, and then the pain inside disappeared and as the pleasure increased she forgot about her back and it got so good that it was hard not to moan, but she forced herself to hold in all sounds for fear of being heard on the other side of the wall.

He heaved on top of her and then he was still. A moment later he withdrew from her body and lay down beside her on the bed. For a moment she couldn't move—as though he'd cast her into a statue's position and she was doomed to remain there—but then she forced her body to roll over on its side and after a moment she was able to slowly unlock her spine and stretch out. Her brassiere was tangled around her neck and arms and she took it off. She pulled up her pants. She turned to look at him; he was looking at his watch.

"Theresita," he murmured, "when I tell you the time you will not believe me."

Nor did she care. But it was different for him, of course. They both had classes at one and he couldn't just cut his, although she couldn't help wishing that he would, just this once.

It was twelve thirty.

"Quickly, quickly," he said. "We must hie ourselves to yon campus."

Obediently she got out of bed and put on her clothes. She felt sweaty and messy and was about to ask him if she could go to the bathroom when she realized it made no sense for her to have to ask. She took in her comb and after she'd washed herself, she combed her hair without ever actually looking at her face in the mirror. When she came back into the study he'd taken the sheets off the bed; only then did she realize that there must have been blood on them.

The next time she came he asked her if she realized that the following week was the last week of school and that she was now marking the last of the papers. She said that she did. He said that she could come the following week, anyway, because he would be preparing to go to the country and there were things she could help him with. Besides, he wanted to talk to her and he didn't see when else they would have time. It was as though nothing sexual had ever happened between them. She thought he must be holding back because of the work to be done, but when she got there the following Wednesday all he was doing was cleaning out some old file cabinets. He asked about her back and she said it hadn't hurt her since that day. He made her promise that if it hurt her over the summer she would go to a doctor; this was a painful promise to make for the implication was that she would not see him before fall, and she'd vaguely hoped for some kind of reprieve. Perhaps their conversation today would be about how they could meet occasionally during vacation.

He sat on the floor in front of the file, handing her things either for the wastebasket or for another file.

"Now tell me why you called it scoliosis instead of curvature of the spine," he said suddenly.

It was the part of their lovemaking she hadn't thought about since. The way it had begun. His interest in her illness.

"It sounded more medical," she said uneasily. *He'd asked his wife.*

"In other words, you were obfuscating."

She was silent.

"Why don't you trust me?"

"It's not that I don't trust you."

"What is it, then?"

"I don't like to talk about all that," she said.

"Oh, all right." But what he seemed to mean was that she needn't talk about it but he didn't feel like talking about anything else. They worked in silence for perhaps an hour and then she could bear it no longer.

"Why do you want to know about it?"

"Because I want to know about *you*. Because I care about you. Because your telling me is an act of faith."

"Okay, then," she said. "What do you want me to tell you?"

"Was it congenital or did it develop from something else?"

He'd had the question all waiting! He'd known she was going to give in! If it had been possible for her to get angry at him she would have been furious at that moment. As it was she just felt hopeless; she might as well do as he wished and get it over with.

"From something else," she said tonelessly. "I had polio when I was little."

"Are you serious?"

"When I was four. It was a mild case. I got better, it just left . . . a weakness on one side. Nobody noticed when it began to happen . . . it was very slow."

"Didn't your parents pay any attention to you?"

She nodded. "But when it was happening, when you could see it . . . my older brother died and they were very depressed."

"Jesus Christ," he said. "Come over here, Theresa."

She moved over on the floor next to him and he put his arm around her. She rested her head on his shoulder, continuing to talk because she knew that was what he wanted her to do.

"By the time we got to the doctor, it was too

late for just a cast, so they used a cast, but then I had the operation, and then I had to be in the cast again."

He kissed her forehead, rocked her gently with him on the floor.

"It didn't hurt most of the time," she said. "Honestly. Or if it did, I don't remember. I remember I thought God was punishing me for my sins. Later I found out other people had committed some pretty bad sins and nothing like that had happened to them. I suppose that's when I stopped believing in God. Or maybe it was earlier. I don't know." The last time she remembered believing in God was when she'd stood in the wet sand with the tide going out and her father had come looking for her. "When I tell you I don't remember being sick when I was little, I'm not lying to you. I don't remember any of it." *Except that my grandmother stopped coming to the hospital.*

No! She sat up suddenly. She couldn't be remembering—everyone knew she didn't remember anything from that time! She looked at Martin, panic-stricken.

"What, Theresa?"

"My grandmother," she said. Once there'd been someone she really loved, who visited her every day and sang to her in Italian and smoothed the hair from her forehead with hands that were cool and papery. That was her mother's mother, Grandmother Theresa Maria, who was very old and thin and wore long skirts and suddenly one day had stopped coming to the hospital and disappeared forever. And when Theresa had asked where she was they'd told her Grandmother Theresa Maria had gone to live in California. "I can't believe I'm remembering it now," she said. *Because you're leaving me, Martin.* "My grandmother died while I was in the hospital when I was four. For years after that every time a TV announcer said a show was coming to us live from California I'd strain for a glimpse of my grandmother."

Martin smiled, brought her back in the circle of his arms. There was a buzzer sound and she started. There was a system between his wife's office and the various rooms of the apartment, but it had never sounded in his study in all the time that Theresa had been coming. He reached up to the desk, just managing to touch the buzzer that signaled he was there without releasing Theresa.

"*Ja wohl,*" he said.

A calm woman's voice said that there was a crisis, a child had just been brought in who had to be treated and Lulu was nowhere to be found and Jed had to be picked up at school at twelve and could Martin do it before he went up to City? He said that he would.

"Thanks, darling," the woman's voice said, and went off.

"So now you know the truth, Theresa," he said solemnly. "I am a married man."

She giggled. "I knew that all along."

"Ah, you see? And I thought I'd deceived you."

"Married men are much more interesting," she said, trying to remember in which of the paperback novels she regularly devoured she had come across the line. "They've done their learning somewhere else." She kissed his neck.

"Hmm," he said. "A woman of the world. Why haven't you dealt with any of your real life in your essays?"

"I was afraid of shocking you." She giggled again.

"What's gotten you giggly all of a sudden?"

"Don't know," she said. "Maybe you gave me some laughing gas."

"What would you say if I told you that it's almost eleven twenty and I should get ready to pick up my son?"

"I'd say make love to me first." In her sudden giddiness it came out without warning and made her more giddy. Suddenly she got up and moved over so that she was sitting in his lap instead of next to him on the floor. She threw her arms around him and kissed him. He was thrown off balance and went down backward but she continued to cling to him, kissing him, rubbing against him until finally he gave in to her and returned her warmth. She felt quite wild and out of control; she was on a tightrope but he was there with her and if she fell, he would fall too. She unzipped his fly, lying on top of him. He asked what on earth had gotten into her but he was laughing and having a good time, too. She kissed him—his face, his neck. Leaning slightly to one side she took his penis out of his pants and caressed it. He put both his hands under his head and lay absolutely still, watching her. She got off her underpants and straddled him as he'd straddled her last time except that she was sitting on his penis, which felt marvelous, and she moved around on it and bounced up and down on it with almost total abandonment to pleasure, only the tiniest corner of her mind telling her that she was crazy, that she was too far out someplace, that when you were having this much fun something terrible had to happen next, be careful, Theresa, something terrible has to happen but doesn't it feel wonderful—oh, oh, oh—

He came when she could have gone on and on and on.

He opened his eyes. She smiled. He watched her without smiling. Suddenly she became self-conscious. A little frightened. She got off him. He looked at his watch. He stood up, fixed his pants. When he spoke his voice was neutral but she was convinced that he was looking at her with hatred.

"I have to get Jed. Slam the door on your way out, don't bother about locking it."

*   *   *
90

LOOKING FOR MR. GOODBAR

On Friday, the last day she was to see him before vacation, a period she was not certain she would survive, he handed her an envelope and told her it contained her payment for the months that she'd worked for him.

She said that she'd thought he'd forgotten about that, that she had never wanted him to pay her. He said that was silly, her services had been invaluable to him, she had saved him countless hours of tedium and stress, and besides, the money was not only tax deductible but was meaningless to him. Which, of course, was why she didn't want it.

He kissed her cheek and told her she was a lovely girl and he was going to miss her. He said he was expecting her to be a marvelous typist by September and then they would begin work on his masterpiece.

In the envelope was a check for $216; in the bottom left-hand corner of the check, where there was a line for explanation, it read: Cler. Assist. 18wks/6 hrs/wk @$2/hr.

She was unutterably depressed.

She took the check home and hid it in a drawer (she'd never told her parents about him), thinking she would keep the check forever. Then she thought he would be angry with her if she did that, so she spent the first morning of her vacation finding the savings bank nearest his home and opening an account there with his check.

* * *

Brigid got married to Patrick Kelly and began having babies.

Katherine was trying to get pregnant and couldn't. With Brooks's encouragement she was going back to school in the fall. She didn't know just what she wanted to do with her schooling, she was just going to go to NYU and start working to get a B.A.

"Unless you get a B-A-B-Y," Theresa said, meaning it as a casual joke, but Katherine burst into tears and ran out of the room.

"Theresa," her mother said.

"I know you didn't mean it to hurt," said Brooks, on his way to find Katherine and comfort her. "But she's very sensitive on this one, Terry."

So would I be if I'd had an abortion.

"I don't know what's gotten into you, Theresa," her mother said, as though she didn't believe Brooks's statement that Terry had meant no harm. Theresa herself was surprised and upset. Joking didn't come naturally to her, she'd begun doing it for Martin's approval, and it was hard for her to believe that she could hurt anyone when she was being playful. Although certainly Martin could hurt her badly with his jokes. Which was different. There was always a heavy element of sarcasm in his humor.

She looked at her father to see if he was angry, too, but he was absorbed in the baseball game. Or pretending to be. Sometimes she thought that the TV wasn't so much an escape as a filter through which he saw and heard everything but was kept from being affected by it too much. Like the beer that went with it. She wanted to run to him and ask if he was angry with her, but of course she didn't; she just glared at her mother and said that Katherine could take a joke better than *she* could. Usually.

Katherine and Brooks were seldom around, anyway. They'd rented a house at someplace called Fire Island and were spending most of the summer out there, except that Brooks came into Manhattan three or four days a week to work. They kept inviting Theresa out there to visit but aside from the fact that she hated the beach, her jobs and her typing class occupied her five days a week. The typing class was from six to seven thirty in the evening and she was still baby-sitting from eight on for two of her regular families— the two that had typewriters. She was determined that by the time of Martin's return she would be a breathtakingly rapid and accurate typist. She was already by far the best in her class.

In the four years that she was going to know him he would change and she would change, but their relationship would never change at all.

He would be pleased that she had become a good typist.

He would be lavish in his praise of her work and her intelligence. He would insist that if she were going to teach at all she must aim for university teaching. (It was the only way she would ever defy him. She kept her education courses down to a bare minimum but was bound and determined to teach young children, no matter what else she might also choose to do.)

When she was ill or unhappy he would be tender and sympathetic.

When they made love he would become hostile.

In the period after Kennedy's assassination she needed to see more of him and instead she saw less, because his family also needed him more. Unexpectedly she found herself drawn into a circle consisting of Carol and Rhoda and Jules, whom she never saw in classes any more but ran across in the cafeteria on the day of the assassination. (She'd gone there because she was afraid to get onto the subway and go home.) She ended up traveling uptown with Jules, the only one of the three who lived in the Bronx. (Carol and Rhoda lived on West End Avenue; she was jealous of their proximity to Martin.) Jules was bright, not a little pompous but funny and fun to be with, and she was surprised and irritated when he asked her to go out with him after a few weeks. She felt he had spoiled something pleasant. She told him she couldn't and he asked if she was having an affair with Martin Engle. She told him to drop dead and he snorted and said, "That's an intelligent answer."

* * *

That year the Engles rented their house in Connecticut to year-round tenants and took a beach house at Fire Island for the summer. Yes, she'd heard of Fire Island; her sister went there. As soon as it was out she was sorry.

"Your sister?"

She nodded.

"Theresa, I have known you for two years and you have never mentioned a sister."

"I have two."

He laughed. "Are you sure that's all?"

"They don't live at home," she said. "They're both married. I hardly ever see them." Brigid had just had her first baby in April. She saw more of Brigid now than she ever had, for the new baby, Kimberley, was adorable, and she loved her.

He asked how old her sisters were and she told him. He asked their names, which she refused to tell him. He asked why she didn't want to tell him and she told him, truthfully, that she didn't know. He asked where her older sister went on Fire Island and she told him, untruthfully, that she'd forgotten. The Engles would be going to Seaview; did that sound familiar? No, it didn't. (Katherine and Brooks had gone to Ocean Beach and were going back there this year.)

When he returned in September he was different, although at first she didn't understand why. He was no longer interested in working on the manuscript they had slaved over months before;

he said they could take their full professorship and stick it. There were more important things in life than professorships, and if he'd ever had any interest at all in the Jewish-Canadian-Socialist-intellectual circle in Montreal in the early twentieth century, he didn't have it any longer. As a matter of fact, what he was considering doing was the lyrics for a musical show. He'd met a very interesting guy out there, a composer, who said that what Broadway needed was a few decent lyricists, and an idea for a musical had immediately popped into his head. He had always smoked a pipe but now he smoked what he called his "home-rolled" and between that and a few articles in copies of the *Village Voice* that Rhoda was always carrying around, Theresa finally realized that Martin Engle was smoking marijuana.

"You must think I'm pretty dumb," she said to Martin, the first time she saw him after that. "Do you think I haven't known all along what you're smoking?"

He smiled. He had grown more consistently benevolent with her. Less likely to be irritated if things weren't exactly right. He offered her a drag and she refused; Rhoda had described the experience—the colors, the dreaminess, the pictures, the not caring—in a way that made Theresa think of going under ether, of losing consciousness against her will, which terrified her.

"Why don't you want to share with me, Theresa?" he asked. She was sitting in the big chair;

he was at the desk but he'd just been sitting there, staring.

"It's not that I don't want to share with you," she said. "It's that I have no interest in trying it at all with anyone."

"It's marvelous for sex," he said. "You might even have an orgasm."

She looked at him helplessly. She'd seen the word once or twice but she really didn't know what it meant; nor had she known she was lacking something. She'd thought the only thing wrong with their sex life was that he made love to her so infrequently. Although lately he had shown a little more inclination to let her lead him into sex. If he was just sitting at his desk, smoking or staring, and she hugged him, or teased him, or sat on his lap, he would come back to the bed with her. But she'd begun to feel that there was something wrong with this. She was *begging*. She grew self-conscious and couldn't summon the abandon she'd once had in seducing him. She would sit in the chair, or sometimes even stretch out on the studio bed in what she hoped was a seductive position, but he would ignore her. Maybe the trouble with her was that she didn't have orgasms. Whatever they were.

ORGASM (F. orgasme, fr. Gr. orgasmos) Physiol. Eager or immoderate excitement or action; esp. the culmination of coition.— orgastic, adj.

The next time she saw him she took a couple of drags on his joint, coughing and choking. He got her water, laughing. She took a couple more drags, went over to the studio bed and went to sleep. When she woke up he was grinning down at her, telling her it was time to go to school. He didn't offer it to her again.

Katherine admitted, when Theresa asked, that she and Brooks used it all the time, that she'd first had it as an airline stewardess. She'd even had acid a couple of times—Theresa would never breathe a word of this would she? No, of course Theresa wouldn't. To whom would she breathe it?

By a year later everyone who wasn't totally involved in conspiracy theories of the assassination (Jules belonged to a group that met two afternoons a week to discuss them) was talking about grass and acid. She and Martin never made love any more. He got calls all the time but not on the intercom. Katherine and Brooks were renovating a brownstone on St. Marks Place and Brigid was pregnant with her second baby.

In a month she would graduate. Martin had never said a word to her about what would happen when she graduated after a conversation the previous fall in which he'd shouted that she would be just throwing away her mind if she went into public school teaching. She knew he was going back to Fire Island this summer, that he would have the children with him, that his wife was planning to be there less than she had the previous summer. He would have a mother's helper living there with him. For a couple of weeks she had been trying to broach to him the subject of hiring her to be the mother's helper. Then she wouldn't have to once again wait out the summer to see him. Not that she could fool herself any longer that he minded their separations. But with her graduation it was going to be so much more difficult to see him; she might have to work for him in the evening. How would he feel about that? She knew relatively little of what his life was like. She knew other girls pursued him; yet after four years she was still here with him. His wife was still there; he had never said anything about her except that she was perfect; yet once when Theresa had asked him after sex why he was angry with her, he'd said he always disliked women after fucking them. She'd blanched because she had never thought of what they did as just fucking. Now she wondered if he fucked his wife at all, and if so, whether he disliked her afterward.

She had learned to use—imitate—a certain ironic tone in bringing up difficult questions. It wore off if he challenged her, yet with other people she could maintain it consistently; in some of her classes now, particularly her Ed classes, she was thought to be a somewhat sophisticated and terribly ironic person.

Now, throwing her legs over the sides of the

chair, curling a lock of her hair around one finger and looking at him with a wry and totally artificial smile, she drawled, "I have an idea. How would you like to have a very intelligent, literate mother's helper who can type this summer?"

"It sounds like an abominable idea," he drawled back. "Why do you ask?"

Tears came to her eyes and she couldn't answer him for fear of crying outright.

She got up, thinking she would just go to the bathroom and cry and wait until it didn't show any more that she'd been crying. But he caught her wrist as she went past him toward the door and pulled her toward him. Making her sit down on his lap. He put down his pipe. (He didn't smoke grass in the morning any more, claiming that it interfered with his work.)

"What is it, Theresita?" he asked gently. "Have you been seeing yourself as my mother's helper—father's helper, we should say?"

She nodded, looking down at the buttons on his shirt.

"Scrubbing the floors, emptying out the ashes?"

"Very funny."

"Cooking the meals? Spending endless hours with my children on the beach, which you hate?"

"I don't even know if I really hate it," she said. "I never go there so how can I know?"

"July second of this year wouldn't be a very good time to find out. Aside from anything else, the sun out there is pretty brutal."

"If you were there," she said, still not looking at him, "I would like it."

"You are very sweet, Theresa," he said. "But I would be doing you a disservice if I let you do it."

She got up but he came with her, his arms around her, push-walking her gently to the bed and down onto it. Then he made love to her, tenderly, for the first time in so long that she really couldn't remember just when the last time had been.

"I love you so much, Martin," she said.

"Ah, yes," Martin said. "Love."

It left her uneasy. But now they began spending the May mornings in bed instead of at work, and then giggling like naughty children because she would have to take home papers to get them done in time. Once or twice he told her not to worry about them but she said she wasn't worried, she just wanted to do them. Things were better between them than they'd been in the whole time they'd been together and she didn't understand why she was anxious, unless it was that he never talked about what would happen the following year. She was afraid to disturb this lovely interlude by asking.

Then, as they were leaving the apartment house on the Friday before the last week, a girl with long blond hair walked into the building and made a high sign to Martin, and when she asked who the girl was he said that she was a teen-ager who lived in the building. When she asked what the sign meant he said it meant only two more weeks until they went to Fire Island, that she was their mother's helper for the summer.

"Teen-ager," Theresa said. "She doesn't look any younger than me."

"That may be," he said. "But in point of fact she's barely seventeen."

"I'm too young to be obsolete," she said, quite seriously.

He laughed. "The one thing you will always have me to thank for is developing a sense of humor behind those sad green eyes."

She said nothing but her anxiety had turned into dread. She was approaching, from too great a distance to know as yet where she was heading, the knowledge that her future did not contain him.

On the following Wednesday, the first day of their last week together for the term, she asked him what his plans were for the following year. He said that he had no plans at all for the following year; that he would doubtless continue at CCNY (which of course she hadn't questioned) although he felt rather strongly inclined to join a couple of young friends of his who were going to set up house in Katmandu; that he might do another musical (the first one had been dropped after almost getting financed for off-Broadway); that he would continue exploring his head for new colors; that he might divorce his wife, since all his friends were doing it, just to see how it felt to have that particular peak experience. Except that this would impose upon him a financial burden which would make it necessary for him to finish his manuscript and get his promotion.

He might divorce his wife just for the experience.

"Why are you looking at me like that?"

"Are things really as simple as all that?"

"No, of course not. Half the members of the Department can't stand me; that's why I don't get my promotion."

She was sure he was willfully misunderstanding her.

"Anyway, the manuscript has no particular appeal to me right now. Maybe because it deals with a group of intellectuals whose only medium was words, and I have no great interest in words at the moment. Or perhaps you've noticed."

She had noticed him paying less and less attention to his classes; to his papers; to what she wrote on them. Or rather, she'd seen without noticing. He never even bothered to change anything she'd written now.

"You haven't . . ." She had to word it carefully, however little interest words had for him now. She was stepping in water that looked calm but was rumored to have fatal currents. "What are your plans . . . for me . . . for next year?"

"My plans for you for next year," he said. "Hm. Well, my plans for you next year, love, are that you shall begin teaching, that you shall go forth

103

from the cloistered world of City College, that you shall live a little and learn a little and get high."

Her body acknowledged what he was saying before her mind did. She began trembling.

"What about working for you?"

"You don't want to do that."

"Yes I do."

"Then you're a foolish girl and I haven't taught you as much as I thought I had."

"When will I see you if I don't work for you?"

"Ah, Theresa, you're making this very difficult."

Then it was true. She could no longer conceal from herself what he was saying. She sank back into her seat and stared at him. He was looking at her. His eyes bored a hole in her and the hole was her whole self. She was an empty whole. For a while she had been attached to something else and a hole attached to something else wasn't a hole any more, or at least it didn't feel its emptiness, but now the something was floating away from her and she was going to be empty again.

"What did I do?" she managed to croak out.

"Oh, for Christ's sake, you haven't done anything, love-child, it's just time."

"I don't understand."

"What is there to understand?"

"Why I'm not going to see you any more."

"Theresa," he said. Very kind and patient. She wanted to kiss him. "You know the Bible . . . For everything there is a season"? He began singing softly, "For everything, turn, turn, turn, there is a season, turn, turn, turn, and a time for every purpose under heaven." He paused. "Do you hear what I'm saying, Theresa?" He had never been so kind, now that he was sending her away forever. "You are a lovely girl and we have had a long and good friendship. And now it's time for us both to move on."

"Will you get someone else?" Licking her lips because they were so dry she could barely speak.

"Of course I'll get someone else," he snapped out. Irritably. Then he caught himself. He became kind again. "I always have someone else, Theresa. It's not that I'm replacing you. I'm not even leaving you. You're leaving me. Because it's time."

She was leaving him. She stood up, gathered two or three books and walked out of the apartment. She said goodbye to the elevator man and walked out to Central Park West. The sun was so bright it was nearly blinding.

The sun spilled onto the sidewalk. Burning her. It was eleven o'clock.

She walked up to Central Park West and 110th Street, where the park ended. It was almost eleven thirty. She walked through Harlem to 145th Street. It was twelve fifteen. She was aware of men saying things to her occasionally but they had no reality. She walked across 145th to Convent and then up to 155th Street. It was a little after two. She walked across the 155th Street Bridge, hearing an occasional hoot or whistle but ignoring it, receiving an occasional offer of a lift and automatically refusing. She dropped her books into the water below the bridge. In the Bronx she walked up to the Concourse and started north without particularly thinking. She'd never been right there before but she knew which way she was going. She reached Fordham Road at four thirty and turned into it, heading toward Pelham Parkway. She'd stopped somewhere along the way but she was no longer sure where or for how long.

At eleven o'clock that night she walked through the living room, where her parents were watching the Late Show, failed to answer her mother's query about where she'd been, got into bed with her clothes on and passed immediately into a sleep so deep that at four o'clock the next afternoon her parents got frightened because they couldn't wake her up, and called her doctor.

She woke up as he examined her and stared at him lifelessly. He asked her how she felt. She said she was just tired but she said it in such a dead, zombie-like voice that the doctor was startled and examined her further for some sign of illness. Her feet were badly swollen.

"I walked home from school," she said. It was an automatic lie; she'd always said she was at school when she was with Him.

Her mother gasped. "What for, Theresa?"

"I felt like it," Theresa replied, and closed her

eyes again. When she opened them it was Monday morning. Both her parents were in the room. Her father was looking at her with such grave concern; her mother had been crying. What for? She stirred and her body ached as though she'd been in one position for a long time. She had a bad taste in her mouth and there was a stale, sour smell that she eventually realized was her own body. If she had felt anything at all it would have been embarrassment at her own bad smell.

Martin. She wouldn't want Martin to change his mind now and come looking for her. She would be mortified if he were to come now.

Her father said, "It's Monday, Theresa."

She understood the significance of what he was saying but it didn't seem to really matter. She'd missed the last couple of days of classes.

"How do you feel?"

"I don't know."

"Should I call the doctor again?"

"No. I'm not sick."

"What happened?"

Everything.

"Nothing."

They stood indecisively at the foot of her bed. Understanding that she wasn't ill, knowing she needed something to be done, not knowing what it was.

She said, "I'll get dressed."

Her father said, "Are you sure you're all right?"

She said, "Yes."

Her father said, "All right, then. Get dressed and we'll see."

She said, "I'll take a bath first."

She waited for them to leave although she was still wearing the clothes she'd gotten into bed with on Friday. A dark-green shirt-dress. (Theresa of the Dark Colors, Martin had called her once, but he hadn't told her to buy other clothes or she would have.) Then she got up, moving slowly but still getting so dizzy that she sank to her knees.

"Theresa?" Her mother's anxious voice, outside the door.

"I'm all right. Go downstairs. I'm going to take a shower."

Slowly she got to her feet, leaning against the dresser until the dizziness had passed. Still very slowly she got her robe from the closet, went into the bathroom, got off her clothes, got into the shower they'd started for her. In the shower she tried to figure out something she could do, someplace she would go, but that turned out to be irrelevant, for when she'd gotten dressed in jeans and a man's shirt and very slowly made her way downstairs, it became obvious to everyone she could barely speak, much less go anyplace.

The sight of food made her ill.

On Tuesday when she still couldn't eat they took her to see the doctor, who again found nothing wrong but said that if this continued for another few days they would put her in the hospital for extensive tests. She knew then that she would have to eat in a few more days because she would never go back to a hospital. She was already ten or twelve pounds below her normal weight and was still losing at the rate of two pounds a day. She was slim for the first time in her life, a fact to which she was totally indifferent. But then she was indifferent to everything. When people talked to her it was as though they were on the other side of a closed window.

On Thursday her mother called Katherine and on Friday Katherine drove up in the little red MG Brooks had bought when they moved from Third Avenue down to St. Marks Place. (When Brooks's children visited them they rented a car large enough for all of them.) Katherine, wearing white bell-bottoms and a black exotic-looking top which everyone a few years later would know was Indian, wore her hair in pigtails and looked like a kid. On most women of her age—Katherine was twenty-eight, for Christ's sake—it would have looked disgusting, but Katherine managed to bring it off.

They had briefly come so close together, the two of them, just before Katherine met Brooks. And then they'd gone their own ways, only to touch, intimate strangers, at times like this. Now they would be close again. They would tell each other secrets the way animals lie down on their backs before each other—You see? I am harmless. I give you this opportunity to hurt me. Then

Katherine would go back to her own life and Theresa would . . . Theresa would stay home. Of course. That was what she always did in the long run. She stayed home.

She'd taken a teaching job near home in preference to one not far from Martin's, even before she knew—or knew that she knew, as she now thought of it. What had been in her mind at the time was to show Martin that she was making no demands on him. That is *she* had thought she could go to him directly after school, that didn't mean *he* had to be thinking the same thing. She could dash down directly on the subway. Or do whatever else he wanted her to do.

From her seat on the front porch she watched Katherine glide up the walk as though it were the aisle of an airplane, then gracefully run up the front steps. Her father was at work; her mother had conveniently disappeared.

"Tessie," Katherine said, startling her slightly because she hadn't heard the name in so long. "My God, you look beautiful! Mom prepared me for anything but this!"

She smiled politely. Thinking how she wished she had told Martin her old name. Thinking that if Martin could see her now she might be able to enjoy the fact that she'd lost almost fifteen pounds in the week since she'd seen him or touched food. (They were making her drink water. If her mother tried to trick her by adding something to the water, she gagged. She was supposed to enter the hospital by Monday if she didn't start eating.)

"It's not just the weight," Katherine said. Katherine had been after her for years to lose weight. "It's your face. You look so peaceful."

In some strange way it was true, of course. If in one brief chat with Martin Engle she'd been robbed of a future, she'd also been robbed of the tightrope she walked toward it.

"What's happening, Tessie?" Katherine asked. "They're so worried about you."

"That's because they're afraid I'm physically ill," she said calmly. "I've told them I'm not ill. I just don't feel like eating."

"When do you think you'll feel like eating?"

"On the day when if I don't start they'll send me to the hospital."

Katherine smiled. "You make it sound so simple."

Are things really as simple as all that?

Theresa shrugged.

"Are you finished with school?" she asked politely.

"Yes," Katherine said.

"Everything went all right?"

"Fine," Katherine said. "I think I'm going to take a Soc major with a Psych minor, but I'm not sure yet."

Theresa nodded.

"You missed your graduation," Katherine said.

"It didn't matter."

111

"You did graduate? Nothing went wrong with school?"

"Nothing went wrong with school."

"Why do you say they're only worried that you're physically ill?" Katherine asked. "I think they care if you're depressed, too."

"Well," Theresa said, "I guess I'm depressed. So I guess they can care."

"Is the doctor giving you something for it?"

"No."

"How come?"

"He doesn't favor pills, and I don't want them, and he was concerned about the effect without food."

"I have twenty different pills right in my bag," Katherine said uncertainly. "If you change your mind."

Theresa was silent.

"I guess," Katherine said, "the truth is, I'm a little hurt. I want to help but I don't know what's wrong and I feel you don't trust me enough to talk to me."

"But I am talking to you."

"But you haven't told me what's wrong."

"You haven't asked me." Not outright. She'd just been sort of fishing around. Never guessing anything to do with a man. None of them would.

"What is it, Theresa?"

"A man."

Katherine sighed. "How could I not have

known? Nobody but men can do that to us, can they?"

There was something at once repellent and seductive about the sentence. Katherine was offering her a haven. Membership in a club. A club where hurt women could lick their wounds together. As though Katherine knew what it was to be hurt; she was the one who did the hurting.

"How long have you known him?"

"Four years."

"Oh, wow," Katherine said. And Theresa couldn't conceal from herself just the faintest hint of pleasure at Katherine's surprise. "You used to say that I was the big liar in the family."

"I never lied," Theresa said quickly. "I just said I was with friends from school. And it was true."

"He was from school?"

"A teacher." She got suddenly irrationally concerned that Katherine would be able to find out who it was. "I never had him for anything, but he taught there."

"What happened?" Katherine asked.

"He went back to his wife."

"Mmm," Katherine said. "That's a rough one." Katherine, the stewardess of life, consulting a flight manual.

Not that she hadn't expected it, Theresa found herself adding. Not that she hadn't urged him to forget her and go back to his wife. After all, he had three children who adored him.

"Oh, children," said Katherine, as though saying now she understood, it explained everything.

"I suppose," Theresa said, "you're going to tell Mom and Dad."

"No," Katherine said, "of course not. But you should tell them something. They've been worried sick about you."

"If I start eating again they'll forget all about it."

"What about in the meantime?"

"Tell them it's because I haven't been to church in too long," Theresa said with a grin. If a little life was returning to her it was returning not to her body or soul but to the sardonic imp Martin Engle had found in her mind. "As a matter of fact, I'll go to church with Mom on Sunday and get cured. I'll walk in very slowly—"

"Theresa!" Katherine protested, laughing.

"Why not? I'll walk in very slowly. I'm pretty weak now, anyway. Maybe I'll take Dad's cane from when he had the sprained ankle. And then after the mass I'll throw up the cane and shout, 'I can walk again!' "

Katherine giggled. "It's not all that bad an idea, though," she said after a moment. "I mean, not all that stuff, but you could go to Church and say you felt better and sort of slowly—"

"Why?" Theresa asked. "Why should I?"

"Because if you're not going to tell them the truth, you have to tell them something else."

"Why?"

"Because they're worried about you," Katherine

114

said, obviously puzzled. "Because they love you."

But she didn't believe that, hadn't believed it in years. How could they? How could they not believe it would have been better for her to have died the first time she was ill instead of turning into whom she had. She might get angry at them when she saw the pleasure in their faces when Katherine visited, but she got angry because they were *right*, not because they were wrong. True, Katherine was a hypocrite who never let them see her real self, but after all, weren't they right to prefer that? What was so great about real selves? About the way people really were when you stripped off the pretty faces and hypocritical manners? Once during a TV newscast years ago on a political scandal in the city she'd heard her father say, "They'll be sorry they opened up that can of worms," and the image had stayed with her. The can was a bright, neat-looking can on the outside but the worms were pink and slimy and looked more like intestines, or something else you'd find if you turned yourself inside out, then like the dry gray worms that crawled through the ground. She remembered now how once, just once, a year or so after the operation, maybe less, she'd looked in the mirror at her back and seen the shiny wormlike scar in her back and never looked again for years. Until the day before she'd begun City and met Martin Engle and by then the scar had imbedded itself much more deeply in her. Now it was just a neat seam where someone had opened her up to get her straightened out.

"I don't think there's much love lost between us," she said. "I just think we sort of accept each other for what we are, now. As soon as I have the money I'll move out."

She had more than seven hundred dollars, of course, from her three years of work with Martin. This year he had paid her by the month.

Katherine sighed. "You're impossible. For years Mother's been telling me when she tries to talk to you, you run. And you won't even sit in the same room with Daddy unless you're eating or the TV's on."

"So what?" That was as much because she knew it was what they wanted as for any other reason.

"So, you don't let them—"

"Listen," Theresa said, with an insincerity so palpable that she couldn't believe Katherine wouldn't see what she was doing. "I'm feeling a little better already, Katherine. I'm really glad we talked."

Katherine was uncertain.

"I really . . . I'll start eating. I'll come out of it. You'll see, as soon as I begin to feel better they'll stop worrying."

The next day she had some pretzels and the following day, dry cereal. Then tuna fish, then peanut-butter sandwiches. But it was a couple of weeks before she could eat meat again.

116

Meanwhile Katherine and Brooks went off to Fire Island for the summer. Katherine wanted Theresa to come with them. At first Theresa refused entirely, but Katherine kept saying she could change her mind at any time. Finally she told Theresa that Brooks's children were going to be there in August and Theresa would really be a big help if she came. She could be like a mother's helper. And if she didn't like it, she could go home any time Brooks went into the city. At first Theresa said she thought not, but then she daydreamed of running into Martin, her new, svelte, peaceful-looking self, and although she didn't believe in the possibilities of the daydream, she said she would maybe try a weekend or two in July with Brooks.

Driving out and ferrying across to the Island turned out to be the best part of the weekends. Brooks was a great talker. Where Martin's conversation had been clever, his conversation a series of feints and jabs, Brooks was fluid and peaceful, his conversation punctuated only by laughter at himself or the world in general.

He was one of those men who'd awakened one day at the age of forty in his home in Scarsdale, turned to look at his wife, a still attractive but very typical Scarsdale wife-mother whose greatest problem in life was getting decent maids, thought about the appointments he had in his law office that day and suddenly said to himself, "Hey!

117

What the hell am I doing here? I'm following someone else's plan for my life!" And a year later, after a lot of bitterness and a lot of anguish over leaving his kids, he'd had a separation and then a divorce. He'd had absolutely no intention of ever getting married again. And then one day on an airplane he'd met this absolutely beautiful girl who had no more interest in marriage than he did. Who didn't even care what he did for a living, for Christ's sake. Who was perfectly happy to see him for dinner, a movie and a good lay without knowing that his father had one of the three biggest Jewish law firms in Boston and he himself was a partner in one of New York's most prestigious firms and had published a law text that was used in half the law schools in the country. Who didn't care if he could even afford the place he was living in.

She didn't have to care, Brooks. If she met you on an airplane doing business, she could take some things for granted.

He had to admit he'd really gone for that, but he still didn't think he'd have gone all the way if he'd never seen the place where Kitty lived.

Kitty. No one had ever called Katherine Kitty before. Theresa wished she had a special name. Not Tessie. Not a baby name.

A *shithouse!* He still laughed when he thought of it. Kitty had kicked out the guy she was living with and two stewardess friends had moved in. The whole place was pretty bad but Kitty's room was unbelievable. He'd never seen anything like it even in his bachelor days (he had to admit he was pretty neat, himself). His ex-wife would have had a hemorrhage. Never mind his ex-wife, the Collier Brothers wouldn't have lived there! Three-month-old take-out Chinese food in the drawers! The only reason the place didn't smell even worse was that she didn't close the drawers and the hot apartment air seemed to be drying the stuff out faster than the bacteria could rot it! He remembered asking her where she kept the thousand-year eggs!

Theresa was fascinated by these glimpses of a Katherine she didn't know, yet resentful of the way Brooks's infatuation with Katherine made him view her as some kind of prize—her failures were her greatest successes! When he talked about her taking eighteen credits her first term because she was so terrified of going back to school that she had to plunge right in, Theresa had to sit on the impulse to say that was just plain idiotic. And what was all this business about Katherine being so scared of school when she was always first or second in her class? Brooks said it was true Kitty was a pretty smart kid, but a Catholic school in the Bronx wasn't NYU. Not that NYU was one big think tank, either, but there wasn't actually a college in the country where Kitty would have to worry about grades if she'd just focus her energy. Concentrate. Do her work.

*   *   *

On the beach they talked politics—the war in Vietnam, mostly—and watched bodies. Theresa was the only one in their group who didn't wear a bikini but then she wasn't really in the group, anyway. She felt like a tourist in a land where everyone was dark and oily and sexy and spoke a language whose words she knew but which, when put together in sentences, had no impact on her. Nor had she experienced any sexual feeling since the loss of Martin. In the evenings they stayed home and smoked grass and played the Beatles and the Rolling Stones and danced (or went to one of the dancing bars). Sometimes they had what they called a party but it was hard to tell those nights from the others. Theresa would sit in the living room where everyone was, but mostly she would stay curled up in one corner with a book, making believe that Martin had found out she was here and even now was looking for her.

Rafe and Marvella, who shared the house with Brooks and Katherine, were, along with them, the hub of the sexual activities—the dancing, whatever was going on. At first Theresa wasn't sure. Both strikingly handsome, with dark hair and deep sunburns, looking like sister and brother, Marvella was a photographer and Rafe an artist. Or so it was said. You couldn't have guessed from anything that happened out here. They smoked all the time and were the only ones in the group who used acid with any regularity. They made Theresa uncomfortable because there was nothing about them that she could latch onto as real. If she'd often had the sense of Katherine as a façade with little solid matter beneath, she knew this wasn't really true, that somewhere beneath the gorgeous groovy surface of her older sister lay a human being with some substance, even if that substance was largely a sense of sin. While Rafe and Marvella seemed to have sprung full-blown from the mind of someone planning the second half of the twentieth century. They were never tense or wound up. They never sat around saying they really ought to be working. They bore no one malice, not even themselves. Their two children, Eamon and Tara, were the darlings of the group. Five and seven respectively, they were almost as cool as their parents, and never bothered anyone. They watched TV during the day when the other kids were on the beach. When Brooks's kids finally came out with them in August it was understood that Eamon and Tara would be their friends, but Brooks's kids always wanted to be out on the beach or making a hut or finding things to sell on a sidewalk stand. They wanted Eamon and Tara to join them but Eamon and Tara would watch them work for a while, then drift back to the house to see what was on TV.

Brooks's children were delightful, too, although they didn't fit with the grownups as easily as Eamon and Tara. But they were quite independent, made friends with other kids on the beach and required little attention. Theresa had only seen them once or twice when they visited their father in New York and of course it had been different there. She was disappointed that they didn't need her more.

When there were parties, if she'd had some wine and someone asked her to dance, she might do it. Otherwise she just read or watched. She refused to smoke. She'd lost the fear since little had happened when she'd smoked with Martin, but there was a great deal of joking about getting turned on by grass and she most definitely didn't want to be turned on. Katherine laughed when she said that, that she didn't want to like sex any more than she did, but it was no joking matter to her; the morning papers weren't into women's sexuality yet and to admit the need when there was no man to fill it seemed to be telling the world that you did forbidden things to yourself to gratify that need.

Katherine and Brooks kept urging her to mingle with a younger crowd, people who weren't married, but she had no desire to do this. She was comfortable where she was, though she wasn't happy. She couldn't even remember how happiness felt.

When she woke up very early one morning on the floor behind the sofa, having fallen asleep during the party the night before while trying to finish a book, and saw four naked bodies lying loosely entwined on the rug in front of the sofa, her first thought was, Oh, so that's what it looks like to be happy—and only later did a variety of other reactions set in.

They were all sound asleep. Katherine was lying in Rafe's arms; Rafe's head was on one of the huge embroidered pillows they kept on the floor. Brooks's head lay not five inches from Rafe's on the pillow, his body going in another direction. Marvella was curled up between them, her head on Brooks's stomach. Not his stomach, really. Her face was touching his pubic hair. Her feet were under Rafe's body.

Tiptoeing out of the room, guilty at having seen them, she went upstairs and got into her own bed. The light was coming through her window and she didn't want to get up again so she buried her head under the blankets, but when she closed her eyes she saw Marvella's face next to Brooks's penis, which jolted her more fully awake than she'd been the whole time until then. The picture drew her so strongly and repelled her so sharply once she got there that the two feelings tossed her between them and she didn't fall asleep again until late morning, when the others had gotten up and were moving around the house.

When she came out to the beach that afternoon Brooks and Marvella were discussing a show some painter they all knew was having at a gallery in Cherry Grove. They were perfectly casual. You'd have thought they were two strangers who'd just met on the sand.

❧❦❧

She was happy in the classroom in a way that she'd never been in her life. She gave and took so much that she came home exhausted at the end of the day but she didn't nap because if she slept then, she couldn't fall asleep at night, and it was too depressing to lie in bed awake for hours when everyone else was sleeping. She still thought about Martin a great deal but it was from a greater distance, now. She still dreamed about running into him whenever she was in Manhattan but she could understand now, if only intellectually, that their affair had had to end. She also understood that she had idealized Martin somewhat. He was the first person she'd ever known who talked—who *was*—the way he was, and one of the effects of the summer, although she hadn't realized it until she got home, had been to make her realize that at least *some* of Martin's virtues, his clever way of speaking, his bored sophistication, were not unique. Not that she ever wanted to know anyone else like him. One per lifetime was enough. She didn't believe she could survive another.

She was friendly in a remote, polite way with the women who taught with her. Once in a while she would leave the building for lunch with one of them. Occasionally one would suggest going to a movie or concert, but she never felt like it. (She had lunch every month or two on a Saturday with Carol; Rhoda was working for a publisher and terribly busy. Eventually she realized that the only reason she wanted to see Carol was to stroke her memories of Martin, so she stopped doing that.) If she hadn't allowed herself to be drawn into the dope-colorful rock-loud lives of Katherine and Brooks, that life had left her with a casual disdain for the ones most of the people she knew were living. She baby-sat for Brigid at least once a week.

Her biggest problem in teaching was the knowledge that she would part from her children at the end of the year. She loved them—corny but true, as she said once to Carol—as though they were her own, even the difficult ones. She had chosen first grade because her most exciting school memory was of suddenly being able to look at a page and understand what was on it, and she had that sense of excitement with her children as they began to read. She was authoritative in some ways, loose in others. She led them into long, marvelous discussions stemming from chance questions or remarks they made. Once one of them asked what he could do that his shadow couldn't do and they spent half an hour moving around the classroom in the sunlight to find out and another half an hour discussing the fine points (What could you really do that your shadow only seemed to be doing?). Another time, when they came in all soaked through on a snowy, slushy day, and found her in the front of the room, looking warm and dry, one of them asked her quite seriously if she was waterproof? From this flowed not only a lengthy discussion of who and what was waterproof, but various other experiments with the nature of water and wetness.

Katherine kept urging her to get a place of her own in Manhattan but it wasn't until the middle of her second year of teaching that she began to feel restless enough at home to even consider it. She sent out letters to a large number of schools in Manhattan just to see what would happen. Of the few that answered, one was on the Lower East Side, not far from Katherine and Brooks's brownstone. Katherine urged her to take it but it wasn't until the tenant in the bottom studio apartment of their house gave notice that this became a realistic likelihood. The tenant had been paying a hundred and fifty dollars a month but they would only take a hundred from her. She accepted the job in May and moved to the new apartment at the end of the school year.

In the back on the ground floor were two very domestic homosexuals who had a beautiful garden and cooked *cordon bleu* meals. Katherine and Brooks were on the main floor and the top floor was occupied by what turned out to be two males and one female, although it was hard to tell, for they were less sexually differentiated than the homosexuals downstairs, each having shoulder-length straight blond hair, blue jeans drawn tightly over no rear end to speak of, and that look that was just becoming commonplace on the streets of New York—of having been some-place that made them realize that Earth was a two-bit town.

Katherine wanted to give her a lot of furniture but she wouldn't take any of it except a double bed. She was apprehensive about moving into the same house as Katherine, determined to stave off any attempts to dominate her life. (In her mind this was a temporary move; she was afraid to move out entirely on her own.)

She spent the entire summer decorating her apartment and took enormous pleasure in doing it—in everything from the painting and plaster-ing to the selection of each and every object she acquired.

It was basically one large room with two win-dows looking up to the street. In the back were a pullman kitchen and a small bathroom. She painted the walls yellow and the ceiling sky blue. Then she pasted star decals onto the ceiling in the patterns of Orion and Gemini and Capricorn and the Milky Way. They shone in the dark after you'd left the light on for a while, and at night she lay in bed gazing up at them, as from the grass, enchanted. An imaginary lover lay beside

127

her; they seldom spoke, they just made love or were together.

From a thrift shop on Second Avenue she had a blue velvet pillow. From a pile of discarded furniture on the next block she got a wooden bookcase which she sanded and antiqued so perfectly as to astonish herself. Thus encouraged she got an oak rolltop desk from a store on Third Avenue that was going out of business; it cost only two hundred dollars because it needed to be refinished. She bought a flowered armchair, new, out of the window of Sloane's, because she happened to pass there one day and see the chair and love it. From Grand Street, which she discovered quite accidentally on a long walk one hot summer day when it was nearly deserted, she bought a blue bandanna-printed quilt that was half price because it was a second. It reminded her of one in Martin's study. She bought a white pedestal table and two matching dining chairs.

She delighted in every object, from the blue drapes she made herself because she loved the fabric (she'd never sewn before) to the tiny wooden Swedish and Norwegian animals she got in the Village, to the old-fashioned print of a clownfish with its ornate frame and quaint caption:

One of the greatest enemies of small fish is the sea anemone, which looks like a flower but has long tentacles that are full of poison.

For some reason the sea anemone does not harm the clownfish. When threatened by danger the clownfish swims in among the anemone's tentacles where other fish will be afraid to follow.

"Fantastic," Katherine said when she saw the apartment. "I love it. It's unbelievable what you've done with it!"

She saw very little of them although Katherine was always inviting her up, when they bumped into each other, for a cup of coffee or to share a pizza dinner. Aside from being genuinely busy and wanting to preserve her independence from her sister, being with them wasn't the way it had been before. If Brooks had once been so adoring of Katherine that he annoyed Theresa, he was now irritated by those very qualities in Katherine —her sloppiness, her failure to cook for him— that had once charmed him so. Not that he complained a lot, but he was quiet and withdrawn and sometimes came out of it with a small burst of temper, which made Theresa uneasy. Katherine was less flighty-casual with him, more deferential, yet there was something going on underneath Katherine's deference that contributed to Theresa's unease. She didn't think about it a lot but she avoided them.

Her situation at school was different, too, not

so much with the students (she'd been relieved to discover that she enjoyed the black and Puerto Rican children as much as the others, and she was, as usual, comfortable and confident in the classroom) as with the staff. Where in the Bronx the staff had been almost entirely made up of middle-aged and older Jewish and Irish women who'd gone into teaching when it was the only decent job they could get and who hadn't stopped at any point since to decide whether they actually liked doing it, the staff here was only half composed of women like that. The remainder were young and often enthusiastic, largely white but sometimes black, mostly female, but there were two men, one black and one white, both dreamy-eyed, both bearded. Their mood paralleled hers in a way she hadn't felt before—idealism about the children and their possibilities, combined with a remote, dope-tempered cynicism about the schools, the government, the country.

Theresa had become much more radical in her ideas without ever getting involved with any group. Gradually she was becoming less frightened of black people—maybe because she wanted to so badly but also because she was seeing more of them than she'd ever seen, close up, at any rate. Her new attitudes made it a little easier for her to be with people like the other young teachers because it relieved her of some of that specific social guilt she'd felt, right through her days at City College, over being a secret racist.

Being really no better than her parents in her ideas.

One evening in November Katherine said she felt like talking and invited Theresa to dinner. Theresa went because she hadn't seen them in so long. Katherine poured wine for both of them without asking if Theresa wanted any. Only one small light was on in the living room but the dim light was pleasant; the apartment didn't look quite as bad as in daylight.

"How's school?" Katherine asked. She was very subdued.

"Great," Terry said, but she volunteered no further information. It was very important to her that Katherine not be a part of her life in school.

Katherine said nothing. She looked depressed. She took a sip of wine and spilled it on herself.

"Oh, God," she said, and burst into tears.

"What's wrong?" Theresa asked.

"I'm pregnant." Looking at Theresa, through the tears, as though she were sure Theresa had a whip and was going to use it on her.

A picture flashed into Theresa's mind. Katherine and Brooks asleep on the rug with Rafe and Marvella. Rafe and Marvella had been back there this year, and God only knew who else.

"Mother of God," Theresa said. "It's the same thing you did last time."

Katherine's face was blank. She stopped crying.

"What do you mean?"

"Not knowing who the father was. Or have you been—?"

"I knew you knew," Katherine said matter-of-factly. "Anyway, it's not the same. It's different."

"How come you got so thin if you're pregnant?"

"I can't eat. I throw up."

"Does Rafe know?" she asked after a while.

"Rafe? Why? Oh, you mean . . . It doesn't matter." Avoiding Theresa's eyes. "He doesn't . . . they weren't the only ones."

Of course.

Brooks called to say he was working late with someone on a brief; Katherine told him to bring the someone down because Theresa was there and they could all have dinner together.

"I know the whole thing must be hard for you to understand," she said to Theresa. "I don't even know how to explain it, it's just something that happened. When I was working for Pan Am I knew there was a lot of sex around but I never did it. Slept around a lot, I mean. I was . . . maybe it sounds silly to you but when I had the two boyfriends, the one in L.A. and the one in New York, I was leading the cleanest, most careful life of anyone I knew. I used to get teased because I was like a nice married lady at both ends of the run."

Theresa said nothing.

"Then we got married and for a while everything was fine. Not that it isn't now, but I mean everything was very regular. Normal. We slept together and we were faithful to each other. . . . Anyhow, I don't even know how all this—I mean, I sort of know. Not just that there was more grass around all of a sudden, people talking about it, doing it in the open instead of waiting for the last two or three couples to be left at the party. It was kind of nice, really. I felt like you were in on this really beautiful secret thing. You'd found this way to like your husband, not to be doing anything sneaky but have the extra . . . you know, the stuff that goes away when you're married for a while. It never occurred to me that I'd . . ." She trailed off.

"What never occurred to you?" Terry asked, hearing her own voice and suddenly hating herself for it. The Grand Inquisitor. She knew that if one of her friends from school, Evelyn, say, had been in the same predicament, she'd have been much more sympathetic. It was hard with Katherine, partly because she knew Katherine would always come out of it all right.

"Never mind," Katherine said. "It wasn't true, anyway. I was going to say I didn't think I'd get pregnant because I hadn't in all this time but the truth is . . . when I thought about it at all I thought, well, maybe if I can't get pregnant by Brooks I can by someone else." On the last words she broke into tears again and buried her head in the blankets.

She's a friend, Theresa. Tell yourself she's like a friend.

She went to Katherine and put one arm around her.

"I didn't know it would work," Katherine sobbed, "and I'd feel this way!"

She cried now as though her heart would break. She cried for so long that when she finally stopped and sat up her face was red and swollen and ugly.

A couple of minutes later Brooks and Carter Story were at the door.

"As you can see," Brooks said, gesturing around the apartment, "my wife has been working like a demon to get the place fixed up for us." It was the kind of thing he'd said during the drives to Long Island but there was a cutting edge to it now.

Carter Story was handsome in an almost pretty way. Waspy. Smooth-faced. With fine straight brown hair that fell over one eye. They drank wine and Carter admired Brooks's water pipe and said he hadn't realized that any of the older men in the office smoked and Brooks repeated "older man" with a groan.

Katherine giggled.

Brooks said that as a matter of fact he had some rather fine stuff in the house right now and maybe he should roll some since his wife hadn't in all likelihood even thought about dinner.

Katherine sat huddled in the chair, looking red and puffy and dejected.

"I'll see what I can find," Terry said.

In the kitchen she found crackers and cheese and fruit and brought them into the living room, where the others were smoking. Sitar music was playing. She arranged the food on the coffee table. Carter dragged on the joint and passed it to Theresa. Not wanting to be out of the group, she took one drag and went back to the kitchen for napkins and anything else she could find. When she returned they hadn't touched the food yet but they were still smoking. She sat and dragged again. She felt quite nice. Contented. She hoped they would all sit around and have a nice time and the men would forget about their work.

"Mmm," Katherine said. "This is fantastic grass."

Brooks cut into the cheese, passed it around with the crackers.

"Mmmm," Brooks said. "Fantastic cheese."

"Marvelous," Carter said. "A toast to the chef."

They drank some more wine and smoked. Off in one side of her head she realized that she was getting stoned, but that it was all right. Carter was smiling. In the dim light his fine features might easily have been a girl's, if he'd only had slightly more hair. Katherine's eyes were closed.

Her head rested on the part of the chair where she'd been sitting earlier.

"I have a funny feeling about that brief," Brooks said.

Carter said he was setting his wrist alarm for four hours from now so that if they all got zonked they would wake up then and do it. Theresa giggled.

They smoked some more and ate some more.

"I want a cookie," Katherine said. "Do we have any cookies?"

As though it were someone else's house and that person should go look. Theresa thought that was rather *dear* of Katherine, to treat Theresa so much as though she lived there.

"I'll see," Theresa said. Happily she drifted into the kitchen, found Mallomars, Oreos and lady-fingers and brought them out in her arms . . . like a baby. She sat down again and slowly with great pleasure began arranging the cookies symmetrically on the clear glass of the coffee table. A layer of Oreos at the bottom, then ladyfingers bridging them, then Mallomars stacked delicately on the ladyfingers.

"Mmm, Mallomars," Katherine said, dreamily taking one.

"Mallomars and ladyfingers," Theresa said happily to her friend Katherine. "Mallomars and ladyfingers and orleos." She giggled because she didn't know where that had come from.

"I knew an Oreo once," Brooks said. "In Baltimore. She was a Baltimore Oreo."

Carter chortled. "She couldn't sing," he said, "but she had some whistle."

"She had lousy teeth," Brooks said, grinning widely; they were all grinning. "But *some* fillings."

"They glowed in the dark," Carter said solemnly.

"Mmm," Katherine said, licking the chocolate off the top of her Mallomar. "That's why she had to keep a lid on them."

Brooks guffawed. "That's good, Kitty," he said. The bad feeling between them was gone now, things were the way they'd once been. "That's really good."

"Good kitty," Theresa said. "Good little pussycat. Meow. Me . . . ow."

"Mmm," Brooks said "Good pussy."

"Good pussy," Theresa repeated. "Pussyfingers and Baltimore Oreos."

They all felt so wonderful now. It was wonderful to not only feel wonderful but to be with other people who felt wonderful. To feel wonderful all together. She smiled happily at Carter, who smiled back at her.

"I have an announcement to make," Carter said. "I didn't want to go home tonight. That's why I made everything happen."

He was beaming at them in general but it seemed to Theresa that he was particularly talking to her. He looked even more handsome now that he'd loosened up so. His features were fine and small and his hair was silky and his eyes were very very . . . whatever color they were . . . and his hands looked as though Michelangelo had taken five years to chisel them for his chapel. Now his jacket and tie were off and he faced her across the round table, grinning broadly, and one of his beautiful hands rested on the table and she wanted very badly to touch it.

"You have beautiful hands," she said, surprising herself but not unhappily.

"Dig that, Car," Brooks said. "It's the first nice thing I ever heard her say to a man."

"Here," Carter said. "Take them. They're yours."

He held them across the table and she took them, examining them. Self-conscious but not embarrassed. It was funny but it was all right. At his part of the table Brooks was rolling joints and she was aware of this while being engrossed in Carter's hands. Brooks passed her a new joint which she dragged on, then passed to one of Carter's hands by placing it between his fingers. Carter tapped Katherine's arm to wake her up and give it to her, Katherine dragged on it, ate another Mallomar and went back to sleep. Theresa gently blew the smoke in her lungs onto Carter's hand, then traced it over the fine ridges formed by his veins and tendons.

"Wait a minute," Carter said, "I'm getting jealous of my hand." He moved around the table so that he was closer to her.

"You took the best," Brooks began singing

against the music from the player, "so why not take the rest?"

"Sssh," Theresa said. "The music is sooooo beautiful." The sitar was still playing but now there was another instrument in with it. She could hear them both together and/or separately. Whichever she chose. Either way the music was quite remarkably beautiful.

"Your eyes," Carter said, "are more beautiful than my hands."

Theresa smiled. "If I was a fortune-teller," she said, "I'd tell your fortune from this side. Not your palm."

"Go ahead."

"Hmmmm. It says you're going to be a lawyer when you grow up."

They all laughed as though it were the funniest thing anyone had ever said. Even Katherine smiled in her sleep. Or half-sleep, as it turned out.

"How about me, Tessie?" Katherine asked. "Will I finish school? Will I have lots of babies?"

Babies. Katherine was asking about babies. "I can't tell about babies from hands," she said. "I have to see your feet."

They all laughed again.

She took some ladyfingers and Oreos and began sticking them upright in the spaces between the fingers of Carter's right hand. Then she took them out and put Mallomars in instead, which was what she'd really wanted to do all along.

"Now let us watch the Mallomars melt between Carter's fingers," she said solemnly.

"He's going to be all dirty when he goes home," Brooks said.

"No," Theresa said, "I will lick him clean."

Brooks whistled.

"Like a mother cat," Theresa said.

"Anyway," Carter said, "I just won't go home. Then no one will know that I'm dirty."

Katherine seemed to have gone into a real sleep.

Carter was watching Theresa very seriously. He was really quite beautiful. She wanted to put Mallomars on his eyes and eat them off. She giggled because she had a picture of Carter with chocolate circles around his eyes where the Mallomars had been. He was lying very still on his back now with his arms on his chest. Like a dead person. Except the unpleasant feelings you would normally associate with such a thought were absent. It was a beautiful picture. There were flowers all around. At first they were mostly banks of flowers, roses and gladiolus, but then they stretched out into paths and lanes, hundreds of thousands of different flowers, like an English garden, lush but still geometrical. The flowers moved gently toward her until it was time for the next set. Then they weren't just in the garden but everyplace. Her whole body felt strange and marvelous. She wanted to gather all the flowers into herself. If she opened her eyes they went away but they came back when she closed her eyes again. She could change them into anything she wanted—blobs of color or brightly colored chiffon veils or bouquets at a wedding. Or on a hearse. It wasn't an ugly black hearse, though. It was white and graceful, more like a bird than a car. It stood next to a lake. The lake where the funeral was being held. The lake was very beautiful, with water like in advertising pictures for the Caribbean, crystal-clear green and blue with darkness way down. Without opening her eyes she crawled into the space between the sofa and the coffee table and curled up on her side.

"Hey," Carter whispered into her ear, sending a thrill through her body, "you left me holding the Mallomars."

She turned onto her back and opened her eyes. The hand holding the Mallomars was suspended over her head. She reached up and took out the first Mallomar and ate it; the others she dropped one by one on the table. From far away some-place Brooks would say, "Bang," or "Crash," or "Thud," each time one landed.

"Poor hand," Carter said when she was finished. "Look at you."

"Poor old hand," Theresa echoed. "I knew you when you were young and beautiful." Tenderly she took the hand in hers and began licking the places where the palm met the fingers, then each finger, from the bottom to the tip. Only when she was finished did she let her eyes meet Carter's. He leaned over and kissed her.

He asked, "Do you live far from here?"

She smiled. "Not very far."

He said, "I'll walk you home and I'll wash my hands."

Slowly she got to her feet. Katherine was asleep but Brooks was just off someplace with his eyes wide open. He ignored them. Carter got his jacket and they left.

"Hey," Carter said when they got to the bottom of the stairs, "where's your coat?"

"I didn't wear one," she said.

"You don't get cold," he said. "Are you a mermaid?"

"Yes," she said, "I'm going to swim home. Gurgle gurgle." She led him to her door, which she hadn't even locked.

"I don't believe it," Carter said. "It's too beautiful."

"Welcome," she said, "to my watery cave." She lit a candle because she was afraid the overhead light would ruin their mood.

"I don't believe the length of time this stuff is lasting," Carter said.

She yawned and sat down on the bed. "The sink's in there."

"They're not all that dirty," he said. "You did a pretty good job." He took off his shoes. "How'd you find this place?" he asked.

"They found me," she said.

"Oh," Carter said, "you knew them before."

"In my other life," she said. "They knew me in my other life."

Carter stretched out on the bed and signaled to her to stretch out beside him.

"Tell me about your other life."

"No."

"Why not?"

"If I told you it wouldn't be my other life, it would be my this life."

"Oh, wow."

Her mouth and lips were very dry; she ran her tongue around the inside of her mouth, licked her lips. Carter leaned forward and licked her lips. They kissed. They moved back so that they were against the pillows, in each other's arms. They started to make love, stopped to get undressed, made love with exquisite pleasure. She came, understood that was what had happened to her but not what was important about it. He came and rested in her. She saw the dictionary page with *orgasm* on it in illustrated script. She smiled. They came apart. She got cold and went under the covers. He got under the covers and they made love again and she came again. She drifted into a perfectly peaceful sleep from which she awakened, confused because she didn't know why she was up. Then she became aware of a tiny insistent buzzing noise close by. Over on the desk the candle was burning very low. Carter stirred in his sleep, lifted his arm. It was his wristwatch. She stared at it. He leaned over and kissed her cheek. "Go back to sleep, love."

Obediently she closed her eyes. When she opened them again it was morning.

She never saw him again.

"How's Carter?" she asked Brooks a few days later in what she hoped was a casual way.

Brooks rumpled her hair. "Don't invest anything in that one, love," he said. Love. Everyone called you "love." "He's a straight, married, settled—"

"I know that," she said. "That doesn't mean I don't want to see him again."

"Listen to me, Theresa," Brooks said. "Forget it. Not forget it exactly, but you have to say to yourself, I had a nice night, that night, I got stoned and I spent some time with this nice guy, wish I could remember his name, this suburban Wasp, a nice guy but just passing through. Both of us. We were just passing through."

"You don't seem to understand what I'm saying," she said. "I don't *care* if he's married, if he stays married, I just—"

"No, sweetheart," Brooks said. "*You* don't understand what *I'm* saying. Forget it."

A few nights later Katherine came down to say she was having an abortion.

"Oh, no," Theresa said.

"It doesn't help much when you make such a big deal out of it," Katherine said.

"I'm sorry."

"You don't even know the worst of it," Katherine said forlornly. She was looking ghastly, Theresa realized for the first time. Haggard and pale. Dressed all in black. "I'm in my fourth month. It's much more complicated to do it now than earlier."

"How does Brooks feel?" Theresa asked, unable to cope with this frightening news.

"He doesn't mind one way or the other. He says it's okay with him whatever I decide."

Poor Brooks. She ached for him in this situation, thought it nearly saintly of him to be willing for Katherine to have the baby even if it might not be his. Then she was confused by her own sympathies. In the abstract it was very clear that the man was at least equally responsible, that no man had the right to make a woman have an abortion, that both Brooks and Katherine had been leading the kind of life that . . . yet her sympathies . . . sometimes she felt certain that Katherine had led Brooks into it all. That he would have been quite contented to just lead a normal married life if Katherine had. That . . . anyway, when she thought about Brooks and Katherine, she felt mixed sympathies at best for Katherine, but nothing but love and affection for Brooks.

Katherine went to Puerto Rico for Thanksgiving week. Brooks and Theresa went up to see her parents for Thanksgiving. The explanation was that Katherine was down with what might be flu.

145

It was very pleasant, actually, although a shadow would cross her mind every time she thought of Katherine in Puerto Rico. Brigid and Patrick were there with baby John and Kimberley, who was now fourteen months old and walking. The conversation was mostly by the men and mostly about football until Patrick announced, with a combination of embarrassment and pride, that Brigid was pregnant again. Brigid was flushed with pride, as though in the latter half of the twentieth century she had not only the right but some particularly good reason to be a Catholic baby-making machine. Theresa thought of Katherine in Puerto Rico and for the first time her heart really went out to her sister.

But Katherine looked beautiful when she finally came back the following Sunday. She had a deep tan and she'd gained a little weight and looked not at all the way one would expect someone to look who'd been raised a strict Catholic and just had her second abortion.

She claimed in the next weeks to be feeling absolutely marvelous and to be capable now of buckling down to schoolwork in a way she hadn't been able to for months. She was particularly excited by the psych course she was taking, not because the material was so great, it was all pretty basic stuff and could've been dull, but the teacher was *incredible*. He took, she explained, the best from each of the schools of thought and added a lot on his own. She had pretty well decided she was going to be a psych major. Dr. Chapman had promised her that he would get her into one of his electives the following year. He'd said there was no sense in someone with her intelligence going through a lot of crap courses without a glimpse of the real thing for another year or two. It was so nice, Katherine said, to be appreciated for her *mind* for a change.

Two months later, when the holiday season had passed, Katherine told Theresa that she and Brooks were going to separate.

"Oh, no!" Terry wailed, thinking they had been looking so much more loving lately. They'd all gone to a New Year's party where Katherine and Brooks hadn't wanted to break their midnight kiss when someone was tapping Brooks on the shoulder, like a joke, cutting in on his kiss. "Why? I don't understand. . . . You're doing it," she said after a moment when Katherine didn't answer. "Brooks wouldn't do it."

"Oh, Terry," Katherine sighed. "What difference does it really make?"

"Plenty." She was nearly crying with her anger at Katherine and the pain she felt for Brooks. "He loves you."

"*Loves* me," Katherine said with more than a touch of scorn. "He doesn't even *know* me."

"What does that mean?" Terry demanded.

"It means we don't have very much in common,

Terry. He's a nice man and I'll always be fond of him, but we're into entirely different things."

"Into," Terry repeated. "What does that mean, 'into things'?"

"I don't mean entirely," Katherine said, "I mean, we're both into music and dope and all . . . but who isn't now? But past that . . . Brooks, well, Brooks hasn't really changed at all since I met him, you know, Terry? He's given up Scarsdale and his teased-blonde wife and all but he's still really very suburban. Law and order. The whole thing. Do you know what I'm talking about?"

"No," Terry said bitterly. Katherine had found the most wonderful man in the world and now she was throwing him away. It was ironic that only women who could do things like that got men like Brooks. She was more convinced than ever that she didn't want to get married, but if she had, someone just like him was whom she'd want.

"The psychology thing isn't just a thing, you know," Katherine said.

"The thing isn't a thing," Terry repeated sardonically.

Katherine looked hurt. Good. She deserved it.

"I mean I'm really into—I'm really *involved* with it." She was very earnest. She looked very young and earnest. She was thirty years old already but probably the people in her classes thought she was just one of the kids. "I'm going to stick with it. I love the field and I love the people who're in it."

"What does that mean, you love the people?"

What was in her mind when she asked was that you didn't go into a field because you loved the people, you had to love what you were *doing*. That was the only safe thing because people could change . . . or go away. . . . But Katherine flushed and then Terry realized she'd hit on something.

"I mean I'm really into—I'm really *involved* with it." She was trembling, "that the people in that field think more the way I do. It's a way of looking at people. At life. A way of digesting experience, as Nick says."

"Who's Nick?"

"Nick Chapman. My psych prof." Katherine proceeded with a description of Nick Chapman's qualities as a teacher, a man, a human being, while Theresa thought about Brooks, upstairs, alone. She ached for him. It was very important to her that Brooks know she wasn't on Katherine's side just because she was Katherine's sister, that her sympathies lay *entirely* with him.

"Is Brooks upstairs?" she interrupted Katherine's narrative on the virtues of Dr. Chapman.

Katherine nodded.

"Is he all right?"

Katherine laughed shortly. "I really think you care more about him than about me."

Terry said nothing.

"All right," Katherine said, "I guess I asked for

that, but for God's sake, Theresa . . . from the look on your face someone would think I'd just murdered him."

I feel as if that's what you did.

"It wasn't the kind of marriage you think, Terry. I don't mean we weren't close. We still are, in a way. I'm very fond of Brooks. But the really deep feelings were never there. It wasn't even a marriage like, say, Mom and Dad's, as bad as that is."

This was something new to Theresa, who'd never thought very much about the quality of her parents' marriage but had simply assumed it was what they wanted . . . that it more or less worked for them, if not for her.

"Why is it bad?" she asked in spite of her determination to be silent.

"Because it's, how, how can I . . . the best way I can put it is the way Nick puts it, he said something once about people being bound together by lovelessness . . . isn't that marvelous?"

Theresa shrugged. She didn't know if it was so marvelous or not, especially if it was about her parents by some snotty NYU professor who'd never met them. If there was one thing that had seemed quite clear to her all along it was that her father put up with her mother because he loved her. Katherine was going on and on about negative bonds and friendship and never getting down deep with Brooks but Theresa thought maybe Katherine had no deep to get down to.

"Are you leaving the house?"

"Yes," Katherine said with a sigh.

"Where are you going?"

"If I tell you I'm moving in with Nick you're going to think I'm leaving Brooks for him," Katherine said. "And that's not true. I would have left anyway. I needed to leave."

"But that's where you're going."

Katherine nodded.

She never liked herself when she was with Katherine. Katherine brought out the Witness in her. The Teller of the Truth. The self-righteous little prig she thought at other times she'd left somewhere between St. Francis Xavier and City College. Now Katherine had caught her unawares again, all out of gear with the time and tides. Weeping for Brooks, who after all had not come to her for comfort.

"I can't think of not being Brooks's friend," she said. "He's been like a—not like a father to me, but like a big brother."

"But nobody's asking you not to be Brooks's friend," Katherine said. Her manner had suddenly changed. She was very appealing. The first female priest. "I *want* you to be his friend, he *needs* his friends now. I'm sure your being here will make it easier for him. He *is* upset. I don't like to admit it because it makes me feel evil, but I know it's true, even if I think breaking up is better for him in the long run, too. I don't even think it's the breakup he's so upset about. It's more being left. However bad a marriage is, however much both people know it should end, the one who does it feels better than the other one."

"I guess," Theresa said.

"Anyway," Katherine said, "I really want you to take care of Brooks for me."

That was strange. As though Katherine had ever taken care of him herself. She'd never done a thing in the house. Was he going to need more care now than he had before? What was she proposing exactly? And how had it gotten all turned around? A few minutes ago Katherine had been jealous of Terry's concern for Brooks and now she was urging her to take care of him. She felt unsettled. Robbed of her own impulses, whatever they'd been. She had a headache. She wanted Katherine to go. She wanted to scream. She wanted to run away. She wasn't sure what to do. She needed to get out but she also needed for Katherine not to see that. *What the hell had Katherine done to her?* She felt as though she'd let herself be tied up, put in a trunk and sent to the bottom of the ocean with a vague promise that someone would get her out later.

She said, "I have to get out of here."

Katherine was startled.

"I've been feeling restless all night. It has nothing to do with . . . with all this." If Katherine knew what it was about she might find some way to change her mind. Katherine was a witch. "The kids have been difficult, I understand it's the

February-March Syndrome, they can't wait for spring to come, they're climbing the walls." She laughed. "They knock me out and I come home and fall asleep and then I wake up full of energy and then *I* start climbing the walls."

Katherine laughed, too. "Listen," she said, "let's go out together. I'll buy you a drink."

"A drink? I thought you didn't drink any more."

"We can have wine."

It was a way to get rid of Katherine. They would go out together and have a glass of wine and then she would say again that she was tired or restless and she would slip away.

"Or we could go dancing," Katherine suggested. "We could go to the Dom."

"I'd rather just have a glass of wine."

Corners, an Old-Fashioned Bar, was like frozen orange juice—the real thing, only more so. The floors were tile, the bar and booths a dark wood, maybe mahogany. The lights were green globes suspended from stiff rods in the ceiling and didn't shed enough light to bother anyone, or even enough to see very well. It was all men, she could just see as they sat down at the bar and she looked around, except for two couples. The two couples were in booths and there were six or maybe seven men at the bar.

"Some nights you can't get into this place," Katherine said.

Theresa felt strange being there. However

153

much she might have read in recent years about women in bars, they were still in her mind very much a male preserve, an almost magical kind of place where men went to get away from women. She could remember the bar way down on Morris Park Avenue where Katherine had once long ago been sent to fetch her father because he was needed for some emergency and the line at the bar kept ringing busy when her mother phoned. Much later she had recognized the name when she was passing by the place, and on impulse, peered into it. It was late afternoon and only two men sat at the bar; behind it the bartender wiped glasses and looked at the TV and whistled. There was still daylight coming in but the dim lights were on anyway, as though you couldn't drink in daylight. The dirt that wouldn't show under the dim artificial light was clear now on the dim windows and the tile floor. She ran out as soon as the bartender saw her.

Katherine was talking to two men sitting on her right; now she introduced Theresa as her sister.

"I wish you wouldn't always say I was your sister," she whispered to Katherine. "It makes me sound like I'm not a person aside from that."

"I'm sorry," Katherine said. "Why didn't you ever tell me?"

Terry shrugged. "Because it seemed silly."

"If it's how you feel," Katherine said soothingly, "it's not silly." Whereupon Terry experienced once again that shift of feelings in which guilt over the way she felt about Katherine when Katherine was so *nice* to her overwhelmed whatever else she'd been experiencing at the moment.

Katherine went back to talking to the men. Theresa stared at the bar and sipped at her wine. To her left, a couple of stools down, sat a man who was alone and who she could feel was looking at her. She glanced at him quickly, looked away. He was very big, with a huge head of dark curly hair and a long straggly beard. The jukebox had stopped and after a moment he got up, put a coin in it, came back and sat down next to her.

He said, "Hi."

She said, "Hi."

He said, "My name's Ali," which seemed funny. The only Ali she'd ever heard of was Cassius Clay.

"Terry," she said. She looked to see if he was really looking at Katherine but he didn't seem to be. Maybe he didn't realize they were together.

"I haven't see you around," he said.

"I haven't been here," she said.

"You live around here?" he asked.

"Sort of," she said.

"I don't blame you for not telling me," he said. "You don't know who you're meeting in a bar."

She smiled, shrugged to show that she was really casual, not worried. "I live on St. Marks Place. I'm a teacher."

"No kidding," he said. "What do you teach?"

"Little kids."

155

"Perfect," he said, "that's who I'd want to teach if I was a teacher. They're so pure."

She searched his face for a hint of irony but couldn't find any. Not that it was funny, or untrue, but somehow . . .

"When do you think they lose their purity?" she asked. "I mean, we lose it."

"I dunno," he said. "My daughter . . . let's see . . . Elana is fourteen and she's a beautiful kid but it's been a long time since you could've called her innocent."

His daughter. He didn't look as though he had a daughter. It didn't matter. She'd known after Carter that nothing was going to matter again.

"How many children do you have?" she asked.

"Four," he said.

"You're kidding," she exclaimed, then she was embarrassed. She'd said it as though it mattered when it didn't. Still, there was something about the situation itself, about the bar, the darkness, that lent an intimacy to their conversation that it wouldn't have had elsewhere.

He shook his head. "I was married for sixteen years."

He looked so young, with his beard and his jeans and his bashful expression.

"You don't look it," she told him.

"I know," he said.

Katherine turned and said something to her that she couldn't catch. She shrugged.

"Am I interrupting you all?" he asked.

"No," she said. Then, suddenly, "I feel like getting out of here, anyway."

He looked hurt. "What's the matter?"

"Nothing," she said. "I'm just restless. I didn't really want to come here in the first place, I just wanted to take a walk."

"If you feel like the company," he said hesitantly, "I'll walk with you. I could use the air."

"Okay," she said. She stood up and told Katherine she was going for a walk. Katherine glanced at Ali, smiled, said, "So long." Theresa watched Ali carefully for signs of interest in Katherine but saw none.

They started uptown on Second Avenue. There was something really comfortable about walking with him. Partly it was his size. It made her think of walking with her father when she was very little. Once in a while when she was maybe in the first or second grade, when she'd recovered from the polio and it was good for her to have the exercise, he would take her for a long walk, perhaps on Pelham Parkway, perhaps across Eastchester Road. She would hold his hand. When she looked up what she could mostly see was his blue sleeve and his shoulder and then maybe a bit of hair or chin. It was the only time she ever got to be alone with him without any of the others, and as they left the familiarity of their own block and began to pass strangers on the sidewalk, she often wondered if these people didn't think they were complete as they were. That there was no one else who belonged with them. That she had no sisters and when she went home that night she would cook dinner for her father.

"How did you get the name Ali?" she asked.

"My name is Eli, actually," he said. Again that shy, sheepish smile. "I felt as if I needed a new name for my new life."

It was ingenuous. The kind of thing she would never confess to anyone.

"You mean when you left your family?"

"I don't like to think of it that way," he said. "I think of it as I left my wife."

"Do you see your children?" she asked.

"No," he said. "My wife won't let me."

"That's horrible," she said.

"You think so?" he asked—almost dispassionately. "You don't think it's fair, even if I walked out on her?"

"Absolutely not," she said, remembering Brooks's delight in his children's visits. What would happen to those visits now? "I have a friend who's divorced and no matter how mad his wife was at him she never came between him and his children."

"I need to hear people say things like that," Ali-Eli said. "When I'm really down, like now. I sometimes think I deserve what she's doing. Even though I know she's a lunatic."

It was as though she'd pressed a button; he began talking, his voice relatively expressionless, at first, but his face intent on his story, chapter and verse.

He had been raised in a super-religious Jewish family, Hassidim, he said, a word she'd never heard. His father was a Hassidic rabbi, his older sister was a Hebrew teacher. He'd gone only to Jewish schools, to yeshiva, when he was growing up. He lived in Washington Heights but he didn't know what pizza was until he was fourteen years old.

When he was nineteen he had gone to the rabbi because he was so horny that he could no longer push thoughts of girls out of his head for long enough to do his schoolwork (he was by this time in his third year of a yeshiva college). One month later he was married to the rabbi's daughter and ten months later he was a father.

His life in the following years was one huge miserable rut. He was super-straight, super-responsible, super-serious. He never laughed except with his children. In 1966 he was still going to synagogue faithfully. There was no way that he could have remained part of the life of that community and *not* gone to synagogue.

But the joke of it, the supreme and horrendous joke, was that this girl, this girl whom it was arranged for him to marry because he could no longer handle his own youthful sexuality and there was no other acceptable way for him to release it, this girl had turned out to be the coldest, dryest cunt on the face of the earth!

Terry felt her face flush but he didn't notice. They were almost at Twenty-third Street but he seemed oblivious to how far they were walking. She was fascinated, both by the story and his ability to tell it to her. A *total stranger*.

She *hated* sex, Rachel did. Their sex life was a series of painful disasters which she allowed in spite of her obvious distaste and discomfort in order to fulfill her wifely obligation to him, primarily *to get pregnant!* Sometimes she pulled herself away so fast afterward that part of it missed and went onto the sheets, after which she would make him get up while she changed them.

Get it over with became his attitude as well as hers. Eventually he stopped believing he'd ever been missing something. When all the sex talk started in the early sixties—even before that, when there was talk, say, of Marilyn Monroe or one of the other sex goddesses—he would think to himself, But look what's underneath! A fraud! The Emperor's New Clothes! This beautiful stuff everyone praised while knowing nothing was really there. He'd forgotten what it had felt like to be horny; for a long time his sexual desires were so totally submerged that they were presumed dead. But then . . .

At Thirty-fourth Street, he steered her west across Second and they continued walking.

When had it begun to change? The truth was, it was when his older children began to grow past childhood. He had seen it in his children, that marvelous vitality, that interest in their own bodies. The seductiveness of his daughters when they looked at him, crawled all over him, begged him when their mother wasn't around to let them take a shower with him.

Rachel had quashed every evidence of their sexuality—the boys' even worse than the girls'. There were many incidents, but one he particularly remembered because it had evoked a long-buried childhood memory, except in this case it was his father who'd done it, not his mother. Found little Eli curled up on an old rug in a closet lying on his back, singing a song and playing with his prick. He'd been beaten within an inch of his life. Gerson had been watching TV when Rachel found him doing it and sent him to his room without dinner. The more things changed the more they remained the same. What difference did the punishment make? It was the same message; your body is unclean, don't touch, don't enjoy, it's not *supposed* to feel good.

He knew it was wrong. He knew it. Yet he had to admit, it had taken the sixties to convince him that he was right. He'd been so cut off, so out of it, that he hadn't known what was happening all around him. Outside of his job, of New City. When Elana first asked him what marijuana was he wasn't sure what she was asking about. He'd gone asking around his office and he'd heard a few things. He'd gotten curious. Started reading the

Village Voice on the sly. If Rachel had seen it in the house she would have had a hemorrhage.

At Macy's he turned her left and they started downtown toward the Village.

He began taking Elana into the city once in a while on one pretext or another. The Jewish Museum. Whatever. He would wander around and talk to people. Eventually he met people who invited him to a party and he smoked grass and from there on it was history. He hadn't taken Elana in with him this time. He'd gone home that night with some girl and smoked some grass and then they'd balled and it was a revelation! All those feelings he'd been sitting on, so to speak, had come back, only this time they'd been satisfied. He'd thought he couldn't get anything faintly resembling pleasure except from jacking off in the bathroom.

Terry felt herself grow weak at this. She had never in her entire life heard anyone confess to masturbating, not in all the sex talk in school, not in the casually intimate revelations between Katherine's friends. Not even Martin Engle! Never!

And the girl had liked it, too, Ali said. Amazing! She made noises so he could tell she liked how it felt! Amazing! She was wet inside! Amazing! *Rachel's* insides felt as though they were covered with *skin*. Could Terry imagine how he felt that night?

She said, her voice shaky, that she thought she

could. They passed Twenty-third Street again. She was exhausted but didn't want to tell him so.

When he went home he felt more like the bearer of good news than the guilty husband. Yes, Rachel, there is such a thing as pleasure and we, too, can have it. He was surprised at Rachel's hysteria when he called her to say he'd been detained in the city, and only realized after he'd hung up that he'd never been away from her for a full night before. Before leaving, he talked to Mary Ann about his wife. Mary Ann went to these great therapy groups and thought his wife sounded like she needed groups. He told Mary Ann he didn't think Rachel would go for the idea but he would try anything. First he was going to try just turning her on. He bought an ounce of grass from Mary Ann and she rolled a few to teach him how.

Theresa might not believe this, but he was unprepared for the scene that greeted him when he arrived. Rachel, distraught, hysterical, her hair uncombed, her face haggard and tear-streaked. Both his parents and her parents were there but the children weren't; Gerson and his sister, who didn't have school, had been sent to a neighbor for the morning so as not to be contaminated by events. At first he was amused—he was so high and happy, he wasn't going to let them bring him down.

"Hi, wife," he said cheerfully, kissing her cheek

163

(she shrank from him). "Who're all these nice people?"

They looked like strangers to him. No, not strangers, exactly, but people he remembered from his childhood. They were all looking at him as though he were quite mad, which was funny. He suggested the others go home so he and his wife could talk.

"*Now,*" said Rachel's father, the rabbi, "*now* he wants to talk." As though some step had been taken that was so large and irrevocable as to make conversation superfluous. It was true in a way, of course, but he himself didn't realize it yet.

"Yes," he said, "I do want to talk. To my wife." Not in his wildest, most innocent dreams had he imagined for a moment that he could discuss a new life with his parents or Rachel's.

"So, Eli," said his own father, the rabbi for the defense—or if not the defending rabbi, at least the mediator, since Rachel's father was obviously the prosecutor—"where were you?"

"Why?" Eli asked. "Could you just tell me why this is a matter for the whole family, not just my wife and me?"

"Oh, my God!" Rachel wailed. "Because I'm terrified, that's why! Because you're crazy! *Because you disappeared.*"

They were at Sheridan Square, now. Without a word Theresa sank onto one of the benches. He sat beside her and continued without interruption.

"All right," he said to Rachel. "I'm really sorry

about that. I'm sorry you were worried. I would've called only . . ." Only he hadn't thought of it. He'd actually, *literally,* failed to think of it until morning. "All right, look, I tried to explain on the phone but you were hysterical."

"Hysterical! I thought you were *dead,* God forbid, I thought—"

"I went to a party," he said.

They stared at him as though he'd very casually announced his attendance at an orgy.

"I met some people," he said. "At the Jewish Museum." Feeling a little disappointed in himself. That he'd had to lend his enterprise a little bogus respectability. "Very nice Jewish people. We got into a conversation. They had some marvelous photographs of the Lower East Side in the old days. We got into a conversation and they invited me back to their place to talk."

"So . . . you . . . just . . . went." Rachel's father. Wonderingly. *So you just picked up the ax and hacked your wife to bits.*

"I tried to call you when I got there," he said to Rachel, "but the line was busy. I tried to call two or three times."

"So we'll let that go for the moment," Rachel's father said. "So what were you doing there without your wife? So why did you stay?"

"I stayed because I had too much wine and I fell asleep on the couch."

"Oh, my God!" Rachel moaned.

"Do they know your last name?" his father

asked, as though falling asleep on someone's couch was something they might blackmail you for later. He had to laugh but their expressions made him stop soon enough.

"Never mind that!" Rachel's father thundered. "There's still the crucial question. *Why were you with them in the first place?* How come a respectable man, a *father*, suddenly ups and goes into New York without his family? Something he apparently did before, his wife was too upset to even mention it to her parents until now?"

"I was restless," Eli said.

"Restless!"

Nobody was ever restless! For thousands of years the Jews had wandered from land to land seeking a home and then they found not only Israel but New City! All this to get restless? Restlessness was anti-Semitic!

"Look," he said, "I think you'd better go now so Rachel and I can talk alone."

He didn't want them to be angry but he was willing for them to be. That was very important. It had something to do with the idea of leaving home. He'd always been afraid to make anyone so angry that he would have to leave home. He'd never been absolutely certain there *was* any place but home. Home in the sense of a life. Yorktown Computer, New City, etc. The outside world had no reality for him. Now he had a new strength. He knew what they didn't know, that there were real people and places out there. If he had to he could leave without stepping into a void. Not that he had any idea of leaving.

Something about the way he said it must have conveyed this new strength to the parents because they did leave, with promises to call Rachel in half an hour.

"Do you want to go back to my place for a while?" he asked Theresa suddenly. "Talk? Have a smoke?" He was staying in someone's loft until he could get himself together enough to find his own place. On Greene Street. It was fun. He was doing pottery. "I'll show you my work."

She wanted to go but felt she shouldn't. "I don't think so."

"I promise I won't rape you," he said, smiling his shy, endearing smile—as though he'd just confessed he was a rapist but was promising not to do it to her.

"I didn't think you would," she said. "I'm just . . ."

"There're other people there, if that makes you feel better. I mean, we won't have to see them, they're up in the front, but they're there."

"All right," she agreed. "For a little while."

He put his arm around her as they cut over toward Greene Street.

Knowing everything Theresa knew, he said, she still would not have believed the fear on Rachel's face as the door closed behind them. Sheer terror. The neighborhood ax-murderer was confronting her in her home. He stood there and waited for her to relax a little.

"Rachel," he finally said, "I want you to know that you're the mother of my children and I love you."

He wanted her to know that even if he was becoming a different person, starting a new life, he didn't want to leave her out of it. He wanted her to come along and change, too. *He wanted to turn her on!*

Rachel was staring at him as though he was speaking Sanskrit when they both knew it was only a written language.

"Listen to me, Rachel. I'm not your enemy. I want to share with you the things I've been . . . what's been going on *inside* me. For a long time."

Silence.

"You know we haven't been happy. That's one thing I'm sure you won't dispute."

She wouldn't bother because it was irrelevant. Happiness? Happiness was for the dumb *goyim* who didn't know any better. Suffering is a privilege.

"All right. I'm going on the assumption that this is one thing we agree on, that there's room for improvement. On both sides. It's not your fault or my fault that we've been miserable. It's just true that we have been."

Silence.

"This has bothered me more and more as time goes by. What am I alive for? Just to do the right thing? Just to have children who'll be as unhappy as I am and have just as little idea what it's all about as I do? There's got to be something good somewhere. Am I right, Rachel? . . . All right. Don't answer. But if you want to argue, interrupt me. Interrupt me if I say something you don't like."

Because that was one funny thing. With all her misery, for all that she might be angry or upset, she never yelled at him or complained. She would never, for instance, tell him, "Don't you dare do such and such," or "No, I won't," or whatever—she would only wait until he'd done it and then at the most give him one of those looks that said, "You see? Anyone could've told you how it would turn out."

He proceeded to tell Rachel that from the beginning she must have sensed, as he did, that something was terribly wrong with their lives. Particularly their sex lives. That when they'd felt those first youthful stirrings of desire they'd never anticipated being rushed prematurely—two horny, scared, ignorant kids—into permanent union with a virtual stranger. Not, he hastened to add, that he thought the marriage was a total disaster, they were both basically good people and must have a great deal in common, their wonderful children, for one thing, but . . . and here, he remembered, he had suddenly thought of a joke which he still thought was pretty good . . . but she had to admit, he'd said, that it was pretty weird in the latter half of the twentieth century, belonging to a group that not only made shotgun marriages but did it before the girl even got pregnant!

Theresa laughed both at the joke and at his renewed enjoyment of it.

"You think it's funny, huh?" Ali said, suddenly not laughing any more. "Would you believe," he asked, with relish, "that that joke would cause a grown woman to get whiter than a sheet, tremble violently and shout—except it came out in a whisper because she was choking. 'Get out! You're crazy! Get out before the children come home!' "

He should have known then, of course. He'd told other people this story in the months since he'd left Rachel and they could never understand why he didn't give up immediately and leave. They didn't know what it was like to have every part of your life wrapped up in a neat little parcel in which you were then enclosed. If he got out he would leave everything. He would be leaving not just his children's lives but his own!

It was almost a year before he got the courage to do it. That morning, when she told him to go, he'd asked where he was supposed to go, and she'd said without hesitation, to his mother's, which of course wasn't really leaving at all. In that year they had counseling from the rabbi. Rachel's father. The less said about that the better. He went to various forms of therapy and tried to get her to join him. He went to a psychiatrist in New York, a psychologist in Nyack and a group upstate where you stripped to your underwear and did exercises to get in touch with your feelings. He spent a great deal of time and energy trying to figure out how he could get Rachel high; he felt if he got her past that initial barrier he might be able to make some headway. He considered lacing her orange juice with acid because that would be easier than getting some grass into her, but it didn't seem morally right. Besides, it was powerful stuff, and how did he know what her reaction might be? She might go totally out of her mind and stay there. He was just beginning to realize, anyway, what with the reading he was doing and the people he was talking to, what a disturbed person lay under Rachel's drab, stable exterior. He was afraid of driving her over the borderline. For a while, when he'd given up all hope that the situation between them could improve, he stayed purely out of the fear that she would go berserk or even kill herself if he left. Then one day when he'd been in that phase for maybe three months he'd said to himself, "Wait a minute. She may go crazy or kill herself if I *leave*, but I might do it if I *stay!*"

They'd reached Greene Street, which was dark and ugly and littered with garbage. St. Marks Place had begun to get too crowded for her taste, with kids and other strung-out types, and too dirty, but this was much worse in its stillness. They climbed onto a huge cement platform to enter the building, which had a strange, musty smell. Then he used a key to open a grate in front of the elevator doors which then opened vertically, or which he pulled apart vertically, bringing to mind guillotines and other unpleasant images. The elevator itself wasn't like an elevator but like a huge warehouse room that moved slowly. After what seemed an interminable time they reached the third floor and he again pulled open the doors.

They stepped into a huge room that was almost empty. There was no light on but the wall at the far end didn't go up to the ceiling and there was a dim light from the other side in addition to the light from the street. In one corner was a mattress with a madras spread and some old pillows; in another some unglazed pots were resting on racks. Here and there a newspaper or magazine looked as though it had been flung on the floor.

"Welcome to the palace," he said. "Wait here. I'll make some tea." He went through the door at the far end.

She took off her coat and sat gingerly on the edge of the mattress but then she was cold and put the coat back on. A few minutes later he came back with the tea and sat beside her on the mattress. They sipped in silence for a while. He seemed suddenly shy, maybe because he had handed her his whole life.

She asked him if there was any chance he'd ever get to see his kids. He said he didn't think so and he didn't want to talk about it, it was too painful. She said she was sorry, that she didn't even know why she'd asked. He took out a plastic bag of grass and some papers and began rolling joints on his leg. When he'd rolled two he lighted the first one and offered it to her. She inhaled deeply. He asked her how she felt and she said she felt fine, which was true. She didn't even feel the need for a joint; she was loose with the wine and with having gotten away from Katherine. She inhaled again. She was getting high very fast.

She wondered if he would try to make love to her and if he did, whether she would let him. It was hard to refuse if someone really wanted to. She tried to remember how she had refused someone in the past and then realized that she couldn't remember because she'd never actually done it. This was unsettling; she looked at Ali suspiciously, now that he briefly seemed to hold her fate in his hands.

"What's the matter?" he asked.

"Nothing," she said. "I just . . . who's in there?" Gesturing with her head over the top of the wall.

"The friends I stay with."

"How many?"

"Three," he said. "It's this woman and her two kids, actually. Her husband left and she's letting me stay here."

"Letting you stay here."

He nodded. "She's a really good friend."

Theresa dragged again. "She doesn't care that

I'm here?" Why was she asking? She herself didn't really care if that woman cared.

He shook his head. "She's not that way. She's not at all possessive." He passed her the joint again. "Why don't you lean back against the pillows? You'll be more comfortable."

She looked back at the wall, then at him, and smiled. "I can't," she said. "It's too far away. It's sooooooo far."

"I'll help you." He helped her back and then stretched out beside her and they smoked the second joint, smiling at each other. He asked if she wasn't too warm with her coat on. She asked if he wasn't too cold with his coat off. He said maybe he was and they took off her coat and stretched it over them.

"Now you won't be cold, Ali-Eli," she said.

"Hey," he said, "I like that."

"What do you like, Ali-Eli?"

She felt like the naughty princess in one of her old fantasies. When she closed her eyes she could see a beautiful girl on ice skates twirling around on her blades while twelve handsome men in tuxedos and Norwegian stocking caps chased her gracefully over the ice. She closed her eyes so she could see them better. Ali kissed her.

"Mmm," she said. "They're making figure eights but there are twelve of them so they don't all fit."

"Mmm?" He was massaging her breasts, now lifting her sweater. He was so big and soft and cuddly. Like a teddy bear. Once there'd been a teddy bear at the ice show; now she could see a hundred of him holding a hundred little girls who were her in his arms as he whirled around on the ice. She let Ali undress her, too limp and relaxed and absorbed in her pictures to do more than help. He grunted as he took off his own clothes. He was so big and white. A white whale.

"Moby-Ali-Eli."

He parted her legs and before she knew it he was in her, but it was all right, she was ready. It felt fine. He came very quickly, and that would have been all right, too, except that instead of staying in her and waiting, he rolled off and lay on his back. She got cold and went under the covers. It wasn't comfortable; the sheet was wrinkled up and full of crumbs and you could feel the mattress buttons right through it. Not nice. But not important. She'd have liked him to stay in her for longer but that wasn't important, either. He was really nice. Lovable. A teddy bear. Moby-Ali-Eli-Teddy Bear. She drifted into a sleep full of teddy-bear images and then he was kissing her. In her sleep she turned to him.

"Terry. Wake up."

"Hmm?"

"I want to take you home."

She opened her eyes, disbelieving. The heaviness that was pleasant when you were making love was awful if you wanted to wake up.

"What?"

"I don't want you to go home alone, I'll walk you."

If he was doing something for her why didn't she feel as though he was doing something for her?

"I'm so sleepy," she murmured.

"Mmmm," he said. "You look beautiful when you sleep. A perfect little *shiksa*, fast asleep."

She sort of liked that. She knew the word from Martin but when he used it there had always been a more ironic tinge.

"You want me to get up?"

"It's better. It'd be uncomfortable in the morning."

"Your friend?"

"Mmm."

"I thought she wasn't possessive."

"She isn't. But you know how it is. *I'd* be uncomfortable."

"What time is it?" A delaying action.

"A little after four thirty."

"How come you're wearing glasses?"

"I took out my contact lenses."

Slowly she forced herself to get up and get dressed. He was dressed already. She was cold. They went back through the big empty room and the triple locks and the awful elevator. She felt as though she were running a nightmare in reverse—too fast and light for it to be really scary but quite unpleasant nevertheless. Only the fact that she was still a little high kept it all from being worse. Downstairs and out again. He lifted her down from the cement platform. There was no one else in the streets until they got to Second Avenue, where a few spaced-out kids stood almost motionless on the corner. In a doorway two of them sat huddled together. Homeless. She shuddered. Imagine if you were always having to leave. Out of one doorway into another. Out of . . . she had the beginning of a thought but it eluded her. She felt lucky to have a nice cozy apartment to go to. It was really cold out. As a matter of fact, she was really glad he'd gotten her up. She wouldn't have liked to wake up in that cold ugly loft in the harsh daylight and make conversation with Ali and his friend.

He came in with her and seemed reluctant to leave. She thought maybe he wanted to be asked to stay and that would be nice, getting into the cold bed with someone to put your cold feet against. She told him he was welcome to stay and he said he wanted to but he'd left his contact lenses under the ashtray and if he didn't get to them before the kids woke up he'd be in trouble. She said okay. He took her number and she waited to hear from him for several weeks and then concluded that he wasn't going to call. This bothered her, not in the way that Carter's disappearance had—she was to be deprived of another marvelous time with him—Ali-Eli didn't particularly even turn her on. But he was a nice, big, cuddly, amusing man; surely they could have seen each other once in a while. Had some fun. Nothing serious. Coming to the conclusion that she didn't really care about hearing from him didn't stop her mind working over the experience like a dog at a bone, though. Looking for some new shred of evidence to explain what was wrong with her that he, that Carter and Martin, that anyone could leave her so easily.

When she wasn't thinking about Ali she thought of Brooks and Katherine. Katherine had moved out. She kept trying to bump into Brooks, who never seemed to be at home, thinking she would tell him how she felt, that she considered him a close friend no matter what, but she couldn't find him to tell him. If she tried to go to sleep at a reasonable hour she would lie in bed, her mind bouncing back and forth between Ali and Brooks. If the phone rang she grabbed it eagerly, hoping it was one of them, although it always turned out to be one of the people she was friendly with at school. There was talk of a big strike the following term, largely over the issue of community control. Sides were shaping up already and the older teachers, who with one exception were fervently with the union and against the community, talked in small groups in whispers.

Finally one night as she lay staring up at the ceiling, worrying about Brooks, she heard a door open and footsteps overhead. Impulsively she got out of bed and got into jeans and a sweater. She almost ran out of the apartment without her key but then at the last minue she ran back, combed her hair, got the key and ran upstairs.

Her heart was beating wildly and she was out of breath, so she waited a moment, then knocked at the door. He opened it without asking who was there. Her heart was still pounding furiously. He looked awful—ten years older than when she'd last seen him.

"Hi, Brooks."

"Hi, Theresa," he said casually. "What's doing?"

They were both embarrassed.

"Brooks, I just . . . I wanted to tell you . . ." He'd lost a lot of weight and lines of exhaustion cut deep into his face. His tan sweater hung limply on his frame. She couldn't speak. Finally he asked her if she wanted to come in for a moment. She nodded.

The only light in the room came from the light machine that was mounted on a shelf facing the sofa. In the moving light she could see that the apartment was neater than it had ever been when Katherine was there. In a strange way the neatness made it worse; while it was messy you'd assumed it would look all right if someone would just straighten it out. Now you could see how little concern had been there from the beginning.

"I've been worried about you," she said. And she hadn't even known what he would look like.

Maybe in the back of her mind she'd even thought he would look better because he'd really be better off without Katherine. "I wanted you to know . . ." What had she wanted him to know? ". . . that I still love you like one of my own family." She'd gotten it out.

"That's sweet of you," he said. He was smiling but as though she were talking to him long distance from California. "I really appreciate that. You're a sweet kid."

Kid. That was a strange thing to be calling her. She felt a little put down by it, as though he were saying she'd offered him something less than an adult could give.

She said, "I'm not sweet and I'm not a kid, I just—"

"Don't you be mad at me now," Brooks said.

"I'm not mad, I just . . . I'm almost twenty-five years old. I'm not a kid."

"Anyone who's sweet is a kid," Brooks said. "That's all I meant. Someone who'd never hurt anybody."

It didn't satisfy her but she felt a little relieved.

"Anyway," she said, "please come down and have dinner one night if you feel like it."

"Sure," he said. "Sure I will, Terry."

She turned to go and as she did a motion at the back archway caught her eye and she turned toward it. In the arch, leaning against one side, wearing a big floppy T-shirt and nothing else, was a very small, slim and beautiful girl with shiny black hair that came down to cover her breasts. She might have been eighteen but fourteen was closer. Terry stared at the girl, who was not the least bit uncomfortable, then at Brooks, who looked the same as he had two minutes before. Tired. Not caring.

"I'm sorry," she said, "I didn't know you had someone here." She felt unreal.

"Don't make no never mind," Brooks said with a fake Southern drawl, raising his hands in a gesture that told her not to leave worrying but to leave. Who was she kidding, he was a part of her family?

She said, "So long," and walked out of the apartment, but as soon as he closed the door she began running down the stairs, tripping when she was most of the way down on a loose tread she usually was wary of, falling but barely feeling the hurt. In the apartment her mind, usually so full of a variety of thoughts she'd just as leave weren't racing through, was quite blank. She started to get undressed and then knew there was no way in the world she was going to go to sleep with the two of them over her. Maybe never. Maybe she would move. It wasn't such a bad idea, anyway. St. Marks Place got less and less appealing as the junkies took over and once or twice she'd talked to Evelyn about moving to the West Village, which was still pretty nice. She got her keys and left the apartment, walking up-town on Second.

She needed pretty badly to talk to somebody but it was almost eleven thirty, too late, probably, to call Evelyn. There was an older woman at school she liked and wouldn't have minded being with right now. Her name was Rose and she was middle-aged and Jewish, like most of them, but she was pretty, with long curly gray hair, which she wore in a bun at the back of her neck, and pale pink lipstick. Rose was benevolent in a way that most of them weren't. The other older women, if they weren't talking about the union and fringe benefits and prices, were bragging about their children and grandchildren with an intensity that suggested some undeclared contest whose winner would someday be showered with all the fringe benefits in the world. Rose had no children. She and her husband, who was a lawyer, were very close. A lot of the other women, when they weren't in a contest to see whose was better than whose, were telling stories to prove who had it worse. Whose husband was more demanding. Rose never complained about her husband. Oc-casionally she would tell stories about their two French poodles. And when she asked how you were, it didn't seem to be just an excuse for tell-ing you how *she* was. She seemed to want to know, though not so badly that she would push to find out. Theresa would really love to talk to Rose right now, but Rose would think she was out of her mind if she called out of the blue and said she needed to talk.

She wasn't far from Corners. She would go there, maybe have a glass of wine, maybe . . . except she had no money. She couldn't go in with no money. But as she told herself that, she had a picture of herself lying in bed with the sounds of mattress-pounding and springs creaking over her head. Not that the picture made any sense, the bedroom in Brooks's apartment wasn't even over her room, but the vision had the same force as reality, so that instead of turning around and heading for home she stood stock still outside of Corners, afraid to go in and unable to do anything else.

A man poked his head out of the bar and said, "Hi, honey."

She looked at him without responding.

"What's the matter?" he asked. "Cat got your tongue?"

"Hello," she said.

"Good. Now tell me what's the matter."

"Nothing," she said. "I just—"

"Why don't you come in and have a drink and tell me about it?"

"That's what's the matter," she said. "I felt like having a drink and I just realized I walked out without my money."

"No need for a pretty girl to buy her own drinks," he said. "Come on."

She let him lead her into Corners. The bar was

crowded but someone got up and gave him what must have been his stool, right at the end where the window was. He beckoned her to it and she sat down. He stood close to her. He signaled the bartender, who came over, smiling affably as if he knew both of them.

"What'll you have, hon?"

She asked for a daiquiri without knowing why. She wanted something sweet, that was it.

He wasn't particularly attractive. Not that he was ugly, but there was something a little strange-looking about him. He looked at once very coarse and very smooth. As though he'd once been made of rough granite and his surfaces had been sanded down. He had brown hair and a strong peasant face but his skin was smooth. He was wearing a nice business suit and spoke well and yet the over-all effect was of the foreman of a construction gang, not a businessman. He was on the old side, maybe in his forties.

"So," he said, "you ran out of the house so fast you forgot your money."

She smiled.

"What happened?"

She didn't feel like telling him anything but she couldn't tell him it was none of his business while he was paying for her drink. She shrugged.

"Fight with the boyfriend?"

"Something like that."

"Didn't feel like it, huh?"

She was beginning to feel a certain revulsion

toward him. She sipped her drink, saying nothing.

"Okay. You don't want to talk about it."

"Right."

"Then talk about something else."

It was peremptory; if she was aware that he
was paying for her drink, he was, too.

"I'm a teacher."

"No kidding," he said. "What're you doing in
here?"

"Having a drink," she said. "Remember? I
took a walk and then I—"

"All right, all right." He put up a hand to signal stop. "So you're a teacher."

"What do *you* do?" she asked so he wouldn't
ask where she taught.

"I sell space."

She laughed.

"You think it's funny." His tone was irritable
and yet she was sure he'd deliberately said it that
way for laughs. "That's because you're a hick
little chicken." His manner was at once belligerent
and seductive. Five minutes ago it would have
upset her more but at his signal the bartender
had just brought her another drink and she was
beginning to feel nice.

"I know what it is," she said. "But it sounded
funny, anyway."

"I don't think it's so funny," he said. "Someone who sells space is basically selling nothing."

She didn't respond. She sipped at her drink.

185

She knew she didn't like him at all but she also knew he wasn't bothering her. The daiquiris slid down like soda.

"Don't you think that's sad?" he pressed.

"If you do," she said.

"If *I* do?" He checked her glass to see if she was ready for another one. Not quite. The whole thing was strange. Here was this strange man being nasty and buying her drinks at the same time. "What kind of answer is that? Don't you have any opinions of your own? How're you going to teach young kids if you don't have opinions of your own?"

Another drink.

The strangest thing was that she was feeling very sexy. It couldn't be him; it must be the drinks. She really felt like crawling into bed with someone. She looked at the bartender. That was who she'd really like to get into bed with. The bartender. Or Carter. Or—

Suddenly he began firing questions at her—where did she teach, her hours, her salary, the names of children in her class—and she realized that he was testing her. She giggled and he asked her what was funny now.

"That you don't believe me," she said.

"What's so funny about that?" he asked, but he was responding to her own flirtatiousness. He was a little less belligerent, a little more sexual.

"You know funny things can't be explained,"

she said, her voice soft with suggestion. "You either get them or you don't."

"What you're getting," he said, "is loaded. I think I'd better get you home before you fall to pieces."

That was pretty funny, too. That he was saying it as though taking her home had something to do with her safety.

I'm only doing it for your own good. Honey.

She finished her drink and ate the cherry with slow relish.

"You're so nice," she said, wide-eyed. "You're only doing it for my own good."

"Right," he said, smiling. "I'm only doing it for your own good."

They left Corners and began walking downtown. He said wait a minute, he'd find a cab, but she didn't want to wait. She wanted to walk. He gave in but she knew that he was giving in because he knew that she had already given in. She sang Beatles songs. She sang "Day Tripper" and "I Want to Hold Your Hand" and "Norwegian Wood" and then she began all over again. He put his arm around her because she was shivering in the cold.

At her apartment she fumbled with the keys until finally he took them and opened the door. The light was on as she'd left it when she . . . a hundred years ago.

She smiled flirtatiously. "Thank you for taking me home for my own good."

He closed the door, locked it and took her in his arms. He smelled of beer. He kissed her for a long time. She moved back away from him—toward the bed. He smiled but he looked like a beast of prey. She sat on the edge of the bed and kicked off her shoes and turned off the light. In the darkness she could just see him taking off his jacket, then his tie, then his shoes.

"Well, doctor," she said, giggling, "*now* what are you going to do for my own good?"

"Only what you want, teach," he said. "I'm only going to give you what you want for your own good."

He lay down on top of her. He was heavy but she didn't mind. It didn't matter, any more than it mattered that she didn't like him. His body was there and felt good. They made love. He wasn't tender but he was competent and when they were finished she fell asleep.

When she awakened the luminous clock dial said it was ten to four in the morning. Her head was throbbing. The moment she saw him lying there she knew she had to get him out. Quickly. Before it was light. She couldn't stand the thought of seeing him in the daylight, she *hated* him. She tapped his arm and he didn't respond. She got panicky and shoved him until he woke up.

"What the fu—"

"You've got to go," she said.

"What for?"

"It's almost morning."

"So?"

She searched frantically for a reason. "My boyfriend'll be back."

That woke him up. "Why the fuck didn't you tell me?"

"I don't know," she said. "I was drunk."

He muttered and cursed but he got up and turned on the light and got dressed. She lay huddled under the blanket, her eyes closed, pretending to be asleep until he left. Thank God. When she'd heard the outside door open and close, she got out of bed and double-locked the door. It occurred to her briefly as she did this that she was locking the barn door after the horse was stolen but she felt too rotten to be amused at her own joke. She was horribly thirsty and she took a glass of water and some aspirin. She got back into bed but she couldn't just lie there, she was too miserable. Her thirst was unquenchable and her headache was worse. She got out of bed and took two more aspirin with another glass of water. She felt as though she'd acquiesced in her own rape, a thought which when it hit her struck her so hard that she leaped out of bed and switched on the TV set in one sweeping motion. Something was on that was so old that she didn't know any of the actors or actresses except Claudette Colbert. She got very involved in it and finally she felt herself getting drowsy. In the moment before she fell asleep, as the screen images faded from her eyelids, his face briefly flickered in front of her; she wanted to scream but then it occurred to her that they didn't even know each other's names. In some way this was reassuring. A little while later she fell asleep.

The next morning she awakened knowing, as though it were something she'd been actively thinking about and planning for a long time, that she was going to move.

Evelyn had a beautiful little apartment in an old six-story house on Morton Street which she shared with her boyfriend, a guitarist who traveled with a group, when he was in town. She checked out apartments for Theresa, as did other people in school, particularly in the West Village, where Theresa thought she really wanted to live, but months went by and nothing turned up, and finally she settled for what was called a three-room apartment because it had an eat-in kitchen that was separate from the main room, in a newer apartment house on Sixth Avenue.

She became quite friendly with Evelyn and saw a lot of her when Larry, Evelyn's boyfriend, was out of town. Evelyn seldom talked about Larry and Theresa wondered if Evelyn assumed that *she* had some very real boyfriend who she just happened to not talk about, either. Sometimes Theresa would refer by name to someone she'd picked up and slept with as though he were a real person—"A friend of mine was just saying" —but she was afraid to use the same name too many times because then Evelyn might suggest that they all get together, she and Larry, Theresa and her friend, and then Theresa wouldn't know what to do.

She wrapped around herself the secret of the way she was living, and if the wrap was necessary, and even comforting, it was also constricting, a barrier, because it placed such sharp limits on the areas of her life she could share with Evelyn or anyone.

Actually, when she thought about it at all, she didn't really feel that she *had* a life, one life, that is, belonging to a person, Theresa Dunn. There was a Miss Dunn who taught a bunch of children who adored her ("Oh, that's Miss Dunn," she heard one of her children say once to a parent. "She's one of the kids. A big one.") and there was someone named Terry who whored around in bars when she couldn't sleep at night. But the only thing those two people had in common was the body they inhabited. If one died, the other would never miss her—although she herself, Theresa, the person who thought and felt but had no life, would miss either one.

⋘⧉⋙

In the fall the teachers' union struck against the schools on the issue of community control. The lines were clearly drawn (more so than they would be a couple of years later, when the complexities of the issue had begun to assert themselves): On the picket lines were the older teachers who'd gone into teaching for themselves, who'd struggled into the middle class and weren't going to let any of what they had be taken from them, who might occasionally have some real feeling for education or children but couldn't believe their own interests should follow either or be subordinate for a moment to the question of self-determination for the black and Puerto Rican communities. (Rose was the only one of this older group who wasn't with them and took an inordinate amount of abuse from women she'd been friendly with for years.) Walking through the picket lines every day, feeling closer to each other all the time, and further from those outside, where the young teachers, white, black, one or two Puerto Ricans, who believed that equality and self-determination came before all the other issues, who had struggled into the middle class and were determined that it was not now going to limit them in their sympathies, their perceptions of justice.

After school they would leave the building together for safety (their minds told them they were not in any real danger from the others but the venom, the invective, the threats were frightening) and often, not wanting to be alone, several of them would go to one person's apartment, most often Rose's, on Eighth Street. There they would talk about the children and how they were being affected by the strike, about what they would all do when it was over, and so on. They felt the strength of virtue and respected themselves and each other for what they were doing. One of the people in the group was Tom Lerner, the gentle soul who taught music and was himself a classical guitarist. Sometimes after the larger group broke up, Tom and Evelyn and Theresa would have dinner together, in the neighborhood or down in Chinatown. Once or twice they went to a movie afterward and then Tom and Theresa would drop off Evelyn at her house, then walk up to Theresa's together. At the door to her house they would stand for a while and chat, and it was obvious that Tom wanted her to invite him up, but she never did. There didn't seem to be any point to it. She didn't really go for him; sooner or later it would have to end and then how would they face each other in school?

When the strike was over the group gradually came apart as naturally as it had come together. Tom never joined her and Evelyn when they went in for a Coke after school, and a while later she heard from someone that he'd moved in with a girl.

Her father was operated on for a massive tumor in his intestine. Brigid called to tell her. Brigid was leaving the children with a neighbor and staying at the hospital most of the time with their mother. (Theresa felt a combination of jealousy and relief. Brigid, who, when they were younger, had only wanted a different family, had managed to remain closer to her own than she or even Katherine, now in India with Nick, who'd taken a sabbatical. Brigid had done the right thing, it was that simple. Brigid had gotten married, had babies, stayed in the neighborhood. Brigid had a real life.)

Theresa didn't ask Brigid for any of the details; she wouldn't have even known what to ask. She never asked questions about things like that. She was never sick herself and moved away if the teachers in the lunchroom started discussing their health. She had never been to a doctor in her adult life, including a gynecologist. She used no contraceptives and didn't consider using them; she knew, as surely as she'd ever known anything, that she would not become pregnant.

She went up to see her father two evenings after the day of the operation, finding herself short of breath as she walked the distance from the train station at Westchester Square to the hospital. Realizing as she walked that it wasn't the exercise that was making it hard to breathe, but the fear of entering a hospital for the first time in years and years.

In the lobby, her mother's sisters cried, while upstairs her father's mother sat at the foot of her father's bed, anxious but dry-eyed. Brigid was gone; she would have been there all day and gone home to take care of the children so Patrick could come. Patrick smiled his usual shy, nervous smile. Her mother. Then, as she came further into the room . . .

They hadn't prepared her. Or maybe she hadn't known what to ask. At first she couldn't even see the person lying under the white hospital blankets, she could only see the tubes and the equipment. Tubes stuck into his nostrils, taped onto him. Tube taped to his arm. On one side of the bed a bottle of liquid suspended high up, feeding the tube to his arm. On the other side of the bed a piece of machinery that looked more like part of the space program than anything to do with medicine. And then there he was. Small under the blankets, and terribly pale.

"Daddy."

She was embarrassed. Her throat ached. She never called him Daddy. She called him Dad or avoided calling him anything. She wanted to kiss him but she didn't know whether it would be all right with all the tubes there. She put her hand on his foot. He smiled at her.

"Are you okay?" she asked, and then thought that of all the dumb questions she might have asked that was surely the worst.

"Fine, except they've got me all rigged up here with these silly tubes. I feel like a TV set."

He sounded like himself, thank God. Just a little weaker.

There was a change of people around them. Patrick and her mother left, some of the others came in. She just stood there with her hand on his foot, watching him. Not talking. She wanted desperately to do something—to bring him something he needed, to make him laugh the way Katherine would if she were there. He asked her if things had calmed down again now that the strike was over; she said they had. He had been on the other side, she knew, but he had never tried to persuade her.

She went every night for the week that he was in the hospital and was there when her uncle Sal drove him home on the following Saturday.

"What a shame," her father said to her, smiling, in a moment when he was settled in his room and no one else was there with them, "I had to get sick for my daughter Theresa to get so friendly."

She stared at him. "I always thought," she said, "you didn't care that much. I always knew Katherine was your favorite."

He looked at her as though he didn't know whether to be more grieved or puzzled. She ran out of the room and wasn't alone with him again for the rest of the visit.

The next day, when she walked into the lunchroom, Rose looked at her and said, "Theresa! What's wrong?" and Terry burst into tears. Mortified, she went into the teachers' bathroom but Rose followed her in.

"I feel so ridiculous," Terry moaned through her tears.

"Because you're a human?" Rose asked.

That made her cry more.

"Come," Rose said when she'd finished, "let's go into my room."

Terry shook her head. "Not necessary."

"Nonsense," Rose said. "From the look on your face when I saw you I wanted to take you home right then and there." She led Theresa into her room, the kindergarten, locking the door behind them and pulling the shade across the window. They both sat at one of the small tables. Terry smiled.

"It feels funny, sitting here," she said. She never sat in those chairs except to work with a child.

Rose nodded. "I had a long discussion with them last week about growing up. What it means, and so on. I sat down in one of the chairs, you know, as if I was a kid. Working at the table. Some of them thought it was hysterically funny, they couldn't stop laughing. But a few were really upset by it."

Theresa smiled. "Probably the ones from strict Catholic families."

"So," Rose said after a moment. "Tell me."

"Oh, there's no point," she said. "It's a bunch of things."

"Boyfriend?"

She nodded, wondering why she was lying. "But not just that. My father's been ill."

"Serious?"

"I don't think so. He had a tumor in his intestine but it was removed."

"It wasn't malignant."

"Malignant?" She knew that meant cancer. Nobody had said anything about cancer. She shook her head.

"But it's hard anyway," Rose said. "Right on top of the thing with your boyfriend."

Theresa nodded.

"What you probably need is just to get back out into the world. Into circulation."

Theresa nodded. Rose gave her a tissue and she wiped her eyes and blew her nose.

"There's someone I've been thinking for a long time I'd like you to meet," Rose said.

Theresa stared at her incredulously.

"I'm not kidding," Rose said. "The only reason I haven't said something before is . . . it's usually very hard to approach you, Theresa. I know it's just that you're shy, not unfriendly, but . . . anyway . . ."

She invited Theresa to come to dinner that Friday night. Theresa said she couldn't, she had to go up to the Bronx to see her father, which wasn't particularly true. The idea of being fixed up was humiliating to her. The idea that everyone knew she couldn't find someone on her own. She refused two more times until finally one day Rose asked her to come to dinner without mentioning James Morrisey, as his name was, and she accepted.

He was there anyway, though, and she sat stiff and tongue-tied on the sofa, able only to nod when Morris offered her a whiskey sour, his specialty.

Rose and Morris had no children, but the poodles jumped all over Terry as soon as Morris opened the door. And then she saw him. James Morrisey. Every Irish mother's favorite son. Pink, smooth-faced, well behaved. Hairless. Neat as a pin.

He was shy and his shyness was excruciating to Theresa, who remained stiff with discomfort until well into her second drink.

He was a young lawyer in Morris's office. From the coincidence of their names had sprung the office line. *There go Morris and Morrisey,* which Morris obviously relished. There were a lot of Jewish bits from Morris. Rose brought out chopped liver and Morris said this was Exercise I in teaching the *goyim* how to live. Theresa smiled and Morris said, "Aha, she's not as innocent as she looks!" Morrisey looked as though he was choking but said it was delicious.

Rose took Theresa into the kitchen on some pretext of needing help and then whispered nice things about James to her. He was a wonderful boy. His father had died when he was in his teens but he'd managed to get a full scholarship to Fordham University and worked full time while he went to college, then law school. Two years through law school he'd found the burden more than he could stand and he'd given up school and sold law books for a couple of years. Then in the course of his selling he'd met Morris, who had talked with him, lunched with him, persuaded him to finish school and take the Bar exam. After which Morris had convinced his partners that they needed a little ethnic balance in the firm. James still lived with his mother in the Bronx. It was almost embarrassing to think about.

Theresa loosened up after a couple of whiskey sours; they all did. Still she barely looked at him. Her eyes would flicker past him when they were laughing at one of Morris's jokes, and she would be aware that he, James, was watching her, and her eyes would bounce away.

James Morrisey obviously liked her, which was funny because he didn't appeal to her at all. At eleven thirty she yawned and said she'd better be getting home and James immediately asked if he could take her. She shrugged and said okay. They thanked Rose and Morris, who beamed at them as though they were going for blood tests.

Eighth Street was jammed with people.

"In my neighborhood," James said, "there's nothing open at this hour but the bar."

"I couldn't stand it," she said. "Living out there in the boondocks."

"Did you grow up around here?" he asked.

"No," she said. "Way out in the Bronx. Way past Parkchester, even." Parkchester was where he lived with his mother.

"What made you move here?" he asked.

"It just seemed like . . . My first apartment was in a house my sister and her husband owned. In the East Village. Then when I wanted to move, this seemed like a good place."

James was taking it all in like a tourist. The Saturday nighters from New Jersey; the strung-out kids; the panhandlers. Old winos and young dopers. Two boys with their hair down to their backsides and dark glasses asked if he could spare the fifty-cent toll for the George Washington Bridge; James was about to give it to them because he was amused by the line. She said, "You've got to be kidding." One of them said, "Motherfucker cunt." James changed his mind. He asked if she wouldn't rather take a cab home and she said no, she preferred to walk. As a matter of fact she'd just as leave roam around for a while (partly because she didn't want to ask him in when she got to her house). That was fine with him. They zigzagged around the Village, James stopping to look in all the windows, most particularly the head shops. She felt impatient when he stopped but she knew this was totally unfair and didn't say anything. He was interested in all of it.

Being with him she lost that pleasant feeling it had taken her so long to acquire, of being a native. Of belonging there. On Sixth Avenue they passed a girl wearing jeans and a beautiful diaphanous Indian shirt so sheer that in the light of the street lamp her nipples were clearly visible.

"So what do you think, tourist?" she asked him.

"I think," he said calmly, "that there's less here than meets the eye."

She laughed, not just because it was good but because it was unexpected. Not that she was about to tell him that.

"Oh," she said, "so you're one of these people who can judge everyone right off."

"I beg your pardon," he said. "I thought you asked me right off."

"True," she said, flushing. "But I only asked because you were gaping." Why was she being like this? She didn't even *know* him, he was just this person who didn't interest her particularly.

"Actually," he said, "I've been taxed with being the sort of person who doesn't gape even when he's gaping."

"Who've you been taxed by?" she asked nastily. Not about to give in. "The federal government?"

"More the local one."

"Fordham must be a Jesuit college."

"Peace."

But he didn't mind her quarreling; he was smiling.

202

"This is where I live," she said without warning when they reached her block.

"Do you mind," he asked, "if I have a glass of water before I'm on my way?"

"Of course not," she said.

In the apartment she turned on the light and looked around with dissatisfaction. She'd never made this one as pretty as the other but hadn't thought much about it until now. He'd probably think she was a slob. Well, that was fine. She took off her coat, kicked off her shoes and went to the kitchen sink for the water. When she returned with it he was standing in front of the clownfish picture.

"That's very interesting," he said. "What do you make of it?"

"I don't make anything of it," she said airily. "It's just this print some—it's just this print I picked up." She'd been about to say this print someone gave me but had changed to the truth at the last moment. Why had she to deny its interest, though? He wasn't aggressive; why was she defensive? She went for her cigarettes. None of them smoked, not James or Morris or Rose, and she'd experienced her smoking all night as an act of defiance. She lighted another one now, half expecting him to ask her why she smoked. Instead he asked if he might see her again and she almost asked why.

Instead she shrugged, "I guess."

"Tomorrow night?"

"No."

"Next Saturday?"

She hesitated, not because she couldn't, of course, but because she wasn't sure she wanted to.

"All right," she finally said. "But you'd better call during the week, just to make sure." He agreed that he would call her on Wednesday or Thursday and wrote down her phone number. Then he said goodnight and left.

❧❧❧

She wasn't at all ready for sleep. She started to get undressed but then it seemed ridiculous when the sleepiness from the drinks had worn off and she was feeling strangely high and restless. She had carried a couple of fairly heavy cartons from the supply room to her classroom the day before and been aware since then of feeling a slight strain in her back. She'd forgotten about it but now it seemed to return, making her want to lie down flat while the rest of her craved to keep moving. She took some aspirin, put her coat back on and left the house. She walked over to Fourteenth and then across, sort of thinking she'd go to Corners because she hadn't been there in a while. But then on impulse she walked up Third, stopping in front of a place called Luther's that looked crowded enough to be comfortable. You could walk right in and walk right out, which was important because she'd once again taken only her keys. She stood outside for a moment. Two couples came out, glanced at her without interest and continued on their way. She took a deep breath and went in, pretending to be looking for someone, walking around the bar, then looking at the tables in the back as though she were supposed to find someone she knew. There wasn't anyone of course. Slowly she made her way back past the bar, still looking. Luther's was darker and lusher than Corners, with dark wood and almost everything else red.

"Lookin' for me?"

She smiled before she even saw him because she knew she wouldn't have to go home.

"I don't know," she said. "Who you?"

He was a punk but a cute one. Very Italian, with dark hair and dark eyes. He wasn't much taller than she was but he had broad shoulders and a narrow torso and the air of a kid who'd had to fight for space to grow up.

"Tony Lopanto," he said. "Pleased to meetcha." Cocky-insecure.

She nodded.

"Glass of wine?"

"Are you from the Bronx?"

"No," he said. "Queens. Are you?"

"No," she said. "I never even heard of the Bronx before."

He looked puzzled for a moment but then he laughed.

"Hey, that's pretty good. I dig that."

The bartender brought them their wine.

"What's your name, hon?" He was very tense. His fingers drummed the bar and his body moved to the Rod Stewart song on the jukebox. Serenely she told him that her name was Sonya Irini Katerina Henikoff.

"You're kidding," he said, laughing uncertainly.

"I'm not, as a matter of fact," she said. "But you don't have to call me the whole thing. I just tell it to people because I like to watch them groove on it. My friends call me Sonny."

"You Russian?" he asked.

"No," she said. "Are you?"

"What are you, kidding?" he asked—that puzzled look again, followed by a laugh as he realized that she was. She wasn't a nut, she was kidding.

"You're pretty funny, y'know? I like you."

"Good," she said, finishing the first glass of wine. "I'm glad you like me because only people who like me are allowed to buy me wine and I'm ready for another glass."

He finished his own and signaled for two more.

"You better watch out," he said. "Red wine makes me horny as hell."

"Okay," she said, clinking her glass against his. "I'll watch out."

"Hey," he said, "you're a doll. Did I tell you that already?"

"I don't remember."

"This friend of mine came in with me before," Tony said. "You should've seen the dog he took home."

She was briefly taken aback by his appraisal.

"Don't you like dogs?"

"No, I mean—" He laughed. "Yeah, I get it. Yeah, I like dogs, but this was supposed to be a *girl*. I kept telling him, 'Forget it, pal, pass it up, something better'll turn up.'" He grinned at her with satisfaction. She was silent, feeling a mixture of emotions from attraction to disdain. How old was he? Maybe not much more than twenty, twenty-two or three at the most. She was too young to be an older woman, surely. She was amused. But beyond all these gentle wine-diluted emotions was amazement at her own distance from them. She could see herself—as though she were both Gulliver and one of the Lilliputians— leaving Luther's with this dopy kid, careening home with him, making fun of him, giggling with him, screwing. Suddenly she laughed, but it was a strange laugh that came from somewhere beneath where the wine soothed her. It unsettled her.

"What's so funny now?"

"I don't remember."

"You still on the dogs? You got it into your head I really hate dogs?"

She giggled.

"Let me tell you something sweetheart," he

shouted over the jukebox. "Sonya! Onya! I *love* dogs. The only thing I love better than dogs is horses."

"Horses," she said. "I've heard of them."

"Aw," he said disgustedly, "maybe we should forget this whole conversation. You don't wanna talk to me, you just wanna give me the business."

She became instantly, genuinely contrite. "Tony, Tony, no, love, you're wrong. I'm not making fun of you. No, that's not true. I mean, I'm making fun of both of us. It's that it's my nature —I'm a clownfish!"

He stared at her, sure now that she was crazy.

"I mean, I joke a lot. It's not about you, it's not about anyone. I joke when I'm depressed. It's just what I *do*."

"What're you so depressed about?" he asked, almost willing to go along. You could see him fighting with himself to believe her so he could keep wanting to lay her.

"I don't know," she said. "That's what the joking's for. It makes me forget."

He watched her suspiciously, his desire for conquest making him want to believe she wasn't getting off at his expense. Some tiny unwelcome pin of intelligence pricking him with the knowledge she had to be. Desire won.

He laughed, "The wine don't hurt either."

"No, love," she said. "The wine don't hurt either."

* * *

He turned out to be a delightful, tender and energetic lover, although he had to have music on the whole time, preferably hard rock at top volume. She laughed when he was fucking her in tune to Chicago and said she hadn't known what hard rock really meant until now, but he was totally into the music and the fucking and he ignored her. That was fine.

He didn't come until what seemed like hours had passed, although he would rest inside her when the music was interrupted by the disc jockey's voice. When he finally did come it was more like a loss of energy than a climax; he just collapsed inside her and became so still she thought he was asleep. But when she got uncomfortable and tried to move out from under him he readily rolled over onto his back and apologized for having to stop for a while. She smiled; now she was peering at him in the darkness to see if *he* was kidding. No.

"Do you mind if I turn down the radio a little?" she asked.

"Nah," he said, "you can turn it off altogether."

But a moment later he reached out and turned it back on.

"I'm sleepy," she murmured.

"The radio bother you?" he asked.

"Can you sleep with it on?" she asked.

He laughed shortly. "I don't sleep either way."

"No kidding," she said. "How long have you been not sleeping?"

"What difference does it make?"

"I was just curious."

"Since I was in the Army." Almost sullenly. "I sleep an hour or two in the morning."

"Were you in Vietnam?" she asked.

"Where do you *think* I was? Palm Beach?"

"I'm sorry," she said, "I won't ask any more questions."

"Ah, that's okay," he said. "I shouldn't of jumped on you. Here, c'mere, you wanna feel something?" He took her hand and guided it to his thigh, running her fingers up and down the skin until she became aware of a scattering of small hard fragments right under it. He'd been soaked with sweat before but now his skin was cool and smooth.

"That's shrapnel," he said.

"Why didn't they take it out?"

"They only get the big pieces."

"Does it hurt?"

"No. Stop talking about it."

"Okay." But she went under the covers to kiss his thigh all over where the shrapnel was. His whole body was rigid. She kissed his other thigh, played with his penis, which was getting hard again, kissed the hair all around it until he pulled her up and they made love again.

"You like that, huh?" he said when she moaned.

She was exhausted. She was sure it was close to morning although it was still dark. The music was bad enough but the artificial high of the disc jockey's voice grated on her ears like chalk on a blackboard.

"Listen," she said, "I have to sleep."

"Okay."

She turned off the radio. He got out of bed and began to get dressed.

"Do you *want* to leave?" she asked.

"Might as well," he said. "Catch a little shut-eye. An hour, maybe."

"You don't take very good care of yourself."

"Cut it out," he said. "I'm not a kid."

"Aren't you?"

"No," he said. "I'm twenty-seven. I done my time. I'm no kid." He sat down on the edge of the bed with his shoes.

"You look younger."

"So?"

"Nothing. You're so touchy, all of a sudden."

"I'm always touchy. It just shows more when I'm tired."

"You have a right to be tired."

He glanced at her to make sure she wasn't teasing. Allowed himself a smile when he saw she was flattering him.

"What kind of work do you do?"

He didn't answer. Instead, he stood up, stretched and jogged a little in space as though he were warming up for a match. He took something small from the floor, she couldn't see what it was, and stuck it inside his shoe or his sock.

"You going to walk home?" She was curious to know where he lived. Not that it mattered. She didn't expect to see him again and she wasn't going to let herself care.

He laughed. "To Brooklyn?"

"I guess not."

He said, "Write down your phone number." She wrote it on the pad near the phone, gave him the page. He kissed her on the forehead and headed for the door.

"Don't you want my name, too?"

"I won't forget it," he said. "Sonya, Moanya."

"No, my real one."

"Cunt."

Silence.

"Okay," he said. "Shoot."

"Theresa," she said.

"I should've known," he said.

"Theresa Dunn," she said.

"Irish cunt," he said. "I'll call ya, Irish."

On Monday night he called and they agreed that he would come over around ten thirty Wednesday night, after work. On Wednesday night she was so eager to see him that she could hardly contain herself and ate constantly from the time she came home until eight thirty, when James Morrisey called. When he told her his name she couldn't place it for a moment; she hadn't thought about him since she'd seen him.

212

"Oh," she finally said. "Hi." Wishing Tony were there.

"Are you having a good week?" James asked.

"Oh, yes," she said. "Definitely."

"Good," he said. "So am I." He started telling her about an interesting case he was working on with one of the partners but she was barely listening. Her juices were running; she couldn't wait for Tony, she might jump out of her skin if he didn't come on time. On time! Another hour and a half! How could she bear it? She would listen to James for a while. James was explaining that the lawyer he was working with was a very strong trial lawyer whose weakness was that he couldn't write a brief, which was why he, James, had been called upon. This was his strong point, while he had little trial experience.

"I can't see you as a trial lawyer," she said.

"Why not?" he asked.

"Because I can't see you giving an impassioned plea to a jury," she said, wondering why she was being rotten again.

"You're thinking in stereotypes."

"True."

"That's not fair to me."

"Why should I want to be fair to you?" Waiting for him to hang up on her because she was being such a shit. Half sorry that he must be about to write her off, because he was pretty smart, after all, and he liked her, and how often did she get to go out on a proper date, to dinner, say, and a movie?

"What would you like to do on Saturday night?" he asked after a long pause.

"I don't know," she said. It was funny the way she was measuring herself out. She had to measure her breath into the telephone in order not to give herself away. It had nothing to do with him, anyway.

"Do you have any preference?"

"I can't think about it right now," she said. "My mind's somewhere else."

"All right," he said. "Then I'll just think of what I like and hope it'll be all right with you."

"Okay."

She tried doing school work but couldn't concentrate. She tried reading and then watching TV. She'd wanted to save a bath for the last half hour of waiting but now it seemed the only thing to do was to soak for a while. She'd bought a bottle of red wine but she didn't want to break into it; it occurred to her that she really should keep a bottle of Scotch or something in the house. A drink right now would be nice.

She had to force herself to stay in the tub for an hour, at the end making up a new fantasy in which she and Tony were making love under water in some position that was at once graceful and passionate when Brooks, having missed her friendship since she'd moved, dropped in and

214

was transfixed, not only by the beauty of the scene but by this new view of her.

Later she got into jeans and a sweater and waited for Tony. Ten thirty came, and then eleven and she gradually decided he wasn't coming. The tension left and its space was filled with a quiet misery, which was maybe just as well because when he finally came she was reasonably relaxed.

"Hi, hon," he said. "Sorry I'm late."

"It doesn't matter," she said. "I fell asleep."

He had a proprietary air that she got a kick out of. He dropped his leather jacket on her desk as though he owned both the jacket and the desk, bussed her cheek loudly, flopped down on the bed, pulled off his boots (the object that fell out was a switchblade knife, she could see now) and stretched out.

"Boy, I'm bushed." But he began drumming on his chest with his fingers. He reached back and turned on the radio, waited to get the feel of the song that was on, and then began moving his arms, and his legs as well, with the music.

"Want some wine?"

"Ah, I dunno. What else you got?"

"Nothing much. Orange juice."

"No beer, huh?"

"No." She was about to say that one of them could run out and get some but he didn't really seem all that interested in the beer.

"Uh . . . okay. Wine."

"Jesus," he said, when she'd brought the wine

and glasses and he'd propped all the pillows under himself, "what a day."

"What happened?"

"It didn't stop. There was no one or two rush hours, it just went on and on all day."

"What went on all day?"

The garage. He worked in a parking garage in midtown. She had to know that. She didn't? Crazy. He worked in a parking garage while he was waiting to get back his license as a horse trainer that he'd lost for some dumb reason. It would take him three years to get it back. That was the only thing in the world he really wanted to do. He must've told her.

"Anyhow, this really great-looking chick pulls in with a white Continental. In front of her is this beat-up black Volks that gets all uptight because every guy in the lot is trying to get to the Continental first. Meanwhile there's this red Chevy Nova trying to." He continued with an incredible elaborate description, by player and position, reminding her for all the world of her father and Patrick going over the baseball game in their ritual fashion. As soon as he finished the description he began his finger tapping again.

"How come you lost your license?"

"How come you ask so many questions?"

"Sorry. Ignore the question."

"Dope."

For a moment she thought he was still calling

her names; then she realized he was talking about drugs.

"What kind of dope were you taking?"

"Boy," he said, "you're so dumb you're almost lovable. C'm'ere."

She put her wine on the floor and moved to him so that his arm was cradling her. He made her get up to give him more wine a second later, then she settled back.

"Buh, buh buh buh," he said to the music. He didn't seem at all interested in making love to her but that was all right, she was contented to just lie there for now, and wait. Except that she was very excited.

"Here," he said, "I'll show you something." He held out his arm, the wine tilting precariously in the glass. "Roll up my sleeve." She rolled it up and he showed her his tracks, which she would never have seen if she hadn't understood what he meant to show her.

"Come on, Tony," she said, "I'm not *that* dumb." But she was enjoying the role. Funny, he was the first one she hadn't told she was a teacher. There'd been no conscious strategy behind the omission but tonight it *had* occurred to her to put away the school stuff before he came. He might be turned off by it. By the suggestion of authority, perhaps, or even intelligence. Not that the teachers she knew were such geniuses, but still . . .

"What are they, then?" he challenged.

"Needle marks."

"Tracks," he corrected.

"Tracks."

The phone rang and she picked it up. It was Evelyn. Apologizing for calling at this hour but she needed to talk. Terry said she was sorry, she couldn't talk right now, she'd call back in the morning before she left for work, and hung up.

"Who was that?" Tony asked.

"Now who's nosy?" she asked.

He got interested in her for the first time. He turned to look at her. She felt shy; she had no idea of how she looked to him. He sat up, rolled up her sweater. But in a strange way. Not as though he was excited and wanted to touch her but as though he were considering whether to become excited. He examined her breasts. One hand still held the wine glass. With the other he played with one nipple, then the other, smiling when they got hard. She was excited but she was also embarrassed. She thought of how he'd kept saying, "You like that, huh?" when he was making love to her. It was one thing to sin and another to enjoy it so thoroughly. One of the characteristics of acts like cursing and petty thievery was that you never really enjoyed them because what was on your mind the whole time you were doing them was what the priest would say if you really confessed. (Masturbating was in a class by itself, too terrible to confess, and so both pleasure and guilt mounted indefinitely until you had to stop for a while lest you explode.)

He spilled a little wine onto one of her nipples, bent over and sucked it off.

She closed her eyes. Some of the wine trickled down her side and onto the blanket but she couldn't worry about it just then. With his fingers he painted the other nipple, then the whole breast with the wine, then sucked that off. She was enormously excited and wanted to pull him down to her but she was afraid that if she moved at all he would withdraw from her. She opened her eyes. He was looking at her breasts as though trying to decide what to do to them next. He was doing his "buh buh buh buh" to the music from the radio. Without turning over she reached back, groping for the light. He told her to leave it on; she brought her hand back to the pillow, some useless tool she'd only thought of using.

"Take off your jeans."

She opened her fly and pulled them down, wriggling out of them without getting off her back. He waved at her flowered bikini pants to signal that those were to go, too. She slipped them down, feeling nauseated by her own shame and desire. He inspected her as though she were a piece of pale freckled meat and he was a government inspector. She closed her eyes again. Felt him painting her pubic hair with the wine. She waited to feel his lips on her again but instead felt the cold splash of wine between her legs.

"What do you think you're doing?" she

screamed, bolting to a sitting position, trembling with rage and fighting back tears at the same time.

He grinned at her like a bad boy caught doing something he'd known was wrong but he hadn't realized anyone else knew.

"Look what you did, you crazy son of a bitch," she screamed, pointing to the quilt between her legs, her beautiful quilt, soaked with wine that looked, because of where it was, like menstrual blood.

"Hey," he said, "what's you screaming about?"

"What'd you do it for?"

"Hey," he said again, softly, coming on sexually now, "relax. Some girls really dig that."

"*Dig what?*" But she felt her anger slipping away from her. "Having their bed ruined?"

"Uh uh. Here. I'll show you." Very sexy now. Turning over to put the wineglass down on the floor, returning to her without his tinted eyeglasses. Gently pushing her back down on the bed, now playing with the wet hairs, sucking them as she'd thought he was going to before. Eating the lips of her vagina and very slowly, too slowly, sticking his tongue, then his finger, then his tongue, then his finger into her. She moaned with pleasure until he finally stuck his finger in all the way without taking away his tongue. She was reaching for him, trying to hold him, but he was too far down on her. And he was dressed. Her face was next to his feet in their smelly socks. She pulled off the socks and let them fall on the floor.

"Don't stop," she whispered.

With his help she got off his pants, fondled his penis, which was huge and hard. She wanted him to come up to where she was and get into her but he kept doing what he'd been doing and so she began doing the same thing for him. Playing with his penis, kissing it, finally sucking it a little. She'd never done that to anyone before and it felt strange. Pleasant but not quite right. In her imaginings of that same act the penis had been soft and fit into her mouth easily, while in point of fact it was much too big to do that and she had to be careful that he didn't thrust too far in and make her gag. Now she was coming. She didn't want to come because she was afraid he would and if she had to swallow his come she would throw up, but she didn't know how to get her mouth out from around his penis without having him stop what he was doing to her. She couldn't bear it if he stopped right now. She made an attempt to get him to switch around but his response to this was to thrust into her throat more deeply. She gagged but he kept doing it and she got really frightened and then all of a sudden he was coming and she was gagging and heaving, a nightmare from which she couldn't rescue herself, it just seemed to go on and on and on. Then, mercifully, just when she was sure she was going to choke to death, he stopped and got soft. She pulled away from him and buried her face in the quilt and spat out what she could, coughing. She moved her face to a dry spot on the quilt.

She thought that if she could have one wish granted at that moment it would be to die instantly. She was fairly certain she would never raise her head from that quilt again. Certainly not while he was there. Certainly she could never meet his eyes again. Or listen to . . . the radio was blaring some particularly loud and inane group. Without raising her head she groped for the dial, turned it off, found the wire and pulled the plug out of the wall so he couldn't turn it on again.

"What was that for?" he asked, sounding innocent of any reason that she might be angry with him.

She didn't answer. If he would just go away. Vanish. Disappear. She could never look at him or speak to him again.

She was getting cold now and she wanted to be under the quilt in the warmth and the darkness, but she was afraid to move. With difficulty, without taking her face out of the quilt, she edged up into the top corner of the bed and squirmed her way under.

"Hey," he said, "what's going on?"

Make him go away. Make it so I don't have to do anything, let him just go.

"Hey! Whosie! Terry!"

He knew her name. It just took a while. Maybe she should be glad she wasn't just some anonymous mouth he'd come into. No. It would have been better if they'd been someplace else and he didn't know her name and she could run away now.

"Is anythinga matter?"

Just go away. The taste in her mouth made her feel sick all over again when she became aware of it. If she only had a pickle to suck on. Or a lemon. Something strong and sour to drive away this taste. She could feel his moving toward her on the bed. She was rigid. Then he was over her, trying to see her face, gently pulling down the quilt so he could see all of it. She hoped he couldn't see how tightly her eyes were closed.

"Ter?"

He kissed her cheek and at the same time pushed the hair off her forehead, the motion so soft and tender that she nearly burst into tears.

"You mad at me?"

Without opening her eyes she shook her head. *What was she supposed to do?* What could she tell him? He seemed to really not know what he'd done to her. Maybe this was a usual thing to him. Maybe she was crazy! She remembered the force with which he'd driven into her mouth, her throat, and shuddered.

"You cold?"

She nodded. He wrapped himself around her quilt-covered body.

Maybe it hadn't been that much force. Maybe

it had seemed worse from her side because she
hadn't wanted it. Maybe if she'd tried to *tell* him
instead of struggling in a way he could mis-
interpret.

"That better?"

She nodded again.

"Okay if I get under the quilt?"

She couldn't tell him it was okay.

"I know you don't feel like talking," he said
gently. "But tell me if it ain't okay."

Since she didn't respond he got under the quilt
and again wrapped himself around her. He was
so warm, so soft and so smooth that she wanted
him to stay there forever, never to move or talk
to her or make her look at him. Nor was there
any way she could reconcile this desire with the
way she'd felt about him a few minutes earlier.
With the way she felt *now*, actually, except that
somehow it had gotten pushed into her mind. Not
even her mind. Her *eyes*. She was *seeing* the way
she'd felt before while all she was feeling now
was the pleasure of having him hold her. She
considered opening her eyes so the *image* of how
she'd felt would be replaced by the room's solid
objects, but then it didn't seem worth it because
the image wasn't even that painful any more. She
was looking at it through the wrong end of a
telescope and it was very far away.

He lifted her hair and kissed the back of her
neck. He reached around under her arm so that
he was holding her breasts. He began moving

gently back and forth against her. She felt his penis growing bigger between her legs and realized, after a while, that she was moving back and forth against him, too, and that her whole body was warm and excited and that once again she wanted him in her. But then the very desire brought back a *feeling* memory of the last time and she froze briefly, then tried to move away from him. Except at the moment she did that he gently pressed her abdomen back against him so that his penis almost naturally without help slipped into her. Then he began slowly moving around inside her and almost instantly she began coming, her whole body heaving with pleasure. He kept his arms tightly around her and pumped inside her, and it was so incredibly good that she thought, as she threw off the quilt because she was burning up, that she wouldn't be able to stand it. Finally she stopped coming and he stopped moving although he was still big inside her.

"You like that, huh?" he whispered.

She reached back and brushed the hair away from her neck, which was wet with perspiration. He blew on her neck. She smiled.

"Still not talkin' to me?"

Talking was so much more complicated than making love . . . fucking, she should call it, since it was hard to see how anything she did with him could be about love. To talk with people you had to ignore the way you felt and speak from the front of your face . . . or else go through the effort of distilling those feelings into something that made some kind of sense, was acceptable in some way. That was what words did, really, make some kind of order out of the dark jumble of feelings and perceptions and nightmares inside you. And there was no way to do that in this situation. No way to explain in an orderly fashion how, without being drunk, stoned or out of her mind, she was having the most incredible sexual pleasure of her life with someone who at best amused her, and at worst frightened her half to death.

Her mind went to the knife on the floor, then skittered away to the quilt. She would have to wash it in the morning. She would put all the linens on the bed into the wash.

The room was very quiet with the radio off. He began to move inside her again. She wasn't really ready. He was probing. Trying to find a place that was particularly good. He wanted to hear her moan again.

"Not yet," she said.

He laughed. "Am I too much for you?"

"Too much what?"

He pushed hard and a little cry of pleasure escaped her. He laughed and did it again but then the next time she fooled him. As he came out of her almost all the way, she pulled away from him and turned on her stomach, hiding her face in the pillow. He rolled over on top of her but suddenly she got scared again; the pressure of his weight hurt her back. She struggled to get him off.

"Get off me," she said. "I can't breathe."

He got up so that he was kneeling, one of his legs on either side of her, very lightly sitting on her. Rubbing his penis into the space between the buttocks. Then it seemed that he was going to try to stick it in there.

"Stop that," she said sharply.

"Okay, okay," he said. "Don't get excited. Some girls—hey, what's this?" He had found the scar that no one since Martin Engle had seen. Her trunk became rigid and her head and arms and legs flew up out of control.

"Hey! What happened?"

"Nothing," she said. "Let me up."

"What are you, sensitive?"

He wasn't getting up. She was caught. Her body went limp with futility.

"That's more like it," he said, kissing her back. "What's it from, hon? You can tell me. You think I never seen scars before?"

"I used to be a fish," she said. "That's where they took out my gills."

"You're cute. Did I ever tell you you was cute?"

"I don't remember."

"And you don't remember how you got the scars."

"Sure I remember, I told you, I used to be a fish . . . no, a mermaid. No, I know, a hand puppet. I was a hand puppet and that's where they stuck their hands in to make me work."

He was leaning over her, fondling her breasts. Kissing her back. His penis was still hard but it rested on her lightly, he didn't push it. Sometimes it rested on the halfmoon, sometimes between her legs. Her heart was beating very rapidly, which was strange because all the worst things had already happened and what could she be frightened of? The knife on the floor? That would be silly. You weren't scared of a switchblade knife just because it was there any more than you were scared of a kitchen knife. Or a scissor. She squirmed around under him so that she was lying on her back, and looked at him for the first time since he had forced her to . . . but already her mind was moving away from the sharp memory. The light was on. With Martin sometimes the light had been on. Never since.

He grinned. "Hi."

She smiled.

He looked different to her now. Not like such a kid. There were lines in his face. Maybe fatigue. He looked like someone who might have been in battle in Vietnam.

"Can I see your knife?"

"Huh?"

"I just want to see what it looks like."

"You never seen a switchblade?"

"Not open."

He shrugged. "Sure." He leaned over without getting off her; she held his thick, muscular thighs so he wouldn't fall off the bed.

"Turn out the light," he said.

"What for?"

"You'll see."

Her heart was pounding again but she couldn't admit that she was scared—after all, *he* had no interest in the knife, *she* was the one who'd asked him to take it out. She turned off the light and suddenly—click—a fluorescent blade glowed in the dark and her heart leaped almost out of her chest.

"Okay," she said, hearing a tiny scared voice come out of her, "you can put it away now."

He laughed. "Whatsa matter? Don't you like my friend?"

"I like him fine," she said, "but put him away."

The blade clicked shut and he let it drop to the floor again. He leaned over her, kissed her cheek. A thrill passed through her body.

"Whatsa matter, fishie? Did I scare you?"

Suddenly the atmosphere was thick with sex again.

"Sure," she said softly. "You terrify me."

"I'm really a nice guy," he said, kissing her neck, then her breasts.

"I'm not so sure about that," she said, her voice catching in her throat as another thrill passed through her.

"Sure I am."

"Did you ever kill anybody?"

"Only in the Army."

And then they were making love again.

A little light was coming through the window when she finally fell asleep in his arms. When she awakened it was eight o'clock Thursday night and she was alone. She had missed an entire day, including school. She ate three grilled cheese sandwiches and drank two bottles of Coke. Then she called Rose and told her she'd taken double tranquilizers and gone into a near coma. Rose said she was so relieved to hear Terry's voice. They'd been worried when they hadn't heard from her and they'd called the apartment a few times in the morning but there'd been no answer. Terry told Rose the ring was pretty low, anyway, so it wouldn't be startling.

On Friday at school she got teased about taking an overdose of sleeping pills. On Saturday night James Morrisey rang her bell promptly at seven.

She'd put on jeans and a sweater, telling herself that nobody got dressed up any more but knowing exactly what she was doing. Knowing full well that James Morrisey would show up at her door in a shirt and tie and suit, as indeed he now had.

"You're disgustingly punctual," she said.

"I didn't know it was a fault," he said.

"Well," she said, "now you know."

"All right," he said. "May I come in anyway?"

A little bit flustered that he wasn't more flustered by the awful way she was acting, or the way she'd dressed, she let him in and closed the door.

"Are we having dinner with the Pope?" she asked, eying his suit.

"Only if you know where he's eating tonight," James said.

Frustrated in her attempts to irritate him, she looked around the apartment.

"What was I in the middle of doing?"

In point of fact she had finished her school planning during a lengthy period of insomnia Friday night, had been too restless to read or watch TV, and had been walking around the apartment trying to decide what she really felt like doing.

"Take your time," he said, sitting down.

She felt irritable and her back hurt a little, maybe a result of her athletics with Tony the other night. She smiled to herself.

"No, forget it," she said. "I'd just as leave go. Where're we going, anyway?"

"I made a reservation at Lüchow's."

She was disconcerted again. When she'd first moved to the Lower East Side she'd passed Lüchow's and heard music from inside and thought it looked nice, a place where it would be fun to be. Then she'd learned that Katherine and her friends disdained Lüchow's, that it was too big, too noisy, too straight and too fattening. A meat and potatoes place, as opposed to rice and bean sprouts, say, which they were all into by this time. A place where the provincials went on Saturday night to drink beer and get red-faced, then shit-faced, and then stomp their boots to German band music.

She smiled condescendingly. "Meat and potatoes."

"My favorite foods."

"So heavy," she complained, thinking that she was not only saying something she'd heard Katherine say but she was saying it with Katherine's intonation.

"They have a wide selection, actually," James said. "Fish and so on."

"How about Chinese food?" she asked, smiling naughtily. She hardly ever ate Chinese food, although Katherine adored it.

He smiled back. "No. They don't have Chinese food."

"That's not what I meant," she said. "I meant how about going for Chinese food?"

"I don't eat Chinese food."

"You're so difficult." Again unable to suppress a smile because she was being such a brat.

He smiled, too. She was amusing him.

"Do I have to change my clothes, then?" she asked.

"I don't know if they have any dress rules," he said calmly. "I can call and ask."

"I wasn't thinking of their silly rules. I meant I didn't want to embarrass you."

"Why would the way *you* dress embarrass *me*?"

She was embarrassed herself now, of course.

"I meant, if that's where your gang hangs out."

"My gang," he said, "if I have such a thing, which I seriously doubt, but the friends I have whom you might call my gang hang out in the Bronx."

"When you say hang out it sounds as if it has quotation marks around it."

"It does. It's your phrase, not mine."

"Don't you ever use slang?"

"Not very often."

"Why not?"

He thought about it. "It doesn't seem to come naturally to me. Maybe because I have rather precise habits of speech and slang tends to be imprecise."

She wanted to smack him. Instead she said, "How about words like motherfucker? They're not imprecise." And watched with satisfaction as he flinched. (In point of fact she'd never said it aloud before and she flinched herself as she said it; she could only pray he hadn't noticed.)

"There are various ways to be imprecise," he said after a moment. "You can substitute the general for the specific, for example. Or you can be very specific but not about the thing you intend to specify. I've heard that phrase used many times but never to describe the situation it very specifically refers to."

She laughed. "What if you were having a fight with someone who'd done that specific thing? Then would you use it?"

"I very much doubt it."

"Why not?"

"It's not my nature. I'm not sure that it's yours, either."

"Would you call yourself a mama's boy?"

"You mean was I born of woman?"

"I mean are you a goody-goody?"

"As opposed to what? A baddy-baddy?"

"Why do the Jesuits answer every question with another question?"

"Is there a better way to answer questions?"

"Oooohhhh . . . I'm going to change my clothes. I feel like it, anyway. I just didn't have time before." She felt uncomfortable saying that to him. The small lies that came so easily with others were hard with him. That exasperated her further.

From the closet she took a kelly green jersey dress she'd bought when her father was still in the hospital but had never worn. Every time she opened the closet she thought about it. She loved it but was embarrassed to wear it. Only after she'd had it a while had it occurred to her that it was the most brightly colored garment she'd ever bought. Now, without letting herself think about it twice, she marched into the bathroom, put on the dress, combed her hair, put on makeup, came out of the bathroom, put on high-heeled shoes, then faced him with a combination of defiance and anticipation.

"All set now?" he asked.

She nodded. She would not under any circumstances let him see that she was disappointed in his failure to react to her improved appearance. The closest she could come to admitting it to herself was to say that somewhere in the mixture of largely negative feelings she had about going to straight Lüchow's with straight James Morrisey on a straight Saturday night date was a tiny desire to have someone tell her she looked pretty.

She got her raincoat and started to march out of the apartment ahead of him. She knew she'd be cold in a raincoat but she always wanted to throw off her heavy, binding winter coat before winter had really ended. He said that it wasn't a particularly warm night and she'd be cold. She said she wouldn't be cold and started out of the apartment again. He asked if she had her keys and she blushed furiously because she didn't.

"Why does that embarrass you?" he asked.

She could see that he wasn't being provocative, he was really curious, but for some reason she felt upset and endangered. She shook her head and fought back tears.

"I'm sorry," he said. "I—"

She grabbed her keys, locked the door and dashed down the stairs and through the lobby without waiting for him, into the blessed darkness.

He asked if she would like to take a cab and she said she would prefer walking. He said that he was sorry he'd upset her, however inadvertently. She told him not to worry about it. She didn't know why she'd been upset. Which was true. She didn't see how it could have had anything to do with that silly business. She said she'd had a crazy week in general, maybe that was it. She was just tense from the week in general. (It didn't sound right but it appealed to her; she didn't want him getting the mistaken notion that anything connected to him could be important enough to bother her.) With Tony she'd been upset and then confused and then ecstatic and then exhausted. Then she'd slept, and since awakening she'd been on what you could best describe as a natural high. Not happy, exactly, but elated. Looking forward to seeing him again. In the whole time with Tony, during the really bad part, she hadn't cried. Or even fought back an impulse to do so. Why now? When all that had happened was that James had made her feel a little foolish about some keys? Maybe she'd held it in. Everyone knew by now, you read it all over the place, that if you held in your emotions at one time, they came out at another.

"Did anything happen during your crazy week that you feel like talking about?" James asked.

"No, not really," she said. "The kids were a little wild yesterday." She explained that she'd overslept on Thursday out of exhaustion, hadn't even remembered to set the alarm. Something that had never happened before. "No one even

realized I wasn't there until nine thirty or so."
The class had gone quite wild and the noise drew
the teacher from the next classroom. They'd
tried to get a substitute but it was too late, so
they'd divided up the kids into different class-
rooms, which totally threw them. Even when kids
had a regular sub they were often a little crazy
and out of control, or so she'd heard—she'd never
been out, so her kids were really unfamiliar with
the whole experience.

They'd been totally uncontrollable Friday morning, as though to express their anger at her for
deserting them. Finally, after lunch, she'd decided to confront the matter head on. She'd had
them gather their chairs around hers for a discussion and asked that each one of them give her
an example of an unpleasant surprise. Something
that had happened that they didn't expect and
that wasn't nice. Something they were supposed
to do and couldn't, someone getting sick, or going
away. Juan said he was supposed to get a bicycle
for his birthday but then his father lost his job
and couldn't give it to him. A couple of others
gave examples and then one of them, Elsie, talked
about the death of her grandmother, who'd always taken care of her while her mother worked.
One day she'd come home from school and her
grandmother wasn't there. Theresa asked how
she felt about her grandmother and it was beautiful—as though Elsie knew her plan and wanted
to help. "I was mad at her," Elsie said. "When I

see her next time I'm going to tell her I didn't like what she did."

"And how did you feel yesterday morning when you came in and I wasn't here the way I always am?"

"I was mad at you," Elsie said, and burst into tears.

Theresa had gone over to Elsie and brought the little girl back to her chair and held her in her lap for the remainder of the discussion. Not only to comfort Elsie but to encourage the others to express how they felt by showing that Elsie was being comforted, not punished, for her honesty. Sure enough, one by one, most of them had admitted varying degrees of anger, fear and confusion at her not being there. Then she'd explained to them that she'd been so tired that for the first time in all the time that she'd been teaching she had fallen asleep wihout setting the alarm and slept right through the night and the morning. She'd told them she was sorry she'd disappointed them, and promised she would do her best to never let it happen again. But if it did happen they'd know it was something she hadn't been able to help.

They'd put back their chairs and been angelic for the rest of the day.

They were halfway across Fourteenth Street, by now, heading toward Lüchow's.

"That's a beautiful story," James said. "You sound like a marvelous teacher."

"I love teaching," she said with a fervor that astounded her. "I'm never happier than when I'm teaching." This was true but it surprised her that she could say it to him. She had times of pleasure outside the classroom, in sex, for example, but happiness was quite genuinely there only when she was with the children.

Talking about it, though. She had never done that with *anyone* outside of school, except Evelyn or Rose, who were already part of school. Mentioning that she was a teacher in her bar pickups (all except Tony) had been a way of saying that she wasn't just some dumb, broke broad hanging around to get a drink or get laid. A status thing. But the thought of sharing with anyone her teaching experiences . . . Still, she had to admit it felt good to hear him say that. He was intelligent, and even if she didn't really like him, it was pleasant to have him recognize her worth when she hadn't even been parading it for him, but only making conversation.

"Until I got to high school, the sisters were the only teachers I ever had," he said.

She wrinkled up her nose to show distaste, though of course it was true of her, too.

"They weren't all that bad, actually," he said. "Although I have to admit I didn't have trouble with even the worst of them." He smiled. "I was a goody-goody."

She returned his smile. He was pretty likable, in a way. It wasn't that she even disliked him,

239

actually; it was that she wasn't attracted to him. She couldn't see ever having sex with him. She could put aside his Irish choirboy face for long enough to talk to him, but she was sure she could never even kiss him and she didn't know how she would handle the situation if he should try.

In Lüchow's they were finally led to seats which James refused because they were so close to the band that you had to shout to be heard. Another table farther back was found and they ordered drinks, Scotch and soda for him, a martini for her. It wasn't very cool to drink any more, but at least a martini was the most sophisticated drink. She had to stop herself from making a face when she tasted the first sip.

"Actually," he said, "I had at least one extraordinary woman as a teacher. She didn't possess the kind of emotional understanding you do but she was extremely intelligent, as I think many nuns actually are. She read voraciously and thought about what she read. Not like most Catholics, who put their minds in straitjackets at an early age."

"Aren't you still a Catholic?"

"More or less, but I don't like to think of myself as that sort of one."

She was silent.

"Anyway, Sister Francine went to Fordham and then out to work in a prison in Illinois someplace. Someone should write about her. Within the strictures of the Church, and certainly they were considerable, before the whole radical Catholic movement had even been heard of very much, she was a tough, brilliant, determined, independent woman."

"You sound like a eulogy. Or an essay. My Kind of Woman by James Morrisey."

"I don't know that I have any *kind* of woman."

The waiter came to check their drinks. James said they would order and asked what she wanted. He did have a certain social grace; it was probably recently acquired. She ordered shrimp and James asked for lamb chops.

"You like strong women," she said.

Something there was that couldn't really be interested in a man who liked powerful, intelligent women. Something there was that wanted a man from Marlboro Country. Smart only in the way he subordinated his girls. Swaggering, suave. With a dick so long that you rode it as though it were a horse. A rocky horse.

He said that a woman's movement seemed to be developing and asked if she wasn't sympathetic to it. She said sure, why not, which wasn't exactly a lie but it was the closest thing to a lie she'd told him. (She wasn't prepared to really think about that one.) The truth was that the new woman's movement made her uncomfortable. The equal pay demand seemed all right but she had that, anyway, and she was upset by the stridency of much of it. The demands. It seemed that men must surely dislike women who were so demanding. Evelyn had begun to talk about a group of women she met with once a week and had invited Theresa more than once to join them, but she'd always made some excuse.

"I don't really belong to it," she said. "I'm not comfortable in groups."

"It's funny," he mused. "I'm most comfortable in a group. Choral group, lawyers' group, church group, whatever you might think of."

She went out with him six times before he kissed her goodnight. She became almost eager for him to do it, not because she wanted to kiss him but to get it over with. His kiss was light on her lips, as she would have expected. She was unmoved by it. As she would have expected.

She smiled naughtily. "Now you're not a virgin any more."

"Ah, Theresa," he said. "You're so cruel to me. Why?"

Because you like me too much, was what came into her head. But of course that was ridiculous. It wasn't that simple.

She refused to see him during the week, telling him that it was impossible for her to go out and get up for school in the morning. The real reason was that Tony worked weekends at the garage, while she never knew just when he was going to show up during the week.

Often one of them was there when the other called. She suspected that if this wasn't particularly a factor in James's interest in her, it was definitely helping to maintain Tony's. For this reason she would force herself to talk to James when Tony was there even if she didn't feel like it. Tony, who might have been complaining of muscle pains, or watching some garbage on TV (with the radio on) would then come over to where she lay stretched out on the bed, pretending to be absorbed in her conversation with James, and start kissing her neck or undoing her blouse or rubbing her thighs. Once he tickled the bottom of her feet and she let out a whoop and told James she had to get off the phone. Then she began pummeling Tony as though she really cared that she'd been given away. He liked that. He especially liked that she'd hung up the phone because of him.

James started calling her earlier in the evening, correctly sensing that she was more likely to be alone then.

"Where's your boyfriend?" Tony asked when there was no call.

She laughed. "He calls earlier now."

"He doesn't want me here, huh?"

"Of course not," she said.

"Well, that's tough," he said. "I got as much right to be here as he does."

He sounded like a little kid staking out territory.

"How come you're not saying anything?" he asked.

"What am I supposed to say?"

"He's not paying for this joint, is he?" Tony asked suddenly.

"No, Tony," she said patiently. "He's not paying for it."

"Who is?"

"I am."

"With what?"

"With my salary."

"How much it cost you?" He was not only suspicious, he was righteous; if he'd been a grown-up she would have gotten angry with him.

"Two hundred dollars a month."

"It ain't worth half that."

She laughed. "To me it is."

"This is a lousy neighborhood. Full of junkies. You oughta live in Queens."

"Queens! Why would I live in Queens? I've never even been there in my whole life."

"That's impossible," he said flatly.

She was silent. This time she couldn't laugh.

"Queens is beautiful," he said. "Nothing like this. My old lady lives in Queens."

"I thought you lived in Brooklyn."

"*I* live in Brooklyn. That don't mean **she** . . . she kicked me out."

"How come?"

"She said it was on account of dope but that's bullshit, she never wanted me there. She didn't want any of her boyfriends to see she had a kid

as old as me. Forty-four years old and she's still
. . . the cunt."

"What'd you expect her to do?"

"Forget it," he said moodily.

She tried to jolly him out of it but he wasn't
having any. She wanted to ask him more questions about his family but his mood got worse
when she tried, so she changed the subject to
horses. Off guard, he began to talk about horses,
about the race track. He had an uncle who was a
jockey who'd brought him there all the time
when he was a kid, that for him was the best
place in the world, the *only* place, from the time
he was five years old. He told her that he'd prayed
when he was a kid not to grow over five feet four
inches because he didn't want to get too big to
be a jockey, and when praying didn't work he'd
aimed for trainer. She asked him about the dope
charges and his license but he got sullen again.

"*You* never tell *me* nothin'," he said.

"What do you want to know?"

"What's his name?' he asked quickly, like a
machine gun firing.

"Who?" she asked, totally unprepared. "Oh, you
mean James."

"James what?"

"Uh uh. No fair."

He looked at her as though to say he'd known
all along she wouldn't tell him anything.

"Would you like it if I talked to him about
you?"

"Sure. Why not?" He was sitting propped up against the pillows, drumming on the night table. The TV was off but the radio was still on. She kissed him, tried playing with him a little. He shrugged her off.

"You feel like taking a walk?" she asked.

"You're not getting me outa here," he said.

"I meant I'd go with you, dopey."

Don't call me dopey!" He raised his hand as though he were going to strike her but held it in mid-air; he was red with rage. She was scared, although she didn't believe he'd hit her.

"If I really thought you were dopey," she said, "I'd be afraid to say it."

He lowered his hand, slightly mollified.

It was a lie, of course. His dumbness was one of his endearing qualities and set him apart nicely from James in her mind. The contrast between them was so perfect that she was beginning to enjoy the arrangement. She could see it continuing indefinitely like this, sex with Tony, dinner and conversation with James.

"Now," she said, hearing herself, very much the teacher trying to bring an errant child back into the fold, "if you feel like taking a walk with me, that's fine. If not, that's fine, too."

"I hate walking."

"Is there anything else you want to do?" Coming onto him, rubbing his thigh, kissing his ear, playing with the lock of hair that had fallen just

246

under the rim of his glasses. Pushing it back, curling it around her finger.

"If you work," he said, "where do you work?"

"On Second Avenue."

"Where?"

Not without some misgivings, she told him.

"What kinda office is that?" he asked scornfully.

"It's not an office," she said. "It's a school. I'm a teacher."

He stared at her openmouthed for a full minute before he said, "You're kidding me."

"No."

"Whaddya teach, for Christ's sake?"

"Little kids," she said.

He stared at her with a mixture of awe and suspicion.

She laughed uneasily. "What's the big deal?"

"No big deal." But he continued staring as though he hadn't seen her before.

She stood up, went into the bathroom, combed her hair, came back out.

"I'm hungry," she said. "Want something to eat?"

"What the hell you doin' fucking around in bars if you're a teacher?"

"Mother of God," she murmured, "I'm hearing it and I don't believe I'm hearing it." But she understood exactly what he was talking about, of course.

He said nothing. His expression was changing

but she couldn't read the new one yet. Less belligerent, maybe. More thoughtful. He was considering. Finally he smiled.

"If that doesn't beat all."

"I'm getting something to eat," she said. "I didn't have dinner."

"You got any hot dogs?"

She didn't because she had them so often for lunch from the Sabrett's cart that she never wanted them for dinner.

"What I could really use," he said, "is a steak and some spaghetti."

She only had spaghetti in a can. He gave her a look of disgust and they both ended up eating peanut-butter-and-jelly sandwiches although he kept asking her if she called this a dinner. She wanted to point out that there were a dozen places in the neighborhood where they could pick up real food but he seemed determined that neither of them should go out. He ate six peanut-butter-and-jelly sandwiches and then said he felt sick. He clutched his stomach and rolled his eyes, and when she asked what she could do, he said he'd better go home to his mother's.

"To Queens?"

"I toldja that's where she lives, didn't I?" Grimacing with a pain that didn't quite come off as pain.

"Yes. But you also told me you didn't live there."

"But wherever my mother lives is my home, right?" It was obviously a rhetorical question as far as he was concerned. "And home is where you go when you're sick, right?"

"I don't know," she said. "It seems to me if I got sick in someone's house I'd lie down and see if it passed. Or throw up, maybe, if I had to."

He groaned. "What'd you say that for?"

One way or the other she would have responsibility for this illness.

He stood up, clutching his side.

"Are you sure you want to go?" If he wasn't sick she wanted him to make love to her, and if he was, being on the train would make it worse.

"I'll call you," he said.

He didn't call for the rest of the week and she was really nasty to James on Saturday night.

Tuesday Tony called.

"Hi," she said, trying to sound casual. To conceal her relief that he hadn't disappeared forever. "Were you sick?"

"Huh?" he said. "Oh. Yeah. But I'm okay."

"Good," she said. "When you coming down?"

"I dunno," he said. "I'm working late this week. The guy who usually has the hours is out sick."

"Mmmm. The bug's passing around." The peanut-butter bug.

"Listen," he said. "Keep a week from Sunday open."

"Okay," she said. "What for?"

"Because I told you to."

"I know that. But you never told me anything

this far in advance and then suddenly you call and say keep open the Sunday after this."

There was a long silence. As though he were overwhelmed by her genius in picking up the discrepancy. Then he said maybe he'd see her next Monday, he wouldn't be working late any more by then. She said okay. But that was a week off and she was already so horny she was climbing the walls.

Into her mind came the time when she had gone month in and month out without sex. When she hadn't even known the need was there. Maybe that was the whole thing. She wondered if Tony really had to work. Probably. He didn't feel any obligation to her that would make him lie to avoid hurting her feelings.

Stop, Theresa.

She could go mad trying to figure out what was happening. She might go mad anyway. Just looking at the walls of the apartment. No. She wouldn't do it. Already the decision was made. She started to get dressed, reminding herself that she'd meant to start working on some drapery material she'd bought the week before. She'd never felt about this apartment the way she had about the first one. It wasn't that she didn't want it to look nice; she just couldn't get absorbed enough in the whole thing to *do* it. Even her schoolwork was often difficult to focus on these days. Partly it was the restlessness that grew each year when spring came in teachers and students alike. But beyond that was some undefinable change in her own attitude toward the school as a place, a home, that had occurred since the bitter days of the strike. And on top of this brew was the perpetual tension over Tony and—no, it wasn't, couldn't be, about James. There was no tension at all connected with James. Just this vague uneasiness about his liking her too much. Not that it was so awful having someone like you. The problem was that she'd come to sort of enjoy having him around to talk to, and she was afraid he would get too serious and then the whole thing would have to come to an end.

Whatever the reason, it had become more difficult for her to concentrate on her work or anything else.

She made up with more care than usual, put on jeans and the black turtleneck sweater, which she'd come to think of as her cruising outfit. It was a fairly warm evening and she would be warm until she got to the cool air-conditioned interior of—where would it be? Mr. Goodbar. It was a comfortable place with old gum-ball machines for table lamps and one wall covered entirely with a shellacked montage of candy wrappers.

In Mr. Goodbar she met a man named Victor who had something to do with advertising for General Motors. He had a wife and five children and lived in the poor section of Grosse Pointe, or so he said with a laugh. He looked like Rock Hudson, except older (he had gray hair), and stammered so badly before he got totally tanked up that it was difficult to see how he could carry on normal business sober. He was rather charming, once you got past the stammer, which he helped you to do by joking about it. Telling you he never stammered in bed, and so on. She went back with him to his room at the Americana and stayed there until Friday morning, calling in sick on Wednesday and Thursday, not without some misgivings.

He bought her a beautiful black nightgown from Bonwit Teller as well as lavender soap and Chanel bath oil. He also brought her magazines to read while he was out doing business, in case she didn't feel like sleeping or watching color TV the whole time. They ate mostly from room service; he had proposed that she be his voluntary prisoner in the Americana until he left New York on Friday. She could leave the room if she wanted to, but not the building. If she wanted anything from the outside she need only ask for it. Did she want some clothes to wear on the rare occasions when they went down to the coffee shop? No, she didn't at all mind wearing the same sweater and jeans. It wasn't as though she were in them the whole time. In the cool half-darkness of the room, with the blinds always more than half closed against the noise and ugliness of midtown Manhattan, she wore the nightgown or her bikini pants. He giggled when she said it wasn't as though she wore them all the time. They giggled together a lot. When he discovered her habit of ordering different drinks all the time and her particular fondness for sweet ones, he took to showing up in the room—late morning, afternoon or evening, with a different kind of liqueur. They drank arak from waxed-paper cups and discovered the strong licoricey stuff had peeled the wax off the inside so the clear liquid was flecked with tiny wax flakes. They drank it anyway, and when they made love later he swore that the wax was now coating her inside and making her more slippery than usual. Sometimes they drank instead of eating.

He told her that he actually didn't do a great deal of this kind of thing, that he was actually a rather straight-and-narrow soul. He asked if she believed him and when she said that she did, he seemed relieved. After that he talked about his family, as though he could trust her because she understood that he was telling the truth. When he talked about them he stammered worse than he had at any time before.

His wife was in a sanitarium in Michigan and had been there most of the time for several years. His children were cared for by the help when he was away. The younger ones, anyway. The oldest had just gone off to college this past year. The next was sixteen. She was the one Terry reminded him of a little. Not just that they both had green eyes; it was something in her expression. Gwendolyn. Gwennie. You could never tell what she was thinking except that once in a while, from somewhere, would come this deeply penetrating, mischievous look, and you knew she knew you were just a lovable fraud and she'd been making fun of you all along. Theresa couldn't recall any moment when she might have been looking at him with anything like that in mind, but it didn't seem to matter. It was his scenario and it didn't have to jibe with hers.

As a matter of fact, she didn't really have one; the fantasy element in the basic situation was strong enough to sustain her interest. That and her pleasure in the idea that if Tony changed his mind and called her, she wouldn't be there. That when James called she wouldn't be there. Not then nor the next night. . . . James would be worried, she suspected. He might even check with Rose and then Rose would tell him that she'd called in sick. He would tell Rose then that it was strange there'd been no answer at her apartment for three nights. Terry would have to make up a story to cover.

Family illness. She hadn't wanted to go into it over the phone but it wasn't actually she who'd been ill, it was her mother. She'd had to stay in the Bronx for a few days. As a matter of fact, that was what she really should do this weekend —visit her parents. She hadn't seen her father since a month or more earlier, when he'd still shown the exhausting effects of his illness.

At eight o'clock Friday morning she and Victor had their last coffees in the room at the Americana and left it together. He hailed a cab for her, kissed her goodbye, opened the door, closed it and handed the cab driver a five-dollar bill. Then he went back to tell the bellhop he was ready to have his own bag put in a cab.

Rose was the first person she saw. Terry could tell that Rose knew she hadn't been home sick but was too polite to say so.

"I wasn't really sick," she said. "I was at my parents'. My mother was sick."

Rose said, "I hope it was nothing serious."

Terry shook her head. "It was just flu. Medium case. But my mother's not used to being sick so it was like the end of the world."

Rose smiled. "You know who was very concerned about you?"

"Evelyn?"

Rose smiled. "James, Theresa. He really likes you, you know."

Terry smiled. "He's a sweet boy."

Rose raised her eyebrows. "The way you say it, it doesn't sound good."

"I didn't mean it that way," Terry said hastily. "I'm tired and I'm . . . I'm really glad you introduced him to me, Rose." She probably never actually said that until now and Rose would want to hear it. She'd been inconsiderate. "I really like *him*, too."

"He's not such a boy, either," Rose said. "Supporting a paralyzed mother and a sister since he was eighteen years old."

Theresa stopped short and stared wildly at her. "He never told me."

"I'm not surprised."

"What is she paralyzed from?"

"A stroke. After his father died."

"I don't know why he never mentioned it."

"He wouldn't," Rose said. "Unless you asked."

No. She wouldn't have asked. In two days at the Americana Hotel with a man she hadn't seen before and wouldn't see again she'd asked more about his family and talked more of her own than she had with James Morrisey in the more than two months that she'd known him.

She felt as unreal as the days she'd just left. Dizzy. Frightened. Not because what she'd done made no sense to her but because it made perfect sense. It was precisely that fact, that she hadn't seen him and wouldn't, that she didn't know him and couldn't, that had enabled her to relax and open up to him. *And that was what was frightening!* It made her feel . . . as though she were standing in shifting sands. She thought now of an early childhood event she hadn't remembered in years—her only memory from before she'd had polio. She had been perhaps two or three years old. It had been a very happy occasion, some grand family picnic with cousins on the Jersey shore, the kind of thing they seldom did after Brigid was born . . . after she herself had gotten sick . . . once her brother had died . . . once all the bad things had happened . . . once the sun had gone down and her hair didn't shine golden any more. . . . It was early evening and the sun was low. They'd cooked steaks and corn and everyone was gathered around the fire and two-year-old Theresa had wandered off by herself down the shoreline a way, watching thoughtfully as the tide, which was going out, briefly pretended to come back in. It nearly knocked her off her feet but she kept her balance by rooting her feet more deeply in the wet sand. Except that suddenly the very sand in which she'd buried her feet for safety began moving fast beneath her, and for seconds that seemed like forever, she thought that she was losing the world. Then her father called her name and came toward her and the spell of fear was broken.

Now she remembered how, writing an essay about that day for Martin Engle years before, she had made the whole incident take place at a later time in her life.

"Theresa?"

"Mmm?"

"Maybe you should think twice before you sign in. Maybe you should call in sick one more day and go home and get some sleep."

"I'm okay," she said. "I really got plenty of sleep."

"Sure?"

"Sure. Anyway, remember the last time I didn't call in early enough to get a sub? I can take a nap as soon as I get home this afternoon."

She told the children, because she knew it was what they'd been told, that she'd been ill but was feeling better. They questioned her rather closely and she was uneasy as she answered, wondering if they would catch her on the fact that she'd been out for only two days and she had no symptoms now. But the time had been immeasurable to them—a few were prepared to swear that she hadn't been in on Monday or Tuesday, either—and most of them accepted her explanation fairly easily, although one or two were suspicious.

The day dragged on. She was tired, having rested a great deal but slept almost not at all during her time with Victor. She was looking forward to her nap after school.

But when she came out of school in the afternoon, talking to Evelyn, Tony was across the street, leaning against the corner building, watching her. Panic. Evelyn was saying she and some friends might rent a house at Fire Island this summer. Would Theresa be interested in a share? It wasn't going to be an up-against-the-meat-rack kind of summer; most of the women were in her group. They were strong and intelligent and had lives of their own and weren't into that other scene.

Theresa stopped short. She didn't really want Evelyn to meet Tony, not only because she was afraid he would like Evelyn (or would flirt with her whether he liked her or not) but because she was afraid he might humiliate her in front of her friend.

"What's the matter?" Evelyn asked.

"Mmm," Terry asked. "Someone I don't want to see right now."

"Do you want to walk the other way?" Evelyn asked.

"No," she said, "he knows I saw him. That would make it worse."

Together they crossed the street.

"Hi, Tony," she said in what she hoped was a casual way. "This is Evelyn."

"Where the fuck you been for three days?" he asked without acknowledging Evelyn's existence in any way.

"I was away."

"Where?"

"I guess I'd better say goodbye, Evelyn."

"You sure?" Evelyn asked with obvious concern.

Terry laughed. "Don't worry," she said, turning away so that her words would be lost on him, "his bark is worse than his bite."

Evelyn left. Theresa looked at Tony, who still stood motionless against the brick wall.

"What are we doing next Sunday?" she asked, which turned out to be an inspiration because it distracted him.

"A birthday party for my mother."

She laughed in disbelief.

"What's so funny?"

"I don't know," she said. "Are you serious?"

"Of course I'm serious, jerk. If I'm kidding I'll tell you I'm kidding so you can laugh."

She said she'd appreciate that. With both hands he did his rapid finger tap dance on the bricks of the building.

"I'm starved," she said, "I want a hot dog. You want one?"

They went to the Sabrett's cart, where they got hot dogs and soda and, when she took out her wallet, he said, "Don't be a jerk. When you're with me, I pay." As though she'd tried to go dutch at the Four Seasons. They walked across Four- teenth Street to the subway, eating and drinking. Tony making remarks about niggers and spics the whole time in a voice almost loud enough to be heard by others.

"What kind of party is it going to be?"

"A party, whaddya think? Food, wine, dancing. Her faggot boyfriend's throwing her a birthday party."

"How come you want to go when you hate him so much?"

"What are you, crazy? You think that faggot's gonna keep me from my own mother's birthday party?"

"No," she said, "but . . . the thing is . . . I'm afraid I'll feel strange. Not knowing anybody."

How will you introduce me, Tony? Mom, I want you to meet this cunt I fuck once, twice a week?

"Don't be stupid," he said. "You know me."

"That's true."

"You're my girl, aintcha?"

She was so accustomed to his insane assumptions that she fielded it calmly. "I don't know. I don't know if I'm anyone's girl."

"Yeah?" he said irritably. "What are you, just a cunt?"

"No," she said, "but what we have—"

"Oh, shit," he said. "What we have." They were almost at the subway. "I gotta get to work."

"When will I see you?" she asked automatically.

"I don't know," he said. "I'll call you. Remember next Sunday."

When she walked into the house the phone was ringing. She picked it up and said hello.

"Hello, Theresa," James's voice said. "It's nice to hear your voice again."

"Thank you."

She hadn't thought much about the conversation with Rose that morning but it had been with her, that and a strange sort of hangover from it, all day. James thought if she were free for dinner he might work a little later than usual at the office and come down and take her out.

Normally she would have just teased him about not going home for a bath first (he always looked as though he'd just been put through some fantastically effective total laundry process, clothes and all). Now she just said that she'd been away so much she didn't really feel like going out again, then, without thinking in advance, said that if he wanted to come down, she would make dinner. He was delighted with the idea and asked if he could bring wine. She said he shouldn't because she didn't know yet what she would be making, but as it turned out she settled on chicken and spaghetti and salad and he brought a bottle of nice white wine.

She found it hard to meet his eyes. She was afraid he would ask her why she was doing this and she would either snap back to her usual sarcastic self or burst out with something incredibly dumb like "I didn't know your mother was crippled." Which was, when all was said and done, the reason she was making him dinner. It was an act of contrition.

He stood at the entrance to the minuscule kitchen and asked if she minded his hanging around while she cooked. She said she didn't. It wasn't true. She never cooked for anyone and she felt self-conscious and awkward in front of him. They opened the wine and each had a glass, she

262

working, he standing in the doorway. She asked if he didn't want to pull over a chair and at least sit in the doorway but he said he'd been sitting in the office all day and preferred standing. She felt uneasy because he seemed to be saying more than that his feet didn't hurt; he was saying that he was happy watching her make dinner for him. She looked at him and looked away quickly. She was fighting tears.

It had been so much easier when she could make mental fun of his bland Irish looks without ambivalence. Without knowing that he didn't live with his mother simply because he was an under-developed choirboy. That he had great burdens which he hadn't shared with her.

She decided to turn the chicken so she would have an excuse for hiding her face from him but as she did it, she burned two of her fingers on the Pyrex dish and burst into tears. He came over, looked at her fingers, got an ice cube from the freezer, wrapped it in a piece of paper towel, wedged it between the two burned fingers and led her out of the kitchen.

"I'm okay," she said, feeling like one of the idiots of the world. "It's not that bad. I just . . . I had a weird week." She was always saying that to him; it was repulsive.

He led her to the bed and with his arm around her, guided her to sit down on its edge with him.

"I wasn't sick," she said, looking at her fingers and the wrapped ice cube. "I told Rose my mother was sick but that wasn't true, either, but I can't tell you what was really true. It's something I can't talk about." He held her. She buried her face in his chest and cried more. He kissed the top of her head. "I never lie to you," she said. "I don't know why."

"I'm sure you're not much of a liar in general," he said.

"That's not true," she told him. "I lie all the time. Not all the time, but most of the time it's just as easy for me to lie as to tell the truth." It wasn't so much that she thought he could tell the difference. It was more that *she* could tell the difference when she was with him, while usually telling a lie felt virtually the same as telling the truth. A lie was something that hadn't happened but might just as well have.

"That's hard for me to believe," he said.

"But it's true." She stood up abruptly. "I better get back to that chicken."

He didn't follow her into the kitchen this time. She did the things that had to be done and set the table, feeling as though she were in a charade. Much more so than at the Americana, where she'd actually been playing no role. (It was rather the absence of her real life that had been striking.) While now there was her real self plus some domestic person she was pretending to be. A sweet little woman who made dinner for her man at the end of his long workday. He wasn't watching television, of course, so it couldn't be a real marriage. Still, if you weren't careful you could end up with a house in New Jersey and six screaming kids. Or maybe five, and one who was too sick to scream and just lay in the bed and stared at you.

He was subdued when he came to the table. She served the food, having trouble with the strands of spaghetti, many of which ended up between the plates instead of on them. With her fingers she transferred them to the plate.

"When I told Rose my mother was sick she told me about your mother."

"Yes?"

"How come you never told me about her?"

"Told you what? You mean that she's paralyzed?"

She nodded.

"I suppose it hasn't come up. It's not a secret but it's not the kind of thing you bring up all the time."

"Some people do."

"I don't know why."

"Looking for pity, maybe."

"Maybe." He smiled. "Pity certainly isn't what I want from you."

She was silent.

He said that the food was delicious and she said thank you.

"Why did Rose bring up my mother, do you think?" he asked. "Was she pleading my case with you?"

"No," she said carefully. "I mean, I wouldn't call it that. She thinks a lot of you. We don't sit around and talk about you, if that's what you're thinking."

"I wouldn't mind if you did. I'd prefer it to your forgetting about me entirely, which is what I usually think happens between the times I see you."

She smiled. "You don't talk about me with Morris, do you?"

"There's not very much we can talk about. Morris finds me mooning, staring out of the window or something, and says I must be in love. The first time he said it I blushed, I'm afraid, which confirmed his suspicions. And now he just asks me Monday mornings if I had a good weekend and gives me a sort of gleeful paternal grin. As though to say that if I'm happy, he's responsible."

"Are you?"

"Happy?" He smiled. "I don't know. How can you tell?"

She laughed. "Don't ask me. I can only tell if I'm high or low. It's not the same thing."

"Where are you now?"

"I don't know. In between, I guess." She was always in between with him. Nervous, on guard, not exactly high or low. "I'm nervous. I guess that's the truth."

"Why are you nervous?"

"It's you," she admitted. Standing back inside

herself. Refusing to believe she could admit it to herself, much less say it out loud to him. "You make me nervous." It was blurted out. The truth. Before she could cave in to the temptation to bury it.

"But why?" He'd stopped eating and he looked upset. As upset as he ever looked. She didn't want him to be upset. She felt confused and guilty and miserable. "It's nothing you do. It's me. I *like* you, James, I just . . ." Her lips trembled and her throat ached with held-back tears. "I can't tell what you were telling me, but please . . . don't love me."

What the hell are you doing, Theresa? All he did was tell this story about Morris. He didn't say he loved you. Idiot. He didn't ask anything of you. Idiot. He didn't ask you to marry him. He's hardly ever had a hand on you. He's . . .

But he wasn't laughing at her. He was regarding her with the utmost seriousness and the little color he usually had was gone from his face.

She was so mixed up! She wanted to scream and to cry at the same time. She wanted him to hold her but she couldn't ask him to hold her because it was wrong when she wasn't at all attracted to him and would hate it if he were to try to make love to her! Victor! If only Victor were here! With Victor she could cry and scream and carry on and tell him to hold her and it wouldn't matter because he'd be going to the airport the next day anyway. And then part of the problem wouldn't even arise because if Victor held her and comforted her and then it turned sexual, they would just go to bed and everything would be all right.

"I'm all fucked up, James," she said. Not having specially prepared the profanity for his benefit as she usually did. "I don't even know what I'm saying. I . . . I don't even know why you want to have anything to do with me. That's the truth. Why do you . . . why do you even want to see me at all? There're thousands of women around New York, it's not as though there's a shortage." She was getting a hysterical edge now. "I'm not kidding, James . . . do you think I'm kidding?"

"No," he said quietly. "I don't think you're kidding."

"Then why?"

"I've liked you since we met, Theresa," he said. "I find you a charming and interesting person."

She stared at him, dumbfounded.

I find you a charming and interesting person.

What could she possibly say to that? He must be blind. Or crazy. Or both. Maybe he was like Victor. Maybe he had some kind of very elaborate fantasy built around her that had nothing to do with who she really was. If he'd said I love you because you're this and that it would have been easier to deal with, because she could have made fun of him. Focused on the word "love." Proved beyond a doubt that whatever he felt for her couldn't be love. This was much more difficult.

Maybe he knew that; maybe he'd said it that way on purpose. He was smart, James Morrisey. She'd never denied that. He had blind spots, but he was smart.

She smiled. "James James Morrison Morrison Weatherby George Dupree," she quoted, "Took good care of his mother, though he was only three."

"Ah," he said, "so we're back to my mother."

"I'm sorry," she said. "It just popped into my head. I read it to my kids in school and I thought of you."

He was silent.

"Will you always live with her?" She had no right to be asking such questions. It wasn't as though she cared.

"Not necessarily. My sister has agreed that if I should need to be free, if I marry, for example, and my wife and I want to live alone, that she would have Mother with their family for as long as possible."

As long as possible. A tricky phrase. His sister could find it possible for two weeks and then say that Mother's presence was putting an intolerable strain on her family life—the children were horribly depressed, having to live with someone who was paralyzed from the neck down.

"What is she like, your mother?"

"She's a very sweet person," he said. "She always was. Sweet, quiet, somewhat stoical. Of course being helpless has tended to . . . she's very religious. She prays a great deal. There's no doubt in my mind that her belief in God and in the hereafter has kept her from going mad."

"Do you still believe in God?"

He smiled. "How could I not believe in the God who's kept my mother from going mad?"

"You might believe in Him as a force in your mother's mind without believing in Him as a reality."

"That's true, of course, but I suppose I don't choose to differentiate. No. That's not true. The truth is that I'm wary of religious arguments. I've heard one too many. A thousand too many. All through school, amongst my friends who've left the Church and haven't, and so on. So I tend to not meet a question like that head on, as I should."

He was so decent. So honest. His decency and honesty were painful to her, as they must be to him.

"The truth," he said, "is that I have chosen to believe in Him. I'm not sure even that's true. I believe in Him and I choose not to challenge my own belief. Because if I found that my challenge was successful . . . I would feel myself totally alone. And then I would know despair."

And then I would know despair.

She looked at him in wonder.

I would be alone and then I would know despair.

"Welcome to despair," she said, feeling her own

bitter smile and then becoming overwhelmed by confusion. "I don't know what made me say that," she blurted out.

He was watching her.

"It's *totally* unlike me to say something like that."

He nodded.

"Now the question is why the fuck I said it."

He flinched.

Well, of course he'd flinched. That was why she'd said it, wasn't it? To make him flinch? To drive him back from the space he was trying to occupy? Into her mind flashed a picture of her father saying some friend of Katherine's had a mouth like a truckdriver and wasn't to enter the house. She smiled.

Ban me from your house, James.

"I don't know if that's the question," James said. "Not in my mind, anyway. You voiced it because you were feeling it at the moment."

"Nonsense," she said angrily. "I was feeling perfectly fine."

"I don't mean you were actively despairing," he said. "It seemed like a more general expression of—"

"Stop it," she said. "I can't stand it."

She stood up and began collecting the dishes. He started to help her but she told him she didn't want him to help, that she'd have another accident if he helped her. An indefensible piece of nasty nonsense. She brought the dishes into the kitchen where, just before she reached the sink, she dropped the whole armload. One dish broke; the other rolled on its edge to the cabinet wall and stood there without visible means of support. The pan had dropped upright so its contents didn't fall out, only the drippings spattered over the floor, but the salad and spaghetti both overturned.

She wasn't going to cry again. She *refused* to cry again. This was ridiculous. She felt him in the doorway without seeing him.

"Go away."

"I thought maybe now that the worst had happened anyway, you'd let me help."

She glanced at him. Just the hint of a mischievous smile.

"No. Go away. You'll get dirty."

"I've been dirty before."

"You don't look it," she said spitefully. "You look as if you've never gotten dirty or messy or wrinkled or . . ." She hesitated, half wanting some restraining hand to clap itself over her mouth and stop her from being such a shit. Such a *bad girl*. ". . . or laid." She looked at him, looked away quickly so his expression couldn't make her stop. Picked up the strands of spaghetti on the floor and put them in the pot. "You look like a virgin! Of everything! Not just sex, everything!" She took paper towels and mopped and scraped the remaining goo off the floor, adding as an afterthought, as though she were afraid she hadn't been quite shitty enough, "But especially of sex."

When she looked at the doorway again he was gone. Maybe he was gone altogether. She suddenly remembered how the evening had begun, how she'd felt *contrite* about her behavior toward him . . . about his mother. She ran to the hallway door and opened it, looking down toward the elevator. But the hallway was empty. She came back in and saw him sitting in the far corner in the armchair. In near darkness.

"I thought you were gone."

"Why?"

"Because I'm such a bitch. I wouldn't blame you." *As a matter of fact I'd probably like you better if you could walk out on me. Or at least smack my face.*

"I don't see how one can afford to walk out every time someone he likes calls him a name. Especially if it's 'virgin.' There are worse things, after all, that you can call someone."

She laughed. "Like what?"

"Liar. Thief."

He meant it, of course. In the year 1969 a twenty-eight-year-old man sat telling her he'd rather be called a virgin than a liar or a thief.

"My God," she said suddenly, "you're not really a virgin. Tell me you're not really a virgin."

"Why do you care?"

"I'm curious. I don't know if I care, I'm curious."

"I don't like to be a curiosity."

"I thought you were so big on being honest."

He smiled. "I seldom lie but I'm often evasive. I'm a lawyer, after all."

"And a Jesuit."

"And a Jesuit in training." A funny expression passed over his face, and since his face so seldom gave away even the lightest secrets, she was intrigued.

"Why did you get that funny look just now?"

"Did I get a funny look?"

"You're stalling."

He laughed. "Not stalling, exactly. I was trying to decide whether to talk or . . ."

"You never talk about yourself," she said petulantly, thinking of Tony saying the same thing to her. "As though you don't trust me."

"You've never expressed interest."

"Well, now I'm expressing interest. I'm interested in whether you're a virgin."

"Because?"

"Because if you are I'll tease you to death. And I'm interested in why your expression got funny when I said something about the Jesuits."

"All right," he said finally. "I have never made love to a woman. When I was at Fordham I had a homosexual affair with a Jesuit priest who was my adviser there. He was the person who really taught me how to think, and in that context, saying I was a Jesuit brought up some very clear and painful memories."

"Why painful?" she asked, almost automatically. A resistance to thinking about the rest of it, which was unexpected and confusing and up-setting.

He thought. He always thought about what he said. As though it mattered to her. No, it went further back than her. As though the truth mattered. God would know. She'd once had that illusion herself.

"Painful," he said, "because it gave me a great deal, then it came to an end. I brought it to an end, and I inflicted pain, which it hurt me to do. I felt, well, it was the end of my incubation, so to speak. Time to go into the real world. Come out from under my protector's wing. However you want to put it. Also . . ." He hesitated. "I . . . sexually it wasn't particularly . . . I'm not sure that I was ever really sexually interested in him. I think I needed, as I say, his guidance and pro-tection. His warmth. He was like a father to me. I went along . . . with the rest . . . in a sense, I suppose, because it was what I could give him in return. It was important to him."

"How come you've never had sex since then?" she asked, unable to say anything about the rest of it.

He smiled. "Have sex. You make it sound as simple as having a drink or having dinner."

"So?"

"Sex for me isn't . . . it's not the first thing I think about when I look at a woman. I know that makes me something of an oddity in this day and age, but the thought of having, of getting into bed with someone I don't love is foreign to me. Unappealing."

"More than the thought of sleeping alone year in and year out?"

He nodded.

His whole confession was extraordinary to her. She didn't know how to react to him. She felt very distant—as though she were looking at him under glass—but also very close.

"It's not really a question of making a choice, a lot of the time," he said. "It's the way it's happened. For a long time I didn't even miss anything. I seldom went out. I was totally occupied, working and going to school and taking care of things at home, once my sister got married. I didn't really have the time or energy for anything else. It's only in the past year or two that I've begun to feel a lack . . . the desire to . . ."

"Mmmmmmmmmm?"

"You're teasing me, Theresa."

"I just wanted to know how you'd finish."

"All right. It's only in the past year or two that I've thought about getting married."

She stared at him incredulously.

He laughed. "I wish you could see the expression on your face, Theresa."

"Why do you call me Theresa? Everyone else calls me Terry, practically."

"I prefer Theresa. Now, since we're studying

each other's expressions tonight, tell me why you looked like that."

"Like what?" She couldn't for the life of her remember what they'd just been talking about.

"You looked aghast," he said. "You looked as though I'd said I was considering rape and murder."

When what he'd really said was . . . married. He wanted to get married. She laughed because she knew it was funny to have reacted that way although she didn't experience it as being funny. She felt acutely uncomfortable.

"I don't know," she said. "I guess I don't think about marriage very much. I guess I'm surprised if someone else does. I mean, I know people get married . . . both of my sisters are married, my older one's been married three times. It's just something she does every time she sees someone she thinks is a little better. But I . . ." *I what?* "I guess I don't think about it because it's not something I want to do. I can't see any reason to get married unless you want to have children and I can't stand children." Thinking of Brigid's children and how she adored them.

"It's funny to hear you say that when you love your work so much and you have children every day."

"Not when they're sick, I don't." As quickly and easily as though it were something she'd thought out years ago and said to herself aloud in front of the mirror every morning since.

"Ah," he said, "is that it, then?"

She didn't know what the *that* was, but she was overwhelmed by the recognition that she'd said something very important about herself to him and to herself. Something she might have been happier to have both of them not know.

I won't cry again.

No one had ever made her cry in her life as much as James Morrisey did. Except that he didn't do anything to make her cry, it just happened to her when he was there.

"Was someone ill in your family?"

She nodded.

"Who?"

"Me."

"You're kidding!" he exclaimed. "I find it hard to associate you with any kind of illness, you're so—"

"I don't want to talk about it."

"All right."

"I had polio."

He was silent.

"And then it went away but later on I developed scoliosis from it."

He nodded. "My cousin had that, but a much worse case, apparently. She has a very unbalanced walk."

"Do I limp?"

"No. At least I hadn't thought of it that way. I noticed you had a nice sort of lilt to your walk."

"I was in the hospital for a year."

"That must have been ghastly."

She shrugged. "I guess. I don't remember too much of it. Anyway, I don't know why I'm talking about it."

He was silent.

"I never should have been there in the first place," she went on compulsively. "If they'd caught it in time I would've had maybe a brace for a while. But my older brother was killed in the service . . . my mother was in a . . . she was depressed . . . they were both depressed and . . . preoccupied. Nobody noticed what was happening."

Oh, God, it was like yesterday! Fifteen years and she was flooded with it. With wanting to tell them how badly it hurt and not being able to because they walked around the house with their eyes on the floor and she knew, anyway, that it was something she'd done that had brought this retribution on all of them. Not just on her. The pain was in some way directed even more at them; what would they do when they found out? So that every time she felt she finally must make them see her pain this other feeling got in the way and she would complain without ever making them *know*.

She stood up. "This is ridiculous. I don't want to get into all that shit. Maybe we should call it a night."

He was startled. "I thought we were just beginning to really talk."

"Beginning. It's almost ten o'clock."

He smiled. "Are you such an early-to-bed person?"

"No," she admitted. And she wasn't sleepy, either. But she couldn't handle what was happening. She couldn't stand always being on the verge of tears. "But I'm upset."

"If you're upset I certainly don't want to leave you."

"Oh, God," she wailed, "don't be such a Pollyanna! I can't stand it when you're so nice to me!" And burst into tears again. If she loved him it would have been all right but how could she accept what he offered when she knew she could never love him?

He guided her back to the armchair and they both sat a little sideways so they could fit, he with his arm around her, she weeping onto his white shirt and striped silk tie—he always wore a striped silk tie, as though he hadn't heard of the sixties. She was doubtless ruining the tie forever. He smoothed back her hair, kissed her forehead when she briefly looked up at him.

"Don't you understand that this isn't me?" she said.

"No, I don't understand that," he said.

"I'm not *like* this. I'm usually very carefree, well, high, anyway, whatever you want to call it. I laugh a lot. Have fun. If I was like this, I'd—" *I'd what? Never go out?* He was the one she went out with on proper dates. *Get laid?* That was for

sure. Surely there was no one of the men she'd
slept with since Martin with whom she could
imagine acting this way for five minutes and then
ever seeing again. And that was fine with her!
He had to realize that. She didn't *want* to be this
way! "There's no *point* to this kind of talk," she
said. "You have the misery once and then if you
talk about it again you have it again."

"You don't think you ease it with talking?"

"Do I look as if I feel better than I did before?"

"I don't know. I can't see your face."

But she didn't want to look up because she was
afraid that if she looked up he would kiss her
again, maybe on the mouth, and she would feel
ill. What she wanted was for him to just hold her
the way he was, and not kiss her or do anything
sexual. Or talk. Just be there.

She liked him, really, that was the thing. He
was such a good person. He'd never hurt anybody.
She would like him always to be her friend.

"Can we be just friends?" she asked tentatively.

"I thought we *were* friends," he said.

"You know what I mean."

"I choose not to know what you mean."

"How can you choose not to know what you
know?" she asked sulkily.

"How can you choose not to talk about what
you feel?"

"If I don't talk about it, I don't feel it."

"Fine. Then let's not talk about just being
friends."

"I hate lawyers," she said. "They always win arguments whether they're right or wrong." But she felt no venom. She was just sleepy.

"Both the prosecution and the defense always win, mm? That's a novel idea."

"You really should go home now." Without moving from her comfortable position. "I'm sleepy."

"Mmm," he said. "You're right. I really should go home."

She fell into a dreamless sleep from which she awakened while it was still dark. Only one small light was on at the end of the room. She was aroused and before she was awake enough to realize where she was or who she was with, she stretched her arm around him to hug him and gently rub the smooth surface of his shirt. He held her more tightly, then, and kissed the top of her head until she turned up her face to meet his. But as she did so the gesture made her know the man and she fully awakened and broke from his grasp.

She sat forward in the chair and rubbed her eyes. She could feel him in back of her. Watching her. She could feel his rapid breathing. Her own body was free of sexual feeling now; it had vanished at the moment she realized it was James in the chair with her. She stood up and looked at the clock; it was ten minutes after two.

"I'm sorry you have to travel home at this hour."

"It doesn't matter."

"Were you asleep?"

"No."

She shook out her arms, rubbed the back of her neck.

"I hope you weren't too uncomfortable."

"If I was I didn't notice."

She turned away from him, blushing.

He went into the bathroom, came out with his hair combed again. He was tieless, for the first time in all the time she'd known him; his white shirt was open at the collar. It made him look vulnerable. He put on his jacket; she sat on one of the chairs at the table, looking at the floor.

"May I see you Saturday?"

"Okay," she said, "unless . . ." Unless what? "There's just a vague possibility I'll go out to Fire Island to look at my friend's house there. She wants me to take a share." Actually she hadn't thought about it since Evelyn broached the subject that afternoon. Not that it was such a bad idea. "Check with me on Friday night, to make sure."

Evelyn hadn't said anything about the weekend, of course. Theresa hadn't even realized she remembered the hasty conversation that afternoon until she needed an excuse for James.

At five o'clock Saturday evening Tony called, not to tell her when he would pick her up the following day but to say he would be down between eleven thirty and twelve that night—as soon as he finished with the Broadway crowd.

"But I have a date," she protested weakly. Knowing that she was going to try to reach James, who was picking her up at seven. Knowing she was relieved to have a reason not to see him. (She hadn't collected herself well enough when he called to lie about going to Fire Island.)

"Tell him you're sick."

She paused. "I don't know if I can reach him."

"Try," he said, and then, as she hesitated, he cajoled in that low, suggestive voice she'd nearly forgotten since her early times with him. "C'mon, Ter, I'm horny as hell. I don't know what I'm gonna do tomorrow, tear up the place or something, if I don't see you tonight."

"All right," she said, hearing the thickness, the eagerness in her own voice. "I'll try. But if I can't reach him—"

"Yeah, right," he said. "I'll call you back in ten minutes."

"Make it half an hour."

"I can't. I'll be getting too busy by then." He hung up before she could respond.

James picked up the phone on the first ring. Only as she heard his voice did she realize, with a flash of panic, that she hadn't prepared what she would say to him.

"James . . . I . . . it's me. Theresa." She had never called him before.

He sounded pleasantly surprised to hear from

her. It hadn't occurred to him yet why she must be calling.

"James . . . I have to—I can't see you tonight."

"Oh. Is anything wrong?"

"No." *Idiot.* "I mean yes, but nothing serious. I don't . . . I just don't feel like going anyplace. I'm . . ."

"Would you like me to pick up something like pizza and bring it to your place?"

"No," she said, "you're sweet, but . . . I'm tired and grumpy . . ." . . . and horny . . . "and I just feel like being by myself for a while."

"I understand," he said. "Can I call you later?"

"No." But the effect on Tony had always been good. "I mean, if you want to. Later. I'm going to sleep for a few hours now, then wake up and try to do some work. I don't think—I still won't want to go out."

"I'll call you just to talk."

"All set?" Tony asked when he called back.

"All set."

"What'd he say?"

"It's none of your business."

"Cunt."

"When are you going to be here?"

"When I get there."

He hung up and she had a brief moment of regret at having told James not to come. What if Tony didn't show up now? If he didn't, she decided, she definitely wouldn't go to his mother's goddamn birthday party tomorrow. Not that she wanted to, anyway, but it was apparently important to him.

James called at ten to eleven and they talked for more than an hour. He'd gone to see a movie by himself since he hadn't particularly been in the mood for company, other than hers. Ingmar Bergman's *Persona*. He had been very much affected by it and would like to see it again some time, with her.

"Theresa? Are you there?"

"I'm here."

"Are you okay?"

"Yes. Except I have a headache."

"If you'd like to take some aspirin or something, I'll hold on."

She laughed without knowing why.

He was silent for a moment. Then, "Or maybe you'd rather I just hung up."

"No," she said. Contrite. "I really feel like talking."

"Good," he said. "Talk to me."

She laughed. "I meant," she said, "like listening."

He talked about the movie and then about other Bergman movies. He talked about his mother and his sister and how in some way the movie had reminded him of them. She looked at the clock and asked him questions about his sister. Patricia. Patricia had three children. Patricia's husband was what you would call a regular guy. Right wing but very decent on a personal basis.

Like so many of the people he'd grown up with. Not nearly as bright as Patricia, but it didn't seem to matter because Patricia had never chosen to develop that part of herself anyway. One of the points in the movie that had touched him deeply was the idea of two women, nurse and invalid, exchanging personalities, not personalities, exactly, persona, and that—

Theresa interrupted him to say that he was making her feel spooky.

He laughed. "I'm sorry. Can I come down and comfort you?"

"It's too late," she said.

"I don't mind," he told her.

"No," she said, although for a moment she'd been thinking maybe . . . maybe Tony wasn't going to show up and maybe she should just give James a try. "Call me later in the week, okay?"

He said that he would.

A short while later Tony was at the door, drumming on it impatiently until she opened it for him, bopping into the room, nearly bristling with electricity, looking around as though he half believed she had someone hidden there. He was wearing a black leather jacket although it was the end of April and the nights were warm. He eyed her critically. She was wearing the usual sweater and jeans.

"I hope you don't think you're wearin' that stuff tomorrow."

She laughed. "If you don't like what I wear I promise not to go."

"Ha ha." He turned on the radio, then took off his jacket. Then he began dancing around the room, doing his "buh buh buh buh" sounds, moving his arms and shoulders widely, bending at the waist sometimes but barely moving his hips and taking tiny steps with his feet. Ignoring her the whole time.

She had a bottle of California Burgundy she'd opened earlier in the evening. She got it from the kitchen with a second glass for him, left his glass on the desk, filled it, then her own, and stretched out on her side on the bed, watching him. When the song ended and the commercial began he stood in the position he'd been in, waiting for the next one, which he began dancing to when it came on. She sipped her wine and kept watching him, at once anxious and lazy. He stopped to drink his wine at one gulp and pour another, then go back to his dancing.

"Too hot in here."

He took off his shirt.

He was sweating from the dancing, but it was also true that he used any opportunity to display his torso, which she had often admired.

"Aren't your pants too warm?" she teased. He took them off and folded them neatly over a chair back. They were army pants; he never wore jeans, which he associated with the hippies he despised. (He'd once told her in all seriousness that dope should be kept from the hippies because it was too good for them.) He wore old-fashioned boxer shorts, which always seemed strange. His legs were hairy and very muscular. She was getting more and more excited as she watched him but she was afraid to let him know because he was always most turned on when she was least interested in him. She put down the glass of wine and closed her eyes. At first he didn't seem to notice; he just kept dancing. She peeked at him through almost closed lids; he had an erection. His dancing had excited him as much as it had her. She closed her eyes again, trying to look relaxed although her heart was pounding. After a while he came over and stood next to the bed. He put one foot up on the bed—on the far side of her body, so that when he nuzzled her with his foot and she opened her eyes she was looking at his erect penis.

"Mmmmm," she murmured, closing her eyes again. "I'm sooo sleepy."

He jostled her with his foot again so that she opened her eyes again.

"What the hell you been doin' that you're so tired?" he asked suspiciously.

"Nothing," she said. "Just the wine."

"Has *he* been here?"

"Sure. He's still here. Under the bed."

This time he kicked her and she grabbed his foot and then they were tussling and he was down on her, she fighting hard because she knew it only turned him on.

They made love and it was the way it had been at the beginning, the music and the "buh buh buh buh" and the changing position slightly until he touched some spot that made her moan and then whispering with a kind of vengeful satisfaction, "You like that, huh?"

It was getting light out when he went home. He'd never come but she was exhausted and didn't mind his stopping. She asked why he didn't stay and they could go directly to his mother's. He asked if she was crazy, thinking he could go there like *this*, without changing into decent clothes.

"I thought you looked pretty decent," she said. Smiling. She felt very loving toward him but knew she must be careful about showing it.

"Not for a party." He was Emily Post and she'd written a particularly dumb letter to the paper. "Maybe you better show me what you're gonna wear."

"Don't worry," she promised. "I'll look respectable."

But when he left she lay awake worrying, for the first time, about what she would wear. Was she supposed to try to look respectable? Pretty? Sexy? She'd assumed she would wear one of her regular dresses, the dresses she wore to school, or when she went out with James. Maybe the bright green one, if she were feeling gay. It wasn't just a question of what to wear, she realized, it was *who* she was supposed to *be!* She hadn't thought about the party—as much, she saw now, out of the fear that if she thought about it too much she would chicken out of going, as for any other reason. Tony would never forgive her if she didn't go, which just added another dimension to her anxiety. If she didn't go he would disappear—and maybe beat her up first. Nights of good sex like this made it harder to think of not seeing him.

So. She was going because she had to. She would wear the green dress. But it was very tailored, not really dressy at all. All her clothing was tailored. They were Italians; when her mother's side of the family had parties they got dressed up like flocked wallpaper. The men wore suits and the women wore crepe and taffeta and velvet as well as enough necklaces and earrings to stock a medium-sized jewelry store. She didn't even have jewelry to make the green dress fancier! She had never owned a piece of jewelry. Maybe she would get up early in the morning and hunt around in some of the little neighborhood stores that were open on Sundays for some jewelry. That was what she would do. Except they weren't open early on Sundays. Oh, well, it was too late to be up really early, anyway. Late morning would do it.

She ended up buying a strand of turquoise beads and some gold earrings. Then, at one o'clock in the afternoon as she began her dash back to shower and change because Tony had told her to be ready at two, she popped breathlessly into a wild little boutique on Eighth Street that had clothes she admired but had never even considered buying, and bought, without trying it on, a slinky-silky black dress with a low, ruffled neckline and long sleeves. It was totally unlike anything she'd ever worn and cost eighty dollars (she had never spent more than twenty-five dollars for a dress). At home she spread the dress and jewelry out on the bed, showered, tried on the dress and looked at herself in the mirror. It fit her as if it had been made to order but she found herself frightened because she looked not like herself but some strange, slutty female she would make it a point not to know. She hung up the dress and put on the green one. Tony arrived at two thirty, took one look at her and said, "That's what you wear to a party?"

"My dressy dresses are at the cleaner," she said.

"Boy, that's great," he said. "You're a genius."

He went to the closet, threw open the door and almost immediately found the black dress.

"What's this?"

Wearily she took it from him, took off the green dress, put it on. Let him zip up the back. Stood back while he scrutinized her.

"Pull up the neckline a little," he said. "You look like a whore." Her face burning, she obeyed. "And change your shoes."

They were plain black pumps. Not the height of fashion, maybe, but the only thing that would be remotely okay with the dress.

"I don't have any others." She waited for him to check the closet again but he seemed to believe her this time; maybe she'd said it differently. He looked over her makeup and they left.

Tony's mother was a small, pretty woman with bleached-blond hair and a flirtatious manner. Her boyfriend was a big, handsome truck driver with a booming voice, who looked like the most jovial easygoing person in the world until he laid eyes on Tony, at which point a remarkable change came over him. His eyes narrowed, his cheek muscles tensed and his whole body stiffened into a boxing stance. He said hello, they both did, with a wariness that suggested each was prepared for absolutely anything. Joe relaxed slightly when nothing happened. He was very charming to Theresa.

The people were mostly friends of Joe and Angela—Angie, as everyone called Tony's mother. Tony kept muttering about the fact that it was more Joe's friends than the family, but when Terry asked who was missing from the family, he could only think of two people and he finally admitted, grudgingly, that they were a very small family for Italians.

He drank a great deal of Scotch. She'd never seen him drink hard liquor before, maybe because she never had it in the house. Everyone danced, mostly foxtrots and old-style dances, but once in a while some rock and roll. The room was crowded enough so that she didn't feel self-conscious about her dancing, and she was loose from three drinks, anyway. She danced with Tony, with some of Joe's friends, with Joe (while Tony danced with his mother). She had begun to feel quite good about dancing and about Tony's being so agreeable, when she found herself standing in a corner of the living room next to Angie, facing Joe and Tony.

A foxtrot had just ended. Tony had danced with Angie and Theresa with Joe. Tony had grabbed another drink—gin or vodka—from the long table that was the only piece of furniture they hadn't cleared out of the room. Tony finished off the drink in one gulp, put his arm around Joe, who was a head taller than he, wiped his mouth, gestured at the two women and said fondly, "Look at them, the two biggest cunts in the world."

Whereupon Joe wheeled around and slapped his face with such force that he staggered back against the wall. Quickly Joe was on him again, getting a grip on both Tony's hands (behind Tony's back) and steering him past the guests and out of the apartment.

It was so fast that Theresa didn't have time to react beyond her initial numb shock at Tony's words. Many of the people in the apartment seemed unaware of what had happened but a few pressed around Angie in sympathy. There were tears in Angie's eyes.

"Again, huh?" someone said.

Joe came back, white-faced and tight-lipped. "That's it," he said. "That's it for good."

Angie nodded.

"I mean it this time. Don't tell me in a month he's your only kid and he's gotta have another chance." He turned to Theresa. "You okay, honey?"

Theresa nodded numbly.

"Poor kid." Angie put her arm around Theresa. "How'd you get mixed up with Anthony?"

"I—I met him at a party." Her mouth was dry. She wasn't sure what to do. She couldn't just stay here without him but she was afraid to leave if he was out there and mad.

Suddenly Tony began banging on the outside door so furiously that all conversation in the apartment stopped except for the low music on the record player. The banging continued.

Joe went to the door and called, "Can you hear me, punk? Bang once more and I get the cops! And your mother won't stop me!"

The banging began again, and then Tony's voice.

"He wants you out there," Joe called across to Theresa. "You don't have to go if you don't want to. We can get you home later."

But there was no point to that. She'd have to face him sooner or later. Still dazed, she moved across the floor. Everyone was watching her. She opened the door and he was facing her, a few inches away, flushed, drunk, enraged. He moved back just far enough so she could come through, although he'd obviously not expected her to do it so readily.

"Call us if you need help, honey," Joe's voice said behind her. Tony made a lunge past her toward Joe, who quickly slammed the door in his face. Tony stood facing the door as though trying to decide whether to break it down. Theresa said, her voice so small and choked as to make her realize for the first time how frightened she was, "Let's go home." And before the words were out of her mouth he had turned on her and slapped her, sending her back against the hallway wall as not five minutes before Joe had sent him back against the living-room wall. Except that she let herself sink down against the wall until she was sitting on the hallway floor in her beautiful sexy black dress. Crying.

The fight went out of him. She could feel it without looking at him as he squatted down close to her. The door opened and someone's voice, Joe's, probably, asked if she was sure she was all right. She nodded without looking up. After a moment the door closed again and she could hear the bolt being drawn.

"C'm'on," he said tenderly, helping her to her feet. "Let's get outa here." They were friends again. Them against the others.

They didn't speak again until they reached Theresa's apartment. She was profoundly depressed without being ready to examine the reasons. It certainly wasn't just a matter of Tony's acting crazy—he'd done that often enough before. Or even of his having hit her; if he hadn't done that he'd come close enough so she'd known the possibility was there. And being hit wasn't the end of the world, either.

Then why this depression? She wasn't angry and she wasn't scared, she was numb and depressed. She flopped down on the bed and stared up at the ceiling. It was cracked and in a couple of places shards of painted plaster had fallen to reveal a layer of ugly yellow paint. That was depressing, too. The whole apartment was depressing. She should either fix it up, once and for all, or move.

Tony turned on the radio, low, got a beer, and then turned on the TV, loud. Vietnam, plane hijackings, the Mississippi flooding. He turned off the TV and turned up the radio.

"You mad at me?"

She shook her head. She wasn't mad at him. She just wished . . . what? She wished she had never known him. Or he were someone else. Someone she could talk to. Like James. Just thinking of them in the same sentence was so funny she had to smile.

"What's so funny?"

"Nothing."

"You're sure you're not mad at me?"

"I'm sure."

She wished James were there right now. She

would love to talk to him. Or just sit and hold his
hand. She wouldn't even mind if he talked about
the office. Very often what he talked about was
interesting, actually. It was just some rotten crazy
quirk in her that wouldn't allow her to listen and
be interested. She really wished James were here
right now. Tony could just go away—not forever,
necessarily, but for a while. Until she could shake
this awful feeling and be interested in sex again.
After a while he lay down beside her, kissing her,
running his hand over the silky fabric of the
dress. At first she was barely aware of him, but
then she felt her body responding. Mildly. She
didn't feel like *doing* anything; if he wanted to
kiss her, play with her, that was all right, as long
as she didn't have to move. Do anything. He told
her to turn over so he could unzip her dress but
she murmured no, she was too lazy. He took off
her shoes and gently pulled down her panty hose,
then her pants. For a while he just rubbed her
gently, played with her, rested his head lightly on
her stomach in a way that at some time would
have affected her. Now she was relieved not to be
responding more strongly.

*Look at them. The two biggest cunts in the
world.*

It popped into her head, disembodied from the
rest of the afternoon. What was so upsetting
about it? He'd called her a cunt before.

But there hadn't been anyone else around,
then. That was the difference. The things he said

298

to her when there were just the two of them in the closeness of her apartment might be crazy but they didn't count like something in the real world, where there were witnesses. She had realized some time earlier that she thought of it that way, that of the compartments into which she'd divided her life, only some were labeled real. School was real. Visits to her parents were real. What else? Tony was unreal. James was . . . James was real. What did she mean by real, then? Tony was no less *himself* than James was James. Maybe it had more to do with who *she* was when she was with them than with who *they* were. She was more herself, the real Theresa, in some ways with James, than she'd ever been with anyone. Maybe that was why it had always been such a strain to be with him; her whole self had been engaged, even if it was usually in keeping him at a distance. Her whole self except for her sexuality. And that had only made it more difficult, more engaging. She'd had to constantly define her boundaries for fear of his stepping over them. While with Tony there was no boundary except around her mind, which was not susceptible to invasion by him.

Or hadn't been, anyway, until there were witnesses. They'd gone out together into the real world, she and Tony. And it hadn't worked.

He was spreading her legs now, sucking her, getting her ready. That was all right. It felt pleasant. He could make love to her if he wanted to. As long as she didn't have to make love back. Or get undressed. Or *do* anything. He slipped off his pants, not bothering with his shirt. He got into her. She was so far away that it took her a while to realize that his erection had disappeared.

She laughed because it seemed like such a perfect ending for the day. Her movement made his limp penis slip out of her.

"Boy," he said bitterly, "you're some doll."

"I'm sorry," she said listlessly.

He got up, put on his pants and stalked out of the apartment without another word. Her first thought was that she was never going to see him again and that was all right. Then she saw that his suit jacket was still neatly hung over the back of one of the chairs, and she thought, with a mixture of relief and regret, that he would have to come back after all.

But she was wrong. He didn't. She hung the jacket in the closet because she was sure that if she got rid of it, he would show up within a week and be furious with her. When summer came and she had her warm clothes cleaned and put them in a garment bag in her big closet, she put the jacket in along with the other things.

Meanwhile, in the next few weeks, she saw only James, at first enjoying him more than she ever had. He sensed her mood in the first week and talked less than usual. Often now, if they sat together in a movie or at the apartment or in a coffee shop, he would hold her hand or keep his arm around her. Sometimes he kissed her cheek or forehead and tried to draw her into an embrace, which she usually avoided.

In the middle of June she went with him to the wedding of a cousin of his. She wore the black dress, partly in a mood of defiance (she wasn't sure it was appropriate, a sexy black dress for a wedding). She swept up her hair and wore a lot of makeup and big silver earrings.

"How beautiful you look," he said.

She stood stock still—a resistance to her immediate impulse to run into the bathroom, change her clothes and wash off her makeup.

He laughed. "You can't stand compliments, Theresa. I've noticed that about you."

"How clever of you," she retorted. It was the first time she'd been sharp with him since the episode with Tony.

He looked at her helplessly.

"Would you like to stand there all afternoon admiring my great beauty? Or do you want to go to the wedding?"

"I'd be quite happy to stay here with you," he said, "but there are people waiting in the car."

People. Car. Panic. It hadn't occurred to her that they would be going with other people. It made sense, of course; the wedding was in New Jersey. She just hadn't thought about it.

"Who?"

"Just family," he said. Sensing—and misinterpreting—her panic.

301

"Family."

Look at them, the two biggest cunts in the world!

His mother. Was his mother out in the car? *Paralyzed?* She really should have bought some nice flowery dress that was appropriate for a wedding. What was wrong with her?

"My sister and her husband, and their two older girls. And my mother."

"Are you sure they have room for me?" Knowing it was a funny question but somehow hoping that she would get by with it.

"It's a van," he assured her gently. "Patricia and Frank's. We have a special contraption in the back," he went on when she didn't respond, "that secures my mother's chair. We wheel her up on a ramp and then secure the chair in the back. Frank is very good about making things like that. The children are sitting in the back seat with Patricia . . ." He sensed her nervousness and he was talking to reassure her. As though she were a skittish horse being soothed into walking into a trailer. "You and Frank and I will sit in the front." When she was depressed she'd appreciated his understanding; now it made her uneasy; if only because it worked. His very matter-of-fact description of the basic physical setup in the van had somehow calmed her slightly.

"Is it going to rain?" she asked.

"No," he said, "I don't think so. But I have a couple of umbrellas in the van, just in case."

She smiled.

"You may not tease me while there are people waiting for us," he said, smiling back.

The blue-and-white van was parked in front of a hydrant. She climbed up with help from James, who then got in and introduced her to the others, except for his mother, who was asleep. (She slept most of the afternoon. In the brief period that she was awake James introduced them and Theresa thought she saw fear in his mother's eyes.) His mother said something unintelligible. It turned out that she was fully paralyzed on one side, only partly on the other.

Patricia looked very much like James except that she had light, reddish hair. The girls both looked like her. Frank looked like James's description of him—homely, gruff, decent. In general she found she knew them better than she would have expected to just from James's descriptions. She thought of him as having perceptions quite different from her own. How then could he look at his family and see what she saw?

Since I met you I have found you to be a delightful and interesting person.

She smiled to herself, and James, apparently deep in a conversation with Frank about the price of replacement parts for the van, turned to whisper in her ear, "Share your joke with me."

She shook her head. "I can't now."

"I'll remind you later."

* * *

The wedding was bearable, the bride feigning shyness and the groom feigning the lack of it. The reception was in a large hall. There was a small band and plenty of liquor and once she'd had a few drinks she found she was having a good time. James turned out to be an excellent traditional dancer, and confessed to her that at some point he'd taken lessons. She was briefly self-conscious when she realized how good he was, but he led her well and strongly and she began to really enjoy herself. Once in a while James went out of his way to introduce her to someone and it finally occurred to her that there was an element of pride in his bringing her to meet people. Naturally. She was such a beautiful, charming, delightful person.

"There's that smile again," James said as they danced away from a cousin who'd said that Theresa and James must come out some Sunday afternoon for a barbecue. "Now you have to tell me what it's about."

"Or else?" she teased.

"Or else I'll do something outrageous."

"Such as?"

"Oh . . . such as asking you to marry me."

"That's not very funny," she said, knowing that it sort of was but being not at all amused by it. Being, in fact, so disconcerted that for a moment she lost track of the step and stood in confusion on the dance floor.

"I'm sorry," he said. "I meant it to be. At least in this context."

"What I was thinking that made me smile," she said suddenly, "is that I was surprised you described your family so well when you have such a distorted view of me."

Now it was his turn to be confused. "I do?"

"When you say things about me I never recognize myself."

"What, for example?"

"Forget it," she said irritably.

"But I can't," he said. "I can't forget it if I've hurt your feelings."

"It's not that you've hurt my feelings," she said. "It's the opposite! You make up these crazy—you make me sound like some kind of ridiculous fairy-tale princess. Beautiful, fascinating, charming—" She stopped because he looked torn between astonishment and laughter and she felt torn between anger and tears. Compounded by a feeling that she was the one who was being absolutely ridiculous in spite of the fact that everything she said was right and true.

People danced around them, occasionally joking about their standing still in the middle of the dance floor.

"I'm sorry," he said after a moment. "I see that you're serious."

She looked down so he wouldn't see that her eyes were filling with tears after all. He tried to lift her chin but she resisted him.

"You understand that I mean what I say about you. You must. Because you haven't accused me of lying, just of having a—a sort of glorified view of you."

She nodded. Her jaw was trembling with the effort not to cry.

"Well," he said, very lawyerish, "it seems to me there are two possibilities. One is that my view of you is simply accurate. Much closer to reality than your own. The other is that I have a somewhat rosy picture because I'm in love with you."

Oh, my God. How had they gotten into this whole conversation, anyway? Why had she come to this stupid-ass wedding?

"Actually, now that I think of it, there's a third possibility. That what I see is true but I see it more readily because I'm in love with you."

She turned and plunged through the dancing couples and ran out of the hall into the parking lot. He followed her. It was raining lightly. He'd been wrong, she thought with a minor twinge of satisfaction.

She ran through the parking lot toward the van, thinking she would just lock herself into it and wait until the others finished. She got in but James followed her, wedged into the seat next to her until she got up and moved over to the driver's seat.

"Theresa."

"Leave me alone." She was crying.

"It's so hard for me to understand you."

"Then don't."

"I'm not demanding anything of you. I'm just telling you how I—the way I feel slips out, I don't even mean to say it, much less to . . . I can wait. I don't want to press you. I know we've only known each other for a few months."

It didn't seem like a few months; it seemed she'd known him all her life. She hated him.

"But you react as though I were threatening your life. As though I were demanding that you marry me instantly or else."

"Don't you ever make grammatical errors?" she asked bitterly.

"I won't dignify that with an answer," he said.

"Love!" she burst out. "I hate that word. I don't even know what it is."

"Maybe you just haven't experienced it yet."

"Maybe nobody has, including you."

He shook his head. "Not true."

"I think it *is* true. I'll tell you what I think. I think you made up your mind a little while ago you were going to fall in love and you better find someone to do it with, and I was just the first person that came along that—"

"You weren't the first," he said quietly. "I'd been out with quite a few women."

"What was wrong with them?" she demanded.

"It wasn't that there was anything wrong with them."

"Then what's so special about me?"

He was silent for a long time. "It seems to me,"

he finally said, "that there's something a little ridiculous about my sitting here defending myself against the terrible charge of having fallen in love with you. You are special to me. I'm not sure if I know all the reasons. That is to say, I know the qualities I—like, enjoy, whatever, about you. But I don't particularly know why they add up to being in love with you—or even if they're the same as the reasons I'm in love with you. I can only tell you that you're not being fair to me or to yourself when you assume that you just happened to sort of—"

"All right. I wasn't being fair. I'm not a fair person."

He smiled. "Here we go again. Theresa telling me what a bad person Theresa really is."

"It's true," she said, but she smiled a little in spite of herself.

"Maybe. It's irrelevant, in any case."

Silence. She stared through the front window. The rain had gotten heavier and there was no way they could get back to the hall now without getting soaked and being horribly conspicuous.

Maybe somewhere there was humor in her having avoided most of her own family's social gatherings since she was an adolescent and now having two disasters in a row at other people's. Nor was it a coincidence, she knew, that it was around their families that the bad scenes with Tony and James had occurred. Families brought out the worst in everyone. She had noticed about herself that she could go for weeks, even months, without thinking of, say, Katherine, but as soon as they were together she was flooded by the old feelings of suspicion and dislike for Katherine, of distaste for herself. (Brigid's having children had somehow changed that relationship for the better; where she'd often pretended Brigid didn't exist, the children now absorbed her attention to an extent where it was unnecessary to prented.)

"I think my sister's pregnant again," she said, startling both him and herself. She was flustered. She laughed. "That was the end of a chain of thought."

He nodded. "Katherine."

She shook her head. "My other sister."

"You've never mentioned another sister."

"That's impossible. Brigid. She's married—she has three children already." She took her wallet from her bag and showed him the pictures of Brigid's three children as though this alone disproved his claim to not having heard of Brigid. He smiled at the picture of the three of them, sitting like angels in front of the Christmas tree.

"You adore them."

She shrugged. "I don't see them very much. They live too far away." She'd said it in all seriousness but now she realized it was weird and she'd better cover with a joke. "The Bronx. That's another country. Or maybe you've noticed."

"Fortunately there seems to be considerable overlap in the language."

He, too, was relieved that they'd managed to get to a lighter plane.

"I wonder if it's raining in the Bronx now," she said.

"Most likely," he said.

"I guess we're stuck here for the duration," she said.

"Unless we want to make a run for it or it dies down. It's a shame I don't have the keys, I could move the van close to the entrance."

She yawned. "And we don't even have the Sunday papers."

"Actually," he said, "there's a *News* in the back."

"You're kidding. Where?"

"I'll get it."

He stooped to go between the seats and around to the back. On impulse she followed him. Behind the back seat the floor of the van was covered with indoor-outdoor carpeting, except for a track where the wheelchair came in and was secured. On the other side was a stack of something which turned out to be slabs of foam rubber, covered by a green vinyl tarp. James had mentioned that Patricia and Frank took their kids camping in the summer. The windows had curtains, which were pushed aside. On the floor the Sunday *News* lay untouched except for the comics, which had been read and refolded on top.

"Mmm," she said, sliding down against the

stack of foam rubber so that she was sitting on the carpeted floor. "How cozy."

He stood bending over in the van. Waiting.

"What's this? Foam rubber? Can I have a piece?"

He pulled over the tarp in such a way that she wouldn't have to move and took down a piece of foam rubber for her. She stretched out on it, leaned up on her elbow and looked at him provocatively. She almost thought she might let him make love to her now.

"Mmm," she said, "this is delicious. I may go to sleep instead of reading the papers."

"Would you like me to close the curtains?"

"Mmm."

He closed them. She lay curled . . . coiled . . . on her side. Teasing. Waiting. Challenging him. *Okay, James, you finally got me in the mood. Let's see what you do about it.* He sat on the edge of the back seat, watching her. She glanced quickly at the magazine section, put it aside, yawned.

"I think I'll take a nap."

"I suppose I'd better get back."

"Is that what you suppose?" Naughtily.

"Do you mind if I leave you?" he asked.

"Yes," she said.

"What would you like me to do?" he asked.

"I would like you to come down here," she said, patting the foam rubber, "and keep me company. Or sing me to sleep. Or something."

He came down to the foam rubber and sat on

the edge of it—somewhat gingerly. He stroked her hair.

"Are you afraid of messing up your good suit?"

"Yes."

She let her free hand rest on his thigh. Beneath the hand his muscles tensed. She stroked his leg lightly.

"Don't," he said.

"Why not?" she asked.

"It gets me too excited," he said after a moment.

"Why don't you want to get excited?"

"Because it's not the appropriate time or place."

"Appropriate time or place," she mimicked. "Life must be so easy when you know all the rules."

"Do you think so?"

She sat up. "All right," she said crossly. "Will you kiss me, at least?"

He laughed. "You said that as though you've been trying to seduce me for months and I've been cold and indifferent."

"I've been trying to seduce you for five minutes and you've been cold and indifferent."

He smiled again. He thought she was being charming.

"Neither cold nor indifferent. I just have certain limitations. I think you knew that when you set out to seduce me. In the back of an automobile. At my cousin's wedding."

"All right," she pouted, scrambling to her feet

too rapidly and banging her head on the ceiling of the van, "let's go, then. I don't care if I get wet." But there were tears in her eyes from banging her head on the ceiling.

Ever since I've known you I've had tears in my eyes.

There were a couple of jokes when they got back to the table because everyone had sat down to dinner and their absence had become conspicuous. But it was pleasant enough, chatting about school with Patricia and Frank (without looking at James's mother as Patricia interrupted her own meal to help her eat). They knew that Theresa was a teacher and treated her with a certain deference, like the parents of the poorer children in school.

When they dropped her off that night James said goodnight to them as though he were going to come in with her but she told him she'd rather he didn't; she was tired and she just wanted to go to bed.

On Monday morning she told Evelyn that if there was still a share available in the house at Ocean Beach she'd be interested. Evelyn said that all the shares had been taken but if someone put her share up for sale she would let Terry know. Theresa was depressed by this news because that house had been in the back of her mind as a sort of escape hatch. The place she could go to if the situation with James became unbearable. The place she could go to if new men didn't appear and she didn't feel like hitting the bars. It was somehow the wrong season now for bars. When she took a walk now in the warm night air she didn't want to close herself off into some dark, air-conditioned hole where she wouldn't even be able to tell that summer was almost here. She called home and asked how her father was. Her mother, after a long pause, said that he was mostly tired. Theresa said she'd been thinking of coming up for a visit; maybe she'd come on Saturday and stay over. Her mother said that would be very nice.

When James called she said she couldn't see him Saturday night because she was going away for the weekend but she would see him Friday.

On Friday night she told him the only thing in the whole world she really felt like doing, aside from having Chinese food, was going to the Fillmore, although she didn't even know who was there or whether tickets were available. Fortunately it was three groups neither she nor anyone else had ever heard of (or would remember a week later) and so they were able to get in and sit in the deafening noise for a couple of hours without any possibility of conversation.

She did her tired routine when they got back to the apartment, but he got her to let him come in by saying the music had made him thirsty and he must have a drink of water before the long trek home. She kicked off her shoes and sat on the bed, her back against the pillows that lined the wall, her knees up and her hands wrapped around them.

"Well," he said, bringing his water back from the kitchen, "what shall we fight about, then?"

"Why should we fight about anything?" she asked. "I thought you were going right home."

"I can't think of any reason," he said. "But on the other hand, I don't particularly want to go right home, so maybe we could have a little fight about that."

He looked a little scared—but determined—as he said it. She had to smile. He was really very dear. She would miss him if she went away.

He set down the glass, took off his jacket and came over to the bed, sitting down on the edge—looking as though he were waiting for an invitation to come closer.

"How did you like the music?" she asked. Naughty.

"I didn't. But I suppose it was an educational experience. I've never been to a live rock concert."

Neither have I.

"How come you haven't thanked me for the educational experience?" Naughty again.

He laughed. "That would be going a little too far."

Cautiously he sort of edged onto the bed so that he too was sitting against the pillows. Next to her. He put his arm around her. She leaned over to turn on the radio but then came back to his arm. She was tense. She leaned forward again and fiddled with the dials until she found some hard rock, but when she saw that he looked amused, she switched to WPAT.

"There" she said. "That's probably more to your taste."

"At the moment," he said, "no music at all is to my taste."

"Well, why didn't you say so?" she demanded.

"I just did," he pointed out.

"Ohhhhhh." She turned off the radio and petulantly came back to the pillows. She could feel him looking down at her, trying to see her face through her hair. She let her face rest against his shirt. She played with his striped silk tie, rolling it up and letting it fall out, then rolling it up again, thinking that if he complained that she was messing up his tie, she would kick him out pronto and never see him again.

Still, she didn't really want to do that. It felt pleasant sitting there, having him hold her. If she could pretend he were someone else . . . Tony, Victor . . . *anyone*, she might even get aroused enough to carry herself through sex with him. She was ready for sex again, that was for sure. She could feel the empty space where Tony had been. Maybe James . . . She shuddered, an almost convulsive motion for which she was looking for some explanation—excuse—when James turned toward her, gathered her into his arms and kissed her at length with a passion she returned because she was off guard. She'd met him with an open mouth and at first he'd sort of met her lips with his but then his tongue had gone into her mouth with an unexpected firmness and she had found herself sucking it with pleasure . . . and that was when her guard had come up again.

"Aren't you afraid of mussing up your tie?" she teased when he stopped kissing her.

He unknotted the tie, took it off and tossed it aside on the bed, opening his shirt collar. Never taking his eyes off her. She grinned but she was anxious. He kissed her again. Very gently he cupped her breast with his hand, held it, murmured her name. She responded in spite of herself. He kissed her again, pressing his body against hers. She could feel his excitement and she could feel his nervousness; his excitement excited her a little but his nervousness made her *very* nervous.

James, let's stop before it's too late. Let's just be friends—anything else has to end in disaster.

It wouldn't be good. His erection would go away at the crucial time, if he got one. Or he would come the moment he entered her. Or he wouldn't even know how. She didn't want him to lean on her! Let him practice on someone else and then come back to her in a few years. He would fumble and she would be humiliated. She squirmed and he moved back.

"Is anything wrong?"

317

"No," she said, "I just—my arm's falling asleep." She changed her position. He looked not quite sure of what to do—as though he'd lost his place—and in a moment of compassion she held out her arms and he came to her, pressing his face into her bosom and then lying still. She stroked his fine, soft hair and thought of a Spanish lullaby Tom Lerner had taught her children, which she had asked them to teach her.

> Aru ru my niño, now what shall we eat?
> We've only a bowl, full of milk warm and
> sweet.

She began humming the melody, thinking of the words.

> Aru ru my niño, now where shall we sleep?
> To serve for a cradle a box warm and deep.

James sat up, blinking.

"What happened?" she asked.

"I don't know," he said. "It was strange. I felt . . . I suppose I felt unmanly." He laughed ruefully.

"I don't know why," she said.

"You don't mind my lying like that?"

She shook her head. "It was nice."

He was bashful now, less excited. He lay on his stomach, his arms folded in front of him on the bed. She smiled and began humming again. He asked what the song was that she was humming and she said she couldn't remember the words. She pulled him toward her and kissed him tenderly—his forehead, his eyes, his nose, his chin. His skin was as fine as a baby's. She kissed his neck.

"Theresa."

He touched her breasts, groped under her T-shirt until he touched skin. Slowly he ran his hand over her skin until it rested partly on her brassiere and partly on the soft flesh above it. When they kissed again she reached around to her back and opened the hooks on the brassiere. He moved his hand so that it was under the loose cloth. Kissing her more urgently now. His body pressing against hers.

She sat up and pulled off her shirt, then her brassiere, as he watched her. She felt languorous and graceful, as though she were in an underwater ballet. She *felt* him wanting her. She was sure. Everything was easy. She lay back again. She opened the fly of her jeans. He was watching her face, now; she smiled. He kissed her. While he was kissing her she pulled down her jeans and pants and kicked them off. He ran his hand down her body, slowly, hesitantly, stopping when he got to her pubic hair. He half sat, leaning on his elbow, without taking his other hand away from her. He looked at her—at her face, her breasts, her stomach, her pubic hair; she wondered if he noticed it was not quite as red as the hair on her head. She stretched. She felt very beautiful.

James took off his shirt and undershirt. If he didn't toss them on the floor he didn't fold them, either, but sort of dropped them carefully. He stood up to take off his neat blue pants, seemed to be fumbling with something in the pocket, put the pants carefully on the floor. His skin was so fair. His body wasn't bad, although it wasn't exactly an ad for muscle-building. His shoulders were too narrow, but he was taller than she'd ever realized, now that she saw him naked. Or almost naked. He started to take off his briefs, sat down on the edge of the bed to slip them off. He had very little hair on his body; what there was of it was light and fine. For a brief moment he sat in seeming indecisiveness, and then he turned around and stretched out beside her, his arm resting across her middle, his penis resting firmly against her thigh. He kissed her cheek but didn't move otherwise; he seemed to be waiting. With her index finger she slowly traced a line down his nose, across his lips to his chin, down his neck, then his chest, down to his stomach, playing in his belly button for a moment then continuing down, touching his pubic hair—even that was almost fine—touched the base of his penis, slowly began to run her finger up along it but felt something strange which she at first couldn't—

Oh, Jesus, no!

He was wearing a condom! She'd never even

seen one before and it threw her. She continued playing with him but she was aware that she was touching rubber, not skin. He wilted slightly for a moment as though responding to her own slight withdrawal, but then as she stroked him he recovered. He started kissing her again but he didn't do anything else. She wanted him to play with her, to stick his finger in her, to *do* something, but she couldn't just *tell* him to do it, she *couldn't*, so she squirmed in frustration, getting angry at him, wishing she'd never let him come this far, wishing she'd never kissed him, never *met* him until maybe ten years from now, until finally he got on top of her, sort of kneeling over her, wanting to get into her but not sure how. Still resentful she rubbed his penis against her vagina, began to guide it in, but then realized that she was dry and closed, not at all ready to receive him. She let go of him, hoping he'd withdraw, but instead he slowly pushed into her until he was all the way in. And the pain was nearly excruciating. She closed her eyes so he wouldn't see how she felt. Slowly, tentatively, he began moving inside her. But it didn't get better; it remained dry and painful. She couldn't believe how much it hurt when he pushed up against the very back of her. There was no pleasure at all mixed with the pain. When he finished, in minutes that seemed like hours, she felt only relief.

He went to the bathroom and got rid of his

condom. When he came back and got into bed he asked if it were all right with her if he stayed the night. She said she had to be up even earlier than usual to pack to go away. He said that was all right with him; he really didn't want to leave her now.

She said, "How come you use condoms if you're such a big Catholic?"

He said, "Isn't it necessary?"

She said she guessed so, rather than attempt to explain to him her deep certainty that she would never become pregnant.

In the morning he acted as though they were husband and wife and she avoided looking at him. He said that he would call her on Sunday night and she made up her mind to come home as late as possible on Sunday.

Her mother worked a great deal in the garden. They'd always had a garden—flowers in the front of the house and vegetables in the back, growing so profusely there were plenty for the neighbors. But always the garden had been an obligation; you did it, her mother made it clear, because you had to, grumbling about it the whole time, and if you sat on the porch when you thought you'd finished for the day and your eye fell on some tomato plant desperately in need of staking which you'd somehow missed when you were down there working, then you might mutter or groan or defiantly announce that nothing would make you go back into the garden before tomorrow morning.

Now, though, her mother seemed to pick a different excuse, each time they settled on the porch, to run out to the garden—a little section she'd failed to weed; she hadn't picked enough peas for dinner, which was hours away—anything. And from the moment she came back and sat down she seemed to be looking for another excuse to go down.

While her father watched with tired, amused eyes and said that this year she would surely get the horticultural award for the entire Bronx.

He had cancer but Katherine had to come back from India before Theresa found that out.

Why did you have to tell me?

Why didn't they tell me earlier?

The two thoughts came into her mind at the same moment, right after the first panic. The wish to have been left in blissful ignorance, combined with resentment that even from India Katherine had managed to remain closer to him.

"Why wasn't I told?"

"They didn't know whether to tell you, Tessie," Katherine said. "They said you didn't seem to want—you didn't even ask if the tumor was malignant."

Resentful. Defensive. "I thought they'd tell me if there was something I should know."

"But everyone knows how you've always been

about sickness, Tessie." Soft. Cajoling. "Not wanting to talk about it."

"He's my father, too," she said, her voice cracking.

"Of course he is."

Silence.

"Theresa? Is there anything else you want to know?"

What else is there to know? How was India?

Nick was staying in India another couple of months. Katherine was going out to East Hampton for the summer with some friends, but would be in to visit their parents. A malignant tumor had been removed but the malignancy had spread to the lymph nodes. It was a question of time. How much time? It could be a fairly good amount of time. He might live five years. Then again . . . Katherine wished she'd come out to East Hampton for part of the summer.

"I can't. I'm busy." Her head was heavy, as from a hangover.

"Once school's finished, maybe," Katherine said. "You could come out and stay. I'd love to get to really talk to you. We can drive in every couple of weeks and see Daddy."

Daddy.

"I can't," she said. "I'm . . . there's someone here I'm sort of . . . involved with."

"Tessie! How nice! Tell me!"

Drop dead, cunt!

It was so inappropriate, so savage; she stared

at Katherine as though Katherine had been directly responsible for her thoughts.

"There's nothing to tell, Katherine, I just . . . we'll talk about it later on."

School ended. Katherine was in East Hampton. Evelyn went off to Fire Island. Summer had really come. Once or twice a week she went up to spend the day with her parents.

She saw quite a lot of James. He would come down and have dinner with her at least twice a week. If the air was reasonably cool they would take long walks; if it was hot they went to the movies. Usually he stayed over. They made love. Usually it didn't hurt. Usually she had no feeling at all while he was in her—as though she'd been given a local anesthetic. The part before sex was nice, though, except for the negative anticipation. And it became very comfortable to fall asleep with him. She was comfortable with him, in general.

She didn't tell him about her father.

On sunny weekends they spent a lot of time at Orchard Beach or Jones Beach, depending on whether they went alone (Jones) or with his sister and her kids or some of his friends (Orchard). Most of James's friends were less interesting than he was. Low-key, good-natured, they talked about baseball, football, occasionally some politics. But they were pretty much off politics since Robert Kennedy's death the year before. James's best friend was Donald, an accountant with whom he played chess. With the others he often played poker; he was apparently an excellent player.

Sometimes they would do Patricia a favor and just take her kids so she would have the day to herself. Then afterward they might take the kids to City Island and have lobster dinners (the kids ate hamburgers) as a special treat.

Twice they went away together for long weekends—once to the Berkshires, where they sat on the grass at Tanglewood and listened to chamber music (neither of them had ever been there before) and once to Pennsylvania Dutch country (James had been there a couple of times). When she asked him why he didn't take a regular long vacation he told her, smiling, that he was saving the time for their honeymoon trip to Ireland. When she gave him a dirty look he chided her for not letting him have his little jokes, but they both knew that he hadn't been joking.

When he was planning to stay with Theresa for the night, James would let his sister know in advance and she would pick up their mother at the time when the day nurse left, taking her back to stay with her own family overnight. Theresa tended to avoid any situation in which she had to be with James's mother. She couldn't meet the older woman's helpless eyes without being overwhelmed by guilt. *Don't worry*, she always wanted to say, *I have no intention of taking your son away from you.*

Toward the end of the summer she let James pick her up at her parents' house a couple of times. (She kept looking for changes in her father but he remained the same.) When her father said that James seemed like a nice fellow, it served to reinforce that fear that had crept up on her recently that she had been sinking, out of sheer lethargy, into the quicksand of Irish Catholic life in the Bronx.

She wished Evelyn were around. She needed very badly to talk to someone who would understand her feelings about James and about marriage. There was no one in her family who wouldn't think she was crazy not to want to marry James—except for Katherine, who would understand for the wrong reasons. (Katherine could never understand James's good points—his loyalty, the quality of his intelligence. Katherine probably wouldn't see why she'd stuck with him for *this* long. She would hate Katherine if Katherine were to make fun of James, or be condescending.)

It struck her now that not since her high school days had she had a really close girlfriend. Someone she could talk to easily, and not just in time of crisis. Talk. Say whatever came into her mind. Of all the women she'd come into contact with, chattered with, had lunch with, Evelyn was the closest, yet even with Evelyn she'd never really let down her guard. Surely she had a much better sense of Evelyn's life than Evelyn had of hers. Evelyn was pretty, and quiet, but with a temper. Evelyn kept her temper in when her boyfriend was in town because her boyfriend didn't believe in hassling. Then he would leave to go on the road (often, she knew, there were girls with him) and she would go home and have a fight with her mother and then she would settle down and gradually she would get peaceful, and then Larry would come back and the whole cycle would begin again. She didn't know what to do about it; if she told him to leave she was sure he would do just that, without a murmur.

But what did Evelyn know of Theresa? To Evelyn's concerned questions after the Tony episode, Theresa had responded with a laugh and reassurance that he was a great lay, and not as dangerous as he looked. She had told Evelyn a little about James but nothing about the rest of her life. She often implied to Evelyn that the demands made by her family on her were bigger than they really were, as a way of explaining why she wasn't around more, more available for movies and other things Evelyn liked to do with her friends. (She had a lot of friends; Theresa didn't like the ones she'd met.)

Now Theresa felt she would really like to be closer to Evelyn, and she was surprised and delighted to hear from Evelyn before school began.

They had dinner. Evelyn was looking lovely. She had a deep tan and her long brown hair was swept up on top of her head. (Theresa had been bright red most of the summer.)

"How was the summer?" Evelyn asked.

"I don't know," Theresa said. "Boring. I . . . I'm having a difficult time with James."

Evelyn sighed, smiled sadly. "Why is it," she asked, "that if you ask a woman how she is, the first thing she tells you is about her husband or boyfriend?"

Theresa was startled into a silence which Evelyn took for consideration of her point.

"Do you see what I mean?" Evelyn pressed. "If you ask a man how he is, he tells you about his work, or something he's *doing*."

"That was what was on my mind," Theresa said. She was upset and a little angry; she had wanted for so long to have this talk.

"I'm sorry I jumped on you that way," Evelyn said immediately. "Please don't be mad at me, I just . . . it just happened to . . . the summer turned out to be so different from the way it was supposed to be, and it was all because men kept . . . *we*, some of us, at any rate, kept letting men fuck up our plans."

They'd planned, for example, to have a rap session at least once a week for all the women in the house, but the only time all of them were always there was the weekend—Friday night to Sunday. The ones who were there all week liked

Friday evening but the ones who were commuting got there on Friday evening all hopped up and wanting to go someplace and dance. Saturday was difficult because at least a couple of the women who went out Friday night ended up not coming home, or just coming home long enough to grab a bikini and go back out with the new guy. Saturday night everyone, or almost everyone, wanted to go to the parties and then Sunday you had the same difficulties, only worse. It was demoralizing to even those people who were most serious about the groups. It was even more demoralizing as a symbol of the way women let men occupy the central place in their lives, giving no thought to their own selves, their cores, their brains.

Terry nodded, resentful because that was exactly what she had wanted to talk about, anyway, *not* letting that happen to her with James.

The reason Evelyn had especially wanted to see Theresa, she said, was that a new group was being put together that she thought Terry might be interested in joining.

Never.

"The first thing about the group is that the women all have real lives of their own. Two of them are writers, one's a lawyer, one's a stockbroker, and then there's me."

Impressive. Scary. It would be frightening to be with a bunch of women like that, she'd never have anything to say. Even Evelyn, though just a teacher like herself, played several musical instruments and had all kinds of interests Theresa knew nothing about.

It would be a consciousness-raising group, Evelyn went on. The idea was that women thought they had their own unique problems, and that the problems were emotional, while in reality their problems were shared and political. Imposed on them by the culture (not just this culture, of course). Theresa pointed out to her that not wanting to get married and have children was the opposite of a cultural problem, that the culture thought it was just fine to do all that, and Evelyn, smiling, said that was exactly the point. Not only did the culture think it was fine, the culture said it was the only thing you *could* do if you were a woman. You had no options. That was exactly what they were fighting. Some of the women in the group were married or living with someone, others weren't, but none wanted to feel that they should be or had to be or that they didn't have an identity that was deeper and more important than their relationship to a man.

For the first time Theresa felt a stirring of interest in what Evelyn was saying. Evelyn picked it up and kept talking but she kept coming back, always, to the group. Theresa had to go to the group to see how many women had the same problems as she did. How many women disliked their own bodies. Theresa looked at her sharply; they'd never talked about anything like that.

Evelyn didn't know about her back, her operation, her scar.

"Women always think there's something wrong with them."

Seldom with such good reason.

"They're too fat or too thin, their breasts are too small or too big, they're too tall or too short, they have a bad complexion or an appendix scar."

Theresa stood up.

"What happened?"

"Nothing," Theresa said. "I just got restless."

"Let me just finish my coffee," Evelyn said. "Then we can take a walk, if you feel like it."

Reluctantly she sat down again.

"The point is," Evelyn said, "we're taught that we have to be perfect. Like objects in a museum, not people. People don't have to be perfect, only objects do."

What if you have a sister who happens to be really perfect? Then how do you handle it?

Evelyn urged her to come to the group and Theresa promised to think about it but she knew that however interesting some of the ideas were to her, she wouldn't be able to sit around with a bunch of women and talk about them.

"I may join a woman's group," she said to James the next time she saw him.

"Oh?" James said. "That sounds interesting."

"Why?"

"Well," he said, "because they seem to be trying to come to grips with a lot of real problems women have."

"Such as?"

"Such as needing a sense of identity aside from being just a wife and a mother. Giving women the feeling of having alternatives, which everyone needs. To feel that it's all right—desirable— to develop their intellects, to be ambitious, competitive, and so on."

"You approve of that?"

"Of course I approve of it. One of the qualities I enjoy in you is that you love your work."

"I don't love it as much as I used to."

"Well," he said after a moment, "that's a problem, too. Finding work you can enjoy . . . that'll continue to be interesting. Making it interesting, ironing out difficulties."

"You're so slick," she murmured.

"I'm not being slick," he said, just a little annoyed. "I'm answering questions as well as I can."

"Now you're angry with me."

"No, I'm not angry. I just want to be taken at face value."

But your face is this bland Irish face.

"The fact that words come easily to me," he went on, "doesn't mean that I'm insincere."

"Prove it," she teased.

"Ah, Theresa," he murmured.

"What else?" she asked quickly, because he was looking at her with that look he sometimes had, a look of longing—of love, if you wanted to be corny about it, a look which if James had been more aggressive she would have had to literally run from, since it threatened to devour her if she ever gave in to it. "What are the other enormous problems we should be grappling with?" she asked. "I mean, if I have my career already I don't have to bother with that one."

"Well," he said, speaking very slowly now, as though trying to disprove her accusation, "there's the question of self-image. Women are always so worried about their appearance. Clothes, makeup, and so on. They feel it's demeaning, they want to be valued for who they are, not for what they look like."

"You mean I should burn my brassieres?"

He blushed. She laughed.

"That's just some silly, extreme symbol," he said. "It seems to me that much too much has been made of it."

"All right, then. I should never wear makeup."

"Not just you," he said. "Even women who look much better with it shouldn't."

"*I* look much better with it."

"To me you're just as beautiful without it."

"Oh, my God," she said irritably, "I can't talk to you. You're crazy. You have this absolutely crazy picture of me."

"You see, Theresa?" he said softly. "That's what the women's groups are for. To give you a better image of yourself."

"Go away," she said. "I don't want to see you. I don't want to talk to you. I don't want to sleep with you."

But he didn't go.

She was restless. School began, and that helped for a few weeks, but then she settled into the routine and she felt it again. She was bored. She felt the need of a man. A Tony, not a James. A good hard fucking and no words. At least a few times a week it crossed her mind that what she really felt like doing was going running again. At Luther's. Mr. Goodbar. Wherever. Just pick up some anonymous muscular type and get laid. And never see him again. Yet something stopped her. There was some inhibition there that she hadn't felt before. Finally she decided that it had to do with James and what James would think if he knew. If he knew about her past life. If he knew she was perfectly capable of . . . Then she got *furious* with him for inhibiting her.

In that mood of anger with him she went to Luther's, picked up a large, fat man who said he was a newspaper reporter, came home with him at three o'clock in the morning—drunk, both of them, out of their minds—and rolled into bed, where he couldn't get an erection and informed her that his wife had castrated him.

Well, call me up when someone sews it back on.

At the door he asked plaintively if she would

hang up on him if he called her. She said she wouldn't, but she wouldn't give him the number, either. She told him to look it up.

James's friends Arthur and Sally, whom she'd met at Orchard Beach during the summer, had a party to celebrate their fifth wedding anniversary. There was a large amount of drinking, dancing and joking, a great number of the jokes having to do with when Theresa was going to give in and marry James.

She laughed uncomfortably. "He hasn't even asked me," she said.

"Will you marry me?" he asked when they got home.

"No," she said.

"Can I hope for the future?" he asked.

"There's no one I'd rather marry than you, James," she said. "I just don't want to get married."

"I hope I can change your mind," he said.

She smiled and knew she was a coward, that she would never marry him. That she didn't tell him so because she was afraid that if he knew the truth, he would leave her. And she didn't want him to do that. Not leave altogether, forever.

She finally went to a meeting of Evelyn's consciousness-raising group.

"I need to talk about my mother," one of the

women said. Her name was Susan. She was blond, very pretty, a stockbroker. Her mother was dying of cancer. "I have this horrible feeling of never having even known her. All my life, my father . . . was like a god to me. I worshipped him. I couldn't understand why he ever married my mother. He was so special and she's just . . . I always thought she was just this ordinary, every-day . . . I had no sense of her dignity, her nobility, really. She raised five kids and kept a house and gave him the support he needed and totally sub-jugated herself to him, to all of us, really, to our needs, and now when I think . . . She's even dy-ing with dignity. She doesn't confess to being in pain, the most she'll admit is that she's tired. But . . . have you ever seen anyone die of cancer?"

"No," Theresa said, because Susan seemed to be looking at her.

"She's actually a very intelligent woman," Su-san went on after a moment, as though the ques-tion had been rhetorical. "She only went through eighth grade; after that she went to work. She got married when she was sixteen. But when I think of it now, whenever we had homework, any of us, she was the one who helped us with it. Not my father, he was hardly ever there when we needed him. And she knew the stuff. Or she knew how to find the answers." Susan burst into tears. "I just realized I'm talking about her in the past tense." One of the other women put her arm around Susan and Susan cried on her shoulder. Terry was at once moved and discomfited.

She went up to see her parents; she hadn't been there since summer. Her father looked the same but her mother looked ravaged. She thought of Susan.

"You must be exhausted," she said to her mother. "If you ever just want to get away for a couple of days, I could come up and stay with Dad."

Her mother looked at her with what she was sure was suspicion. "I'm fine," her mother said. "There's nothing wrong with me. You want to come up and visit, come up and visit."

Her mother was making Thanksgiving dinner, as usual. So was Patricia making it, for James's family. They were both invited to both dinners.

James suggested, half jokingly, that the families combine.

"Ha ha," Theresa said.

They decided to have dinner with Theresa's family, then go to Patricia's for the evening. Theresa asked James if his mother wouldn't mind this terribly. He said he'd thought about this; he felt she would mind, but not terribly. That she would have Patricia's family with her, and other members of their family as well, and that in recent months she'd gotten accustomed to having him around less than before.

"She doesn't like it, though," Theresa said.

"I think she cares more for my happiness than her own," James said.

"Doesn't that make you feel guilty?" Theresa asked.

"No," James said, "strangely enough, it doesn't. Patricia's the one who feels guilty toward my mother."

"That's because you've done so much more." *And maybe because she knows she doesn't really want to have her living there.*

"Maybe," James said. "But after all, Patricia's always been there when she was needed."

Brigid and her family came, of course. And Katherine—without Nick. They'd had an argument. It didn't matter, Katherine said, what the argument was about. It would pass. Basically everything was perfect between them. Everyone knew by now that it was the couples who didn't fight who were really in trouble. Katherine paid a great deal of attention to James, and seemed fascinated by everything he said.

"Don't you think my sister is gorgeous?" she asked when Katherine went into the kitchen to help.

"She's an attractive woman," James said.

"She's also more intelligent than I am," Theresa said.

"Oh?" James said. "How can you tell?"

Brigid's children also seemed quite taken with

James. At first Theresa suspected that they gravitated toward him in very much the way children always gravitated toward the one object in a room that wasn't supposed to be touched, soiled or broken. Then she realized that as usual she was being unfair to him, that neither he nor any of the children was the least bit concerned over his white sweater and well-tailored gray flannel pants, that they simply liked him because he didn't press them but waited for them to come to him and then gave them his full attention when they did. James and Patrick and her father talked a great deal about football and seemed to enjoy themselves. Brigid's due date was just a few weeks away and she sat, mountainously contented, on the sofa, never moving except to the table for dinner, and then back at the end. As they sat at the dinner table, laughing gaily and eating, all of them, like some scene out of a Dickens novel, Theresa found it increasingly difficult to breathe. She hadn't eaten all day but she barely ate now because the breathing difficulty made her feel that she would choke as the food went down. When Katherine commented that she was barely touching her food, she said that she had a huge, rich dinner the night before and was feeling a little sick now. Only after she'd said it did she begin to feel that she wanted to throw up. But when she went into the bathroom to vomit, almost nothing came up because she hadn't eaten all day. As she sipped at her coffee in the living room, her hand trembled so that she had to be careful not to spill the hot liquid, and the breathing difficulty continued until she told James that she thought she might be ill and she wanted to go. He insisted on calling for a cab.

"I don't want you to take me home," she said, although she was in a cold sweat and her hands were trembling. "I can get home by myself. You go to Patricia's."

"I'll take you home and then, if you're all right, I'll go to Patricia's."

"I'll be all right," she said, "once I get home."

They were silent in the cab, he with his arm around her, concerned; she, sick and upset. In the apartment he helped her off with her coat, pulled back the covers so she could lie down on the bed.

"I'll be all right," she said. She was chilled and she pulled the covers up over herself.

"I'm sure you will." He pulled over a chair and sat down next to her bed.

"Patricia and the others are going to wonder about you."

"You're right." He went to the phone, dialed, told whoever answered that Theresa had gotten ill and he might be up by himself later.

"You can go *now*," she said, her teeth chattering. "I'll be okay."

"I liked your family," James said. "Particularly your father."

341

"He's going to die," she said. "He has cancer." And began crying.

James came to the bed, sat down, took her hands.

"Theresa," he said, "I . . . did you just find out?"

"No," she said through the tears. "I've known for months."

"Why didn't you tell me?"

"I don't know. I couldn't talk about it."

"Is that what . . . did it sort of well up on you today?"

"No," she said. "I don't know. Maybe. I'm not sure what happened. I felt as if I couldn't breathe."

"Can you breathe now?"

"Yes. I'm just cold."

He got under the covers, stopping only to take off his shoes, and held her. Gradually she stopped shivering.

"You're going to wreck your clothes," she said, although she was still in hers.

"Don't do that," he said shortly.

She squirmed around under the covers so that she was facing him.

"I'm sorry."

He smiled. "I accept your apology. Under the circumstances."

"What circumstances?"

"Whatever circumstances."

She wanted to take off her dress but she didn't want this to be an invitation to him. After a while, though, he got up and took off his jacket, then his pants.

"You'll never get up to your mother's," she said. "I mean Patricia's."

"That's all right," he said. "I want to stay here with you."

"I don't need you to, if that's what you're thinking."

"I want to."

She got out of bed and went into the bathroom to put on her flannel granny gown. She washed and got back into bed, sitting propped up against the wall. He sat at the foot of the bed in his neat white underwear and his dark blue socks that clung wrinkleless to his legs.

"Theresa," he said, "why did you never tell me about your father?"

I don't know. I didn't want you to pity me. To sense a weak spot.

"Why did you never tell me about your mother?" she countered.

"I would have. I hardly knew you, then."

"I don't feel as if I know you well, now."

Pain and astonishment played on his face. "Do you mean that?"

She nodded. "I don't mean that I'm not fond of you, James," she said, "because I am."

He smiled wryly. "Well, that's something."

"But *knowing* you. That's something different. I don't understand you. I don't sense your dark side." *If you have one. If you don't, well that's worse.*

"You mean you think I'm all sweetness and light? What a lovely thought."

"You've never gotten really angry at me even though sometimes I'm a perfect shit." *If you could give me a good beating when I acted like that, I would like you better for it. I might even be able to enjoy sex.*

"I don't get angry at people I love. At most I suppose I get a little irritated. Or hurt . . . It hurts me that you didn't tell me about your father."

"I didn't tell anyone."

"I would assume"—he was choosing his words particularly carefully—"that I was . . . closer to you than most people."

"You mean because we sleep together?"

"In a way. Except that's a bit simplified . . . or backwards, even. We sleep together because we became very close."

"I've slept with men I hardly knew."

"Is that true, or are you saying it to shock me, the way you sometimes do?"

"It's true."

His face was expressionless. She got scared. Then angry. *Who the hell was he to pass judgment on her?* She'd had more fun in one night in bed with some of those men than in all the months with him. Then scared again.

"You don't like that."

"No. To me it implies . . . a lack of self-regard, I suppose. Not valuing yourself enough to—"

"Jesus Fucking Christ!" she exploded, seeing the flinch she'd once enjoyed so much. "You sound like something right out of the nineteenth century!"

"Maybe," he said. "Actually when I read novels about the nineteenth century, the eighteenth, even, it doesn't seem to me that people were really so different from the way they are now, that is—"

"Maybe *you're* not," she retorted. "Plenty of people are."

"In behavior. That's true. But deeper down—"

"Deeper down," she repeated. "Screw deeper down."

He was silent. She'd really turned him off, now. Well, if that was the way it had to be, then it was. He'd have had to know sooner or later. In a moment he would put on his pants and jacket and go home. She would never see him again and that was sad, in a way, but also a relief. If he left right now maybe she'd drop down to Mr. Goodbar and see what was doing. Or maybe go out and get something to eat. That was what she really wanted, as a matter of fact. She was *starved*.

"I'm hungry," she announced, without premeditation. "I've got to get something to eat."

"Shall I take you out?" He seemed almost relieved.

"I don't know. I don't know if I feel like getting dressed again."

345

She looked in the refrigerator but there was nothing but some white bread and a pitcher of orange juice.

"Yich," she called in from the kitchen. "Nothing here!" She was high now but not at all in a good way; she felt in danger of falling off whatever she was on and breaking her neck.

"Why don't I run down and pick something up and bring it back?" he called in.

"Are you serious?" She couldn't believe he would do that now.

"Of course. That way you won't have to get dressed."

"But *you* will."

In a moment he'd slipped into his pants and jacket.

He smiled. "No problem. What would you like?"

"Mmmm." She thought about it, dancing around the room because she couldn't stay still, she was too tense, too high. "Let me think." She turned on the radio but didn't even note whether it was talking or music that was on. "I know, hot dogs. Three hot dogs with mustard and sauerkraut, and some French fries. And Doctor Pepper."

He was smiling at her. He was an idiot. He was a love. He was crazy. It was music. She danced. What did she care if he was crazy? That was his business.

But as the door closed behind him she had a moment of overwhelming fear: He was leaving. He'd used the food as an excuse to get out and never come back. He was gone. She was alone again. Alone. She would be alone for the rest of her life.

Now you're the one who's being crazy, Theresa.

James would never do that. If James didn't want to see her again, he would say, in that calm, precise way of his, "I'm leaving you now, Theresa. I love you but I can't cope with your being a whore." No. Prostitute. No. What was the right word for someone who did it just for fun, not money?

She giggled.

Still, it wouldn't be funny if he didn't come back. She looked at the clock; it was just past seven thirty. She went into the bathroom and looked searchingly at her face—as though trying to see in it the answer to whether James would come back to her. She looked ghastly. If it were *she* coming back, she wouldn't. That wouldn't really help to find out what James would do, though, since he thought she was beautiful. The idiot. The crazy idiot. She put on some makeup. At twenty to eight she admitted to herself that if James disappeared from her life he would leave an enormous gap that couldn't easily be filled, something she could not honestly say about any of the others. A cocksman could always be replaced, even if not immediately with one of the same quality. But James was something else. She felt a surge of almost sexual feeling toward him. If James came back, if she ever saw him again, she would try much harder to . . . to what? She would be nice. She would be reasonable. She would try to . . . she would make a real effort to like sex with him. Maybe she should try to turn him on. Or at least turn herself on. She'd hardly had grass in the months that she'd been seeing only James. Why hadn't she thought of it before? She was an idiot. Except it wasn't going to matter because he wasn't coming back. At a quarter to eight she started getting dressed and at ten to eight she went downstairs, wearing a jacket over her sweater and jeans, carrying only her keys. She met him in the lobby.

"Theresa," he exclaimed, "what happened?"

"I thought you weren't coming back," she said with what she hoped came off as nonchalance.

"Are you serious?" he asked.

"Yes," she said.

"Why wouldn't I?" he asked.

"Because you were disgusted with me," she said. Flip. Now that she knew he was here.

"Disgusted?"

"Deeeeesgusted."

He shook his head. He couldn't imagine how she would think that. He never got disgusted with people he loved.

He held up a paper bag. "I had to go to Fourteenth Street for the hot dogs," he said.

"You're a love," she said.

"That makes it all worthwhile," he said with a grin.

* * *

348

She got some grass. He didn't seem particularly surprised when she offered him a joint, but he didn't want to try it, either. She smoked one by herself and experienced mild pleasure instead of total anesthesia. She got into the habit of smoking a joint just before they went to bed. He asked why and she said it improved sex. She asked teasingly if he didn't want to try it; he said that sex was quite good enough already, thank you. She said, "Don't mention it," and they both laughed.

For Christmas he gave her a ring. Not a diamond ring, he was too smart for that, but a thin gold band with a small ruby surrounded by seed pearls in an old-fashioned setting. It had never occurred to her that it would be a ring, not even when she saw the little box—a jewelry box, was what she'd said to herself. She was overwhelmed. She felt everyone watching her and she looked up and blushed.

They were at Patricia's. The kids had gotten all their presents and were occupied with them except for the oldest, Eileen, who was almost a teen-ager and was developing an interest in romance. She was watching. Involuntarily Theresa's eyes went to James's mother, who sat, half asleep, half smiling in her wheelchair.

She said, "Thank you," in an almost inaudible voice. There were tears in her eyes and she pretended to be looking at the ring so no one would see them.

"Do you think you can get her to try it on, Jim?" Frank asked.

Everyone laughed.

She started to say she couldn't just now, but somehow the laughter at the idea of her not putting it on had made that impossible. She took it out of the box and very slowly (she was having that same difficulty breathing, as though she were putting something around her neck instead of her finger) slipped it down on the fourth finger of her right hand.

"Wrong hand," Patricia said.

"Ssshh," James said. "She can wear it wherever she likes."

It seemed to just fit and yet it felt strange. She'd never worn a ring before, she'd seldom worn any jewelry, but most particularly not rings. She kissed James's cheek. He looked very pleased— proud, even.

She had bought him a rather wild but quite beautiful batik tie which she thought he would never wear. He immediately put it on over his turtleneck sweater.

She kept slipping the ring off and then putting it on again. It didn't seem tight and yet it squeezed her finger, made it itch when it was on for any length of time.

They went for a while to her parents', then back to her apartment. It was well past midnight. She put the ring in the top drawer of the dresser. It

briefly crossed her mind that maybe her apartment would get broken into and the ring would
be stolen (there was little else of value) and she
wouldn't have to wear it any more.

The phone rang. The first thing that entered
her mind was that something had happened to
her father. He'd been visibly tired, more so than
her mother, for the first time since she'd known
of his illness.

"Hello?"

"Merry Christmas," said a voice. "Where the
hell you been?"

Tony.

James was looking at her. She avoided meeting
his eyes.

"Out."

"You busy now?"

"Yes."

"Tomorrow?"

"I don't know," she said. "You can call me."

"Okay, love,' he said. He made a long, low,
suggestive noise in her ear, a sort of sucking-
inhaling noise, to which her mind reacted with
irritation and her body with a thrill that left her
momentarily weak. She hung up. She went into
the bathroom to take off her clothes. That was
what she often did before going to bed with
James, no matter how often they'd seen each
other naked. She went into the bathroom to strip
and put on a robe. There was something very
yich about it. They might as well be married,

some farty old married couple, for all the real
sexuality and romance in their—what?—friendship?

James was sitting in the armchair, fully
clothed, pretending to be absorbed in a magazine.
She put on the radio but there was nothing but
Christmas music, which irritated her for some
reason, and she turned it off. She would have to
get a record player. She had never owned one
and suddenly that seemed ridiculous. Not ridiculous, pathetic, really—a symbol of so many things
she'd never had that she still wanted. If James
started with her again about marriage she would
ask him how she could possibly get married when
she'd never even had a record player. He wasn't
looking at her.

She took off her robe and got under the covers,
leaning on one elbow.

"What are you sulking about?"

"I wouldn't call it sulking," he said. "I confess
to feeling jealous of anyone who feels free to call
you at this hour."

"He feels free to call anyone at any hour. That's
the way he is."

A pause. James was having great difficulty.
"Do you like him?" he finally asked.

She shrugged. "He's a good lay."

He blanched, if you could say that of anyone
who was so pale to begin with. He regarded her
gravely.

Gravely. Because I just buried myself.

The hell with him! If he doesn't like me he can go and take his ring with him!

"Have you been . . . sleeping with him all along?"

"I feel free to." Not wanting to admit that she hadn't. Needing to make the point of her freedom.

"That doesn't answer my question."

"I feel free not to answer your question. And you can take your ring back if you don't like it."

"This has nothing to do with the ring, Theresa. The ring was a gift. Because I love you."

"Love," she said bitterly. "Is that what love is? Thinking you own someone?"

"It's not a question of ownership."

"It's not a question of this or that," she mimicked. "Or the other thing. What is the question exactly?"

"When you love someone," he said, very slowly, his voice trembling, "it is very painful to think of her making love with someone else."

"Well, then," she said, softly now, because there were tears in his eyes and she was already regretting what she was about to say, "maybe you'd better forget about me. Maybe it'll be much less painful if you fall back out of love."

He lowered his eyes so that she couldn't see the tears in them, which now welled in her own throat. He was still wearing the batik tie, neatly knotted over the white turtleneck. He looked very dear and she wanted to run to him, sit on his lap, press his face to her bosom, but she knew she couldn't do that because he would misunderstand.

Time went by. Ten minutes, fifteen, twenty. Neither of them moved. It was good that Tony had called. That this happened. It had to happen sooner or later, better to get it over with.

James stood up. Slowly. He looked very tired. His body. His face. He had aged many years since he lowered his eyes from hers.

"I think I'd best go home, Theresa," he said. "I need to be by myself for a while. Think."

*I really love you, James, I just—*She was confused by the unbidden thought. But that was silly, she understood what she'd meant by it. She did love him, in a way. Just not the way he wanted her to.

She nodded.

He put on his coat. It was a very well-tailored camel's-hair coat. It was always clean. At the moment that didn't seem so ludicrous as it sometimes had.

"I'll call you," he said. "I'll call in a few days."

She lay where she was, staring at the door motionless, for a couple of hours. Sometimes she was thinking but sometimes her mind was totally blank. Often, after a blank period, Rose's face would suddenly come into view. During the few chats they'd had since the school year began, Rose had been cold to her. Not cold, exactly, but—as though she'd given up on Theresa. She wanted to tell Rose not to give up on her. She wanted to tell Rose that there was hope. That she was, after all, only twenty-seven years old, and she hadn't even *tried* to change. Her throat ached a little as she thought of how unfair Rose was being, to view her with such skepticism. As though, if James wasn't what Theresa wanted, there couldn't possibly be *anything* she wanted.

What *did* she want, anyway? She tried to think of some specific thing she wanted, in the present or in the future. She'd never really thought in those terms and it was a problem for her to do so now. When she tried to focus on what she wanted, her mind bounced away to things she ought to do during the Christmas vacation, like take her winter coat to the cleaner's and pay some bills. Of course there were things anyone would like to have, that went without saying. A fur coat. A warm body beside you in the bed. But as for the future . . . realistically, how could you know what you'd want in the future? You could only know who you were and what you wanted *now*. How could you be so sure you would exist in a year, much less that you would want what one year back in time you'd thought you would want?

The phrase "controlling your own destiny," which Evelyn had used more than once, had a delightful ring to it, but there were huge limits, after all. You couldn't control which men you met, or which ones liked you. You could make sure you didn't have a baby, if you worried about that sort of thing, but you couldn't make sure you *did*. (How many years had Katherine been trying, on and off, to get pregnant, and she could never do it at the right time?) If you drove a car you could make fairly sure that you wouldn't smash into something else, but you could never control whether someone smashed into you.

Controlling your own destiny.

Actually she was sorry she hadn't continued to go to Evelyn's consciousness-raising group. The same thing would have happened with James, but she would have felt much better about it. They would have supported her. They all supported each other in their determination to become more independent, less subservient to men. She could use the group's support now. She had no illusions that James would come back to her and she missed him already. She wished he hadn't said he would call; it would have been preferable to know for once and for all that they were finished. If she knew for sure, then she could make plans. Sally and Arthur were having a New Year's Eve party, to which she and James had planned to go. Now she probably wouldn't be going. Evelyn was also having a party; they'd thought maybe they would go there first.

Maybe she would call Evelyn in the morning and ask if she could still join the group. She'd responded to so many different points, really, at that first session, it had been foolish not to go back. Just sitting there listening to each woman discuss what was wrong with her own body had been a revelation. One of them had felt as self-conscious, as deformed by an appendix scar, as she herself did about the scar that ran down her back. The other woman's scar wasn't comparable, but still, it was interesting. She would definitely call Evelyn in the morning. If she didn't do something like that she might spend the entire Christmas vacation just lying here in this helpless way.

So much of her life she had felt strapped down.

She looked at the light fixture in the ceiling. Of the three bulbs, one had burned out months earlier and a second had died recently. She would change it during the vacation. Better yet, she would move.

That appealed to her. She had never loved this place as she had the first one. Even the way she'd decorated showed that. So little thought. Her old possessions were there and she still loved them. But the things she'd added—the flokati rug, the fur pillows, the thirties mirror with the blond wood frame and the frosted designs on each side —they didn't look as though they belonged in the same apartment with the other stuff. As though two people with different tastes and personalities had pooled their belongings in one room. A bad marriage. When she moved she would get someplace with a separate bedroom with four walls and a door. And a living room. She needed more space. She didn't know how she'd survived this long with barely space to breathe. She would spend tomorrow looking for an apartment. Maybe on the Upper West Side, this time. That was someplace she knew nothing about. It would be an interesting change. She would spend all day tramping around looking for an apartment. That way she would be too tired, by nighttime, to pace around the apartment waiting anxiously for Tony to make up his mind to pick up the phone and call.

He didn't.

She'd called Evelyn. Evelyn wasn't sure how the group would feel about having someone new come in at this stage, but she'd ask next week. She hoped Terry would be at the New Year's party. Terry said she wasn't sure but she'd try.

She'd looked at apartments all day but seen nothing remotely reasonable. She looked again the next day. But she had trouble sleeping at night, which sapped her energy during the day. She took aspirin but they didn't help. She called Katherine because Katherine always had storehouses of tranquilizers in the apartment. She'd forgotten that Katherine and Nick had gone to Aspen. Maybe she'd try to find a doctor who would give her a prescription for tranquilizers. The trouble was, she'd never gone to a doctor in the whole time since she'd left home, and she was afraid to start now. (She always had the sense that if she was ill and she went to a doctor he would find more things than she'd ever suspected were wrong—a veritable Pandora's box of secret ailments that would cost a fortune to correct.)

She dreamed that she was on her knees in a cold, dark place. Her chin was resting on something padded. She couldn't move. Things were being done to her but she didn't know what they were because she could almost but not quite feel them.

She woke up and turned on every light in the apartment, then was upset by the glare and turned off most of them.

Maybe she should go to a shrink. Not the kind who really messed with your head but the kind Katherine had been seeing for years, who helped you understand some of your real motives. Katherine was exactly the same person she'd been years ago but she seemed to have much more understanding—a whole set of satisfying explanations to prove how different things were this time around.

In her next dream she was trying to get home to her apartment on St. Marks Place. She was crawling, on her knees. It was hard to find the apartment because the whole street was covered with some kind of dark material that turned it into a tunnel so you couldn't see the sky. And the sidewalks were covered with jive-ass spades with knives, hustling everyone, except they didn't see her because she was on her knees. Just as she was finally getting close to her house a huge red Checker cab chased her right up onto the sidewalk and out of the dream, but not quite into consciousness.

In a later dream she was telling a shrink about the first dream. She was sitting facing him but he had no face. Just a pair of glasses resting on a sharp nose on what was otherwise a blob of pink skin. They were in a store on St. Marks Place—on the same block as the Circus—except that the front of the store had been torn away, maybe by a bomb or some kind of explosion, so you could see the whole street. Except it didn't look like St. Marks Place. There was a river and some dark woods and the BMT subway was running through and there were trapezes in some of the trees. She started to tell the shrink about the first dream, about the tunnel and the people with knives, but as she talked she realized that the shrink was getting bigger and bigger and was now easily twice her size. She began to laugh because it struck her as very funny that a *shrink* should be getting *bigger and bigger* instead of *shrinking*. And then the next thing she knew she was lying strapped down to his couch, and a voice that wasn't a human voice (because he didn't have a mouth) but came from some mechanical device inside him, was saying, "We're

360

going to straighten you out, Theresa. We're going to have to straighten you out."

She awakened, struggling against the straps that were binding her. Crying. At first she wasn't certain she was out of the dream but even when she was sure that she was awake, her anguish remained and she cried and cried. Her pillow was soaked with tears and still she couldn't stop crying. It was four o'clock in the morning. She put on a sweater and jeans and her winter coat, took keys and money and left the apartment.

There was no one at all on Sixth Avenue; at first she thought she was the only person awake in the world, although here and there an apartment light was on. But then she saw a few people—men, mostly. Staggering along. Curled up in doorways. One throwing up in a wastebasket. Creeps. So bad even the Statue of Liberty wouldn't let them huddle under her robes. A very young queen, his arm around an elderly dwarf, smiled at her as they passed. A dwarf out of the circus. The mention of the circus stirred some memory but she couldn't place it.

Fourteenth Street, devoid of its shoppers, its hangers-out, its cheap wares spilling out of large brown cartons on the sidewalk, was unbelievably ugly. The garbage stood out on the street as though some maniacal artist had gone around outlining it with a black crayon. She returned to Sixth Avenue and headed uptown. Two small, thin, bleary-eyed Puerto Ricans made their clucking, sucking noises at her, obviously too spaced out to care if she responded. A cab driver slowed down to ask her if she was crazy, walking around the streets like this at this hour. She shook her head. He said she should get in the cab, if she didn't have money he would take her where she was going. She told him she didn't know where she was going. He was reluctant to drive off and leave her.

"I'm all right," she said. And thought of James. She wished James were with her right now. Not even talking. Just walking, with his arm around her. She couldn't think of anyone else it would be pleasant to be with right now. The taxi drove off. Somewhere a police siren wailed. She was beginning to feel cold.

She didn't see another person walking between Eighteenth Street and Thirty-second.

At Herald Square she dropped onto a bench and closed her eyes. She was cold but she didn't care that she was cold. She didn't want to go home yet. She wanted to walk so far and so long that when she got home and fell into bed she would be too tired to dream.

She was there for a long time before she realized that two benches down a man, or the body of a man, lay curled against the slats. She stared at him, or it, wondering if he was dead or alive. At some point a police car went by, its siren at a low wail, and it occurred to her that she should tell them about the man, so if he were alive . . . if he were alive, what? They would wake him out of what might be a not-too-bad sleep and take him to a jail or a hospital and he would be no better off than he was now. He would feel the cold for the first time. The thought of the hospital brought back, for the first time, the dream, memory, whatever it was she'd had of herself on her knees . . . in the cast . . . during . . . or before . . . when? *The operation on her spine.* At the split second that it hit her, she rose from the bench and moved swiftly across the enclosed park area, climbing over the benches on the other side, half walking, half running across the street, until she was in front of Gimbels. Where to now? Downtown? Across?

Suddenly it occurred to her that for much of her life she had been running away from that table. From the helplessness and the humiliation. She could see herself walking . . . on Rhinelander Avenue, on Pelham Parkway, on Convent Avenue, on St. Marks Place, on Eighth Street. Once her mother had called the doctor to see if Theresa wasn't hurting herself with all this walking, and the doctor had said that if it hurt her, she probably wouldn't be doing it. But that wasn't actually true. Sometimes it hurt and she did it anyway because the need to move far outweighed the pain. The need to know that she *could* move. That she wasn't being held down. She was free. Freedom was no vague philosophical concept; it was movement, pure and simple.

She admitted her tiredness to herself for the first time but she wasn't ready to give in to the extent of taking one of the cabs that still zipped by, probably on their way to Brooklyn. It was almost five in the morning. Slowly she started walking downtown.

Maybe the idea she'd had earlier and then forgotten wasn't such a bad idea. She would go to a shrink. If she didn't do that she would have to do something else drastic. Take a leave and travel. Something. Or go back to school. Or take a job abroad. A shrink was probably the best idea. What she needed now was to come to a better understanding of some of the events of her childhood that had affected her life so strongly without her realizing it. She'd never thought in terms of a cause-and-effect relationship—this had been done to you and therefore you did that—so that it had been unsettling, fascinating, though, to suddenly *feel* that very distinct relation between being confined in a cast and needing to move. It would be quite an extravagance, of course, seeing a shrink. Particularly for something that probably wouldn't really change her life in any way. On the other hand, she could stop any time she was feeling a little better . . . or if she didn't like the way it was going . . . or if she liked it but it was going too fast, if her money was going too fast.

By the time she'd reached home and climbed the two flights of stairs to her apartment she was exhausted almost beyond belief and thought she would fall asleep instantly. But as her head hit the pillow, the thought *I can't ask Katherine and how else will I find someone?* jolted her awake, so that while the exhaustion was still there, she couldn't sleep, but lay awake trying to think of different people, aside from Katherine, whom she might ask about a shrink. Finally it occurred to her that she might, once school began, ask not only Evelyn but also Rose. The more she thought about it, the better an idea this seemed. Not only because Rose was basically sympathetic, however distant she'd been out of concern for James, or because she and Morris were Jewish and most shrinks were Jewish, but also because it would be a way of acknowledging to Rose that her failure with James was at least partly her failure, not all his. Rose would appreciate that; it might make her feel more friendly toward Theresa again. Theresa felt she could use a friend like Rose.

As the sky began to lighten she fell into a sleep punctuated by dreams that were frightening enough to make her want to wake up, which her body wouldn't allow her to do, so that she would struggle almost to the surface and fall back into blackness again.

Tony called and asked what she was doing New Year's Eve. She said she thought she was going to a party with James but she wasn't sure. He said he'd call her that night and check her out. She told him she didn't believe him because he hadn't called the last time he said he would. He said he couldn't help that, he'd had to go out of town on a business deal.

"For the garage?" she asked sarcastically.

No, he said, he wasn't working at the garage any more. He was into something big, he'd tell her about it when he saw her. She told him he should come up right now and tell her or forget about it.

"Whatsa matter, love?" Tony said. "Ain't James giving you what you need?"

She hung up, sorry she'd even asked him to come. She wasn't even horny. Hadn't been for a while. Maybe it was the depression; her juices weren't flowing.

She stayed up all night and slept during the day, in her mind marking off the days until the end of Christmas vacation the way a prisoner marks off the days to his release. She felt totally alone.

James called late in the afternoon of December 30th, awakening her from a strange dream in which she had found a beautiful new apartment on the Upper West Side, signed a lease, painted and decorated the rooms, then moved uptown to find herself back in the same old place. She picked up the phone without being fully awake and said hello without thinking of who it might be.

"Hello, Theresa. It's James."

"James," she said, her voice and mind hazy, "James, I—"

"Is this a bad time for you?"

"No," she said. "I was asleep."

"Shall I call back later?"

"No," she said. "I'm all right."

Shoot.

"I've been thinking a great deal," he said. "As you might imagine." His voice was almost the same as usual—perhaps just a tiny bit more reserved. "I spent a good deal of time, at first," he went on, "trying to see this thing from your point of view, an independent woman who always had a great deal of freedom, and so on. Trying, well, as I said, to see it your way. But after a couple of days I realized that what I was doing was futile. Not that understanding and compassion are futile, but that in the long run, no matter how well I understand your feelings, I have to act from mine, so that the only thing I I could really do was to understand exactly how I feel about our—about you and me—and act on *that*, and that you would act upon your own feelings."

I love you so much, James. She kissed the receiver. *I wish you were my brother. I wish Thomas were alive. Why did you have to die, Thomas?* She stared at the receiver in astonishment, as though it were responsible for her suddenly thinking of Thomas.

"You know that I love you, Theresa. And that I want to marry you."

Even now, James? I love you. I despise you for loving me even now.

"I'm not quite certain . . . I feel that you're fond of me . . ." He seemed to be waiting for her to interrupt. After a moment he went on. "I can't tell . . . I'm not sure whether your reluctance to get married is a general reluctance . . . or you simply don't want to commit yourself to me . . . or it's that—a couple of times you gave me the impression that it was children that were the problem. That you didn't want to have children. The thing I want to say about that . . . is that I can live with that, with not having children. I had sort of looked forward to having children but it's not the deepest desire of my life. I can give it up, if it's a question of having you or not having you."

James! I don't know what to say! I don't know what to do!

"Theresa?"

"I'm here, James. I'm listening."

"All right." She could hear him draw in his breath. "What I can't live with . . . I'm not going to apologize for this, it's the way I am and it barely matters whether it's archaic or foolish or anything else you might think of . . . I can't live with knowing you're with another man . . . men, whatever. I'm not even talking about being married, now, I mean even as we are. It has nothing to do with morality, immorality, anything. That phone conversation was like a knife in my heart."

And she had twisted it.

"I'm sorry."

"Don't apologize."

"I was a shit."

"You were honest. I think I needed that. I was being somewhat unrealistic."

Silence.

"In any event, this is what I've decided to do." He laughed uncertainly. "I seem to be making a rather long speech . . . a summation to the jury, or some such thing, but there doesn't seem to be any getting around it."

"I don't mind it," she said. *I like hearing the sound of your voice. Later I'll try to remember the words.*

"In a month, at the end of January, I'm going to take a vacation. My overdue vacation. I'm going to go to Ireland. I would like the trip to be . . . I would like you to marry me before then and come with me. I'm making it that far away to give you time to think. The reservations I've made are for two people but I told the agent I might be changing it to one. I will go one way or another. I . . ." But he had run out of things to say.

Will we go to the New Year's Party, James? Or will I be alone? New Year's was a very significant time. On other nights you might be alone out of choice, but if you were alone then, it was because no one in the whole world wanted you.

"When will I see you?"

"I don't wan't to see you, Theresa, until you make up your mind."

"Should I send back your ring in the mean-time?" Silly. Petty. She hated that ring, it had started all the trouble.

"It's not my ring, Theresa. It's yours."

"James? I just—" She stopped, confused, be-cause she had been about to tell him she'd taken a new apartment when she realized it had been a dream. "I'll call you, James. Happy New Year."

She went back to sleep. She was in the new apartment with James, but it was empty because there'd been some complication and she hadn't been able to get her furniture out of the old one. In order to get her furniture there was something she had to find. The fact that this apartment was empty should have helped but it didn't be-cause there was no lights, it was terribly dark— and besides, she didn't even know what she was looking for.

She awakened ravenously hungry. It was al-most nine o'clock. She walked over to the super-market, bought herself a huge steak and some salad vegetables and a six-pack of beer. Also two fashion magazines, two movie magazines and the *Village Voice*. At home she turned on the TV while she made dinner, kept it on while she ate it. Two more days and three nights to get through before school began, before she could talk to

Katherine, or Evelyn, or Rose. Before she could start to change her life. She was really feeling quite good, better than she'd felt in days. Hopeful. Almost high.

The *Voice* fueled her high, for almost every page offered some possibility for changing your life in large or small ways. You could learn an instrument, meet people, stop smoking, go back to school, join a group, buy a farm, learn to belly dance, move your furniture cheaply (she must make a note), scan 5,000 photos to find your new mate, get an abortion, furnish your entire living room in Brazilian leather for six hundred dollars (she'd have to remember that one, too; if she had a separate bedroom in her new apartment that was where most of the furniture she had now would go), learn Tai Chi or Kung Fu, palmistry or urban conversational Spanish, or get in early on the grooviest pad in Kismet.

She watched the Late Show and the Late Late Show, then fell asleep, her hand still on the *Voice*.

On the morning of December 31st she called Katherine's apartment on the off chance that one or both of them had come home early from Aspen and she could get some tranquilizers to get her through the day. A sleepy voice answered that they were expected the next day. The two days and two nights stretched before her, a vast tapestry of time which she couldn't possibly fill.

Don't panic.

But it was difficult. She felt as though she were walking a tightrope and certain moves would send her plunging, but she had no way of knowing exactly what they were. She forced herself to look for apartments, because it seemed the kind of activity in which there wasn't too much terrible that could happen. She left her checkbook home to make sure she wouldn't do anything too impulsive. At night she smoked a lot of grass and listened to music and managed to fall asleep at eleven or so, knowing that if Tony hadn't called by now he probably wasn't going to call. She pretended to herself that it wasn't actually New Year's Eve, but just any night of the year. When James came into her mind she shoved him out. That would be the first thing she had to talk about . . . to a group, to a shrink, whomever . . . this terribly nice man who wanted to marry her. Sexually he was like a dose of anesthetic, he made her go dead all over, but he was so nice! She smiled to herself as she fell asleep.

She spent New Year's Day cleaning her apartment from top to bottom, telling herself that it was a good investment of time even if she was going to move. She sorted things and put them in neat piles. She threw out things she'd held on to for years, knowing she'd never use them. She washed the windows and scrubbed the floors. She called Katherine's apartment but Katherine wasn't there yet. She called Evelyn to say she was sorry she'd missed the party. Evelyn said she was sorry too, it had been a good party. Theresa said she'd see Evelyn the next day and Evelyn said, "Why did you have to remind me?" That depressed her a little, that Evelyn's life was so full that she hated the thought of returning to school; while her own was so empty that she needed school to fill it up.

It was eight o'clock. She was dirty and sweaty from her work in the apartment. She took a bath but then she didn't feel at all tired, so she got dressed. Katherine and Nick were probably home by now but if she'd gone this far without them she could go the rest of the way, and they would never have to know how miserable she'd been.

Suddenly it occurred to her that she should begin a diary. It was something she'd never done. This was the beginning of a new year, good things were going to happen, it would be nice to have a record. She went out and bought a hardcover black-and-white notebook at the drugstore, then on impulse went over to the liquor store and bought a jug of California red. She got home, opened the wine, poured herself a glass, sat down at the table. Wrote her name on the front, then January 1st, 1970—And suddenly thought of Martin Engle.

You get the St. Francis Xavier Ginzberg Award for Penmanship.

She took a sip of wine. Pleasant. She hadn't

thought of Martin Engle in a long time, though there were moments with him, things she'd said or done, that could still make her flinch when she thought of them. She brought the pen to the first page of the notebook and again wrote the date, but then she was paralyzed; where should she begin? How could you begin a diary not long before your twenty-seventh birthday without ever saying anything about what had happened before? And what could she say about what happened before? What was there to say about her life? Agitated, she stood with the glass of wine, turned on the radio, quickly drank what was in the wineglass, poured some more. Then, as though she needed to reassure herself that she had indeed had a life, she went to the phone and called Katherine.

"Ter," Katherine said, "how are you? It's not Dad, is it?"

"What?" she said. "No. No, I saw them for a while on Christmas." Christmas a hundred years ago.

"How was he?"

"Tired."

Katherine sighed.

"I just called to say Happy New Year."

"You're a love," Katherine said. "We just walked into the house."

"I'll talk to you," Terry said. And hung up. The phone rang a moment later but she knew it was Katherine, wanting to say she hadn't meant to be abrupt, Terry should come over if she felt like it, really, they'd love to see her. So she didn't pick it up. After the fifth ring, it stopped. She smiled. That made her feel good, in a way, that she'd let the phone ring like that. She'd never done it before. Maybe it was a small omen for the new year.

She finished the wine, which was making her a little sleepy. She took off her clothes, got into bed and lay there for a while, listening to the music. It was only when she found herself playing with the lips of her vagina that she realized that it wasn't sleepiness she'd felt at all. She was horny. What she needed was to get laid. This threw her into a state of confusion because she didn't immediately know what to do about it. She hadn't been in a bar since she'd gone out of anger toward James. Actually, the anger was well deserved, because the more she thought about it the more she knew that in some way he'd spoiled that whole scene for her. Not that he'd said anything about it; he didn't even *know*, of course. It was more that going into the bars, fucking around, had once been a simple act for her. She was in need. She wanted a man but didn't want to get terribly involved. She found a man and got laid. Of course, having the need filled seemed to make it grow instead of taking it away, but that was a separate problem. The real problem was that since she'd known James the act of picking up a man and fucking wasn't simple any more; a whole dialogue had been set up in her mind in which he argued against it and she argued for it and even when she won it didn't matter, because enough of his view lingered in her mind to take the edge off any possible pleasure.

Damn you, James!

He had made her uncomfortable with her old life, and then he'd left her. Of course, he hadn't exactly left her, but it amounted to the same thing. If she married him she would have to be faithful to him, there was no doubt about it, and how could she be faithful to a man for whom she had no sexual feeling?

She got up and got dressed, not in the clothes she'd been wearing before, except for the jeans, but in a bright yellow sweater she'd worn only once or twice. One of her kids in school had said they should call her Mrs. Sunshine when she wore that sweater, and she'd wondered about the Mrs., whether it was significant that he had called her that.

On the way out of the house she put in her pocketbook a copy of *The Godfather*. Someone had given it to Evelyn, who hated it, and who'd loaned it to her weeks earlier, telling her not to hurry to return it.

Goodbar's was less than half full.

"Long time no see," the bartender said.

"I was going with someone very straight," she said.

"Cut him loose?"

"You'd better believe it," she said. She liked the way she sounded. Tough.

"That's not for you, huh, Irish?"

"Not for me," she said, and he insisted that her first glass of wine be on the house.

She'd automatically taken her favorite stool, the one that was up against the wall at the end near the entrance. Now she hung her coat on the rack and sat down again, taking the book from her bag. She had ten dollars or more in her wallet and she felt very independent. She could sit there for hours if she wanted to and never have to talk to anyone. Unless, of course, she saw someone she really dug. And there was no question that she was in the mood to dig someone.

Amerigo Bonasera sat in New York Criminal Court Number 3 and waited for justice; vengeance on the men who had so cruelly hurt his daughter, who had tried to dishonor her.

The dim light made it difficult to read, but for a while she kept on, compelled by the story and by her desire to be reading, not to be anxious. Hungry. After she'd finished the first glass of wine, she let the bartender pour her another.

Around the curve of the bar some men were

talking. One of them she'd seen around a few times earlier in the year, a homosexual who was usually in a group. Once she'd seen him on the street in drag, but in here he was relatively straight and subdued. The guy sitting next to him was blond, very clean-cut and handsome, wearing a denim workshirt and, no doubt, faded jeans. The fag was talking to two other men who didn't seem particularly interested in the conversation. He held his drink with both hands and stared into it. He must have sensed that someone was watching him because he looked up, their eyes held for a moment, then they both looked away. A thrill went through her. She picked up the book again so she wouldn't seem too eager.

In a garishly decorated Los Angeles hotel suite, Johnny Fontane was as jealously drunk as any ordinary husband. Sprawled on a red couch, he drank straight from the bottle of scotch in his hand, then washed the taste away by dunking his mouth in a crystal bucket of ice cubes and water. It was four in the morning and he was spinning drunken fantasies of murdering his trampy wife when she got home. If she ever did come home . . .

A blond girl asked if Theresa had seen four people come, a very tall girl and three men. Theresa said if they had, she hadn't noticed. The girl looked vexed and Theresa suggested she try the back, where the tables were. Theresa sensed that the handsome man in the denim shirt was watching them; she wanted the other girl to go fast. Someone called the girl from the back.

"Ciao," the girl said.

Fuck you, ciao. Ciao was the way Katherine and her friends said goodbye and it always struck her as a perfect symbol of their attempts to be what they weren't.

The handsome one was looking back into his drink. The bartender, Steve, came around, mopping the bar. She really liked Steve, he was kind of big and bearish, a perfect antidote to James. Maybe, if the handsome one wasn't interested, she'd take Steve home with her tonight.

"Who's the guy with that fag who's always here?"

"Don't know him," Steve said without turning to look. "Don't think he's been in here before. You like him?"

"Mmmmm."

"Let's see what I can find out." He moved away from her, mopping up the bar as he went, filling an order from a man on one of the stools between her and the others. She could feel the man looking at her as though he wanted to talk, but there'd be time enough to talk to him if the other one didn't work out. She looked at her book.

"This is the one looks familiar, huh, Terry?" Steve called out.

She looked up. "Hmm?"

"This mug over here's the one you think you know?"

She smiled. "I'm not sure, really. I think maybe we've met someplace."

"Well, move over, darling," the fag said, "and let's find out, by all means."

She moved over.

"I'm George," the queer said, "and this is Gary."

"Hi," she said, "I'm Terry."

George nodded. "And you don't know me, Terry, but you think you know Gary."

He was trying to trap her into lying. Maybe he was making a play for the other one.

"I've seen you before," she said. "Around here . . . around."

"Ah ha," George said.

"But I had the feeling maybe I knew Gary from someplace else. Like way back, maybe high school or something."

George laughed. "I don't think so."

Gary glanced at George in a way that seemed calculated to show Terry that George disgusted him.

"I didn't go to school in New York," Gary said to her with a thick, strange accent—Southern, but strange.

"Oh, wow," she said, smiling. "I can hear that now. Where'd you get that accent?"

"In the South," he said. He didn't particularly want to talk about it. "I grew up in the South."

They chatted for a while about schools in the South and in the North. She told him that she was a teacher; he didn't register any surprise, which she liked. She liked him in general. Aside from his good looks and hard, muscular body, he had a manner she found very endearing, shy and serious but with a hint of fierceness when George, whom he obviously disliked, butted into the conversation. After a while George followed the two other men to the back. Steve came by to check their drinks. Gary was nursing his but she pushed her glass toward Steve and immediately paid so Gary wouldn't be embarrassed if he didn't have money.

She was a little nervous and talked a lot because he would seem to go into himself for minutes at a time and she felt she'd lose him entirely if she didn't keep talking. He reminded her of Angel, one of her favorite kids in school. Angel's father was white and blond and his mother was dark, pretty and Spanish. Angel had huge dark eyes, skin in between his two parents in color, and kinky blond hair. He was quiet and dreamy, seldom fighting with the other boys. But on the rare occasion when he got pulled into a scrap, he fought like one possessed, and he would tremble with rage if pulled apart from his opponent, needing to be held down by force until his rage had passed. Gary looked like Angel when one of his rages had just passed—shy, a little sheepish, very dear.

She yawned. "I think I've had it."

381

"You going home?"

"I guess. I'm a little restless, I could take a walk, but I'm tired. I didn't get much sleep last night." He wanted to come with her, she felt, but didn't know how to go about suggesting it. "I have some wine at my place, if you'd like to come up for a while."

He glanced at George, then stood up. "Yeah. Sure."

He didn't say anything to George before they left. On the street, she asked him if he knew George from work. He said no, he didn't know George at all. George was just a friend of a friend of his who'd suggested they have a drink together. He hadn't realized until they were in the bar that George was a queer.

In the apartment she didn't turn on the ceiling light, but walked over to the night table while Gary stood in the doorway, and turned on the light there. Then he came in and she locked the door behind him. He looked around and took off his jacket. She went into the bathroom and combed her hair; she was worried about how she looked to him. She couldn't tell if he was attracted to her or had just come along because he had nothing better to do. When she came out of the kitchen with the wine she found him sitting in the armchair. She settled against the pillows on her bed. She was high and horny and she was waiting.

Waiting, she thought, smiling to herself, to begin the New Year with a bang.

He stared into his wine as he'd stared into his beer at the bar.

"You're talking too much," she said. "I can't keep up with you."

He looked up. "How come you was reading in the bar?"

She shrugged. "I like to read and I like to sit in bars. I'd go nuts if I had to stay in here every night and look at the walls."

"You should try jail," he said. "You'd really go for that."

"Have you been in jail?" she asked with interest. A little excited by the possibility. He didn't *look* like a con. If anyone ever looked as if he'd come straight from rustling steers in Marlboro Country . . .

He nodded.

"What for?"

"Petty larceny. Possession. Assault."

She whistled, impressed. "Who'd you assault?"

"A cop. I was trying to get away."

"I once hit a cop," she said, wondering why she was lying. "In Washington. In a demonstration." It was Evelyn who'd done that.

"You get busted?"

"We all got taken in but they didn't book all of us."

"How come?"

She shrugged.

"You have the limp then?"

She stared at him. He'd asked it quite casually. Only two people in her life had ever talked to her about her walk—and they'd both known her well. She'd assumed for years that most people thought she had this sort of sexy walk, and now here was this stranger asking as though it were her most immediately obvious trait. It cut the ground from under her high. It was a warning. There were people who could start new lives and people who couldn't.

"I have an ingrown toenail," she said.

He shrugged. "I just meant maybe that's why they let you off."

"Maybe," she said. "Except the whole thing never even happened. I was just trying it on for size."

He stood up and began pacing around the room.

She was feeling a first small dislike for him but she didn't want to acknowledge it. If she acknowledged that she didn't like him she might have to tell him to get out, and she wouldn't get laid, and she was depressed, and she wouldn't be able to go to sleep if she didn't get laid, and then she might not ever get to school the next day, and she *had* to get to school, school was the oasis.

He stood with his back to her, looking at the clownfish.

She said, "You queer like your friend?"

"No, cunt," he said. "I'm not queer like my friend."

She put down her drink, yawned and stretched. "I think maybe you are. I think maybe if I feel like fucking tonight I should go back downstairs and find someone straight."

He came over to the bed and stood over her. "You're not going nowhere."

"Mmmm," she said, "maybe you're right." Her heart was beating furiously but her manner was indifferent. "I'm tired. I'm going to sleep." Slowly and deliberately she pulled off her shoes. Then her socks. She stood up not two feet from where he was and unzipped her jeans, watching herself, thinking, *I can't believe I'm doing this. This isn't me, it's someone else.* She let her jeans drop to the floor and kicked them aside. She reached for the bottom of her turtleneck, the bright yellow turtleneck, her heart beating so furiously she could barely breathe. The air between them was crackling with electricity. She pulled off the sweater. "Would you slam the door when you go out, please?"

He pushed her back onto the bed and came down on top of her heavily, kissing her, pressing her lips so that it hurt. His penis was hard against her. She struggled out from under him because she could hardly breathe. He moved up, too, but he wasn't so heavy on her now. She was enormously excited and when he groped for her breasts under the brassiere, she reached back to open the clasp, to help him. She pulled at his shirt to get him undressed but he moved away from her and did it himself while she pulled off her pants, and then he was in her, and she was moaning with pleasure, coming and hoping that he wouldn't come soon because she wanted him to go on and on and on.

Which was what happened. He never came in her. He would get tired and stop for a while and maybe they would change their position . . . at one point she sat on him and she really liked that, but he didn't and made her get off . . . and then they would begin again in some other way, maybe a little better than the last, maybe not quite as good, but always good. So good that sometimes she would shake her head—no, no—because it was so good she might not be able to stand it, she would burst. And then she would come again and the excitement would die down and he would go down some and lie inside her. But he never came.

Finally they stopped. He rolled off her and they lay silent on their backs for a while, not looking at each other. She felt contented and sleepy but she didn't want to go to sleep, yet, because she wasn't sure she wanted to fall asleep while he was still here. He'd given her a lot of pleasure but she wasn't totally easy about him. About the idea of turning over a new leaf in the morning with him in her bed. She was cold. She got under the covers. He didn't, which was a relief. Maybe he would just go and she wouldn't have to worry about it. She looked at his handsome face. He was staring up at the ceiling. He still had his erection but he didn't seem aware of it. As though it were part of someone else's body. He turned over so he was lying on his side, facing away from her.

"Hey," she whispered, "don't fall asleep," but he didn't seem to hear her. Then, as she waited for some response from him, she realized that he was masturbating to get off, that he was going to come all over her quilt, and she was seized first with revulsion toward him and then with the fear that he would know that she knew. She didn't know which feeling was worse. She lay on her side without moving, facing his back, barely breathing for fear that he would become aware of her awareness. As ashamed as though it were *she* doing this disgusting, humiliating thing in the bed next to someone else. She was enraged—with herself even more than with him, for letting herself be put once again into a helpless, vulnerable position.

His body shuddered and then relaxed. Slowly she let herself breathe again. He was still. She waited a few minutes.

Then she said, as calmly as she could, "You can go, now."

He was silent.

She tapped his arm. "Hey, don't fall asleep."

He said something she couldn't understand. He was obviously half asleep already and that frightened her because there was no way in the world she could spend the night here with him in her bed.

"Hey," she said, "don't fall asleep. You're not sleeping here."

He didn't turn around but she could see his body tense.

"Why?"

"Because I don't want you to."

"Why don't you want me to?"

Because you're a pig. You came all over my beautiful quilt, you filthy pig. Because you're a bum with a record. Because—

"Because I hardly know you. Because it's one thing to fuck someone you don't know and another thing to look at him over coffee in the morning."

"I won't have coffee."

"You know what I mean."

"I just fucked you pretty good, didn't I?"

You fucked yourself better, you pig.

"You were okay."

"Fuck you," he said, "I ain't going nowhere."

"What are you talking about?" It came out in a scream although she hadn't meant it to. She was really frightened now. She could see she might have to get him out by force and she didn't know how she'd do it. "Where the fuck do you think you are?"

"I'm right here, cunt," he said "and I'm staying until I get some sleep."

She pushed at him but he was like a mass of stone, there was no way she could ever get him out. Panic was accelerating to hysteria now—she would never get him out and she would never get her sleep and she would never get to school.

"If you're not up in one minute I'm calling the cops."

There was a moment when neither of them moved. And then suddenly she reached for the light switch and he whirled around on the bed, grabbed the phone off the night table and hurled it across the room. Terrified she leaped out of the bed and ran across the room toward the door but he got her and dragged her back. She screamed and he covered her mouth.

Wait a minute! Something's gone wrong!

She was kicking and struggling with all her might but it was no match for his. He pulled her back to the bed, struggling all the way, his arm around her face so that she couldn't breathe, all she could think about was *breathing*.

Wait! Just let me breathe a minute! Help! Mommy, Daddy, dear God, help me!

He threw her down on the bed and sat on her, his hand over her mouth when she tried to scream.

James! Dear God!

Then suddenly the pillow was over her face and terror blotted out her mind entirely so that her body kept struggling but her brain wasn't working at all. It snapped back for a moment because the pillow loosened on her face and she could feel his fingers between her legs, invading her vagina, and she caught her breath and heaved under him and somehow the pillow was off and he was a huge mass, looming over her, sticking his penis into her, and she began screaming again and he tried to cover her mouth but she kept screaming, and then he had the lamp in his hand, raised over her head, and it was going to come down on her head, and *Help Mommy Daddy Dear God, help me—do it do it do it and get it over w—*

THE MOST FABULOUS
WOMEN'S FICTION COMES
FROM POCKET BOOKS

- ____ ROCK STAR Jackie Collins .... 70880/$5.95
- ____ LUCKY Jackie Collins .... 70419/$5.95
- ____ HOLLYWOOD HUSBANDS Jackie Collins .... 72451/$5.95
- ____ HOLLYWOOD WIVES Jackie Collins .... 70458/$5.95
- ____ A GLIMPSE OF STOCKING Elizabeth Gage ...... 67724/$4.95
- ____ SMART WOMEN Judy Blume .... 72758/$5.50
- ____ FOREVER Judy Blume .... 69530/$3.95
- ____ WIFEY Judy Blume .... 69381/$4.95
- ____ KINGDOM OF DREAMS Judith McNaught .... 72764/$4.95
- ____ SOMETHING WONDERFUL Judith McNaught ... 72906/$4.95
- ____ ONCE AND ALWAYS Judith McNaught .... 73282/$4.95
- ____ TENDER TRIUMPH Judith McNaught .... 73514/$4.95
- ____ WHITNEY, MY LOVE Judith McNaught .... 70861/$4.95
- ____ DOUBLE STANDARD Judith McNaught .... 73392/$4.95
- ____ INHERITANCE Judith Michael .... 68885/$5.95
- ____ DECEPTIONS Judith Michael .... 69382/$5.95
- ____ POSSESSIONS Judith Michael .... 69383/$5.95
- ____ PRIVATE AFFAIRS Judith Michael .... 69533/$5.95
- ____ SAVAGES Shirley Conran .... 72719/$5.95
- ____ PRIME TIME Joan Collins .... 67962/$5.50
- ____ ANY DAY NOW Elizabeth Quinn .... 65893/$4.50
- ____ LOOKING FOR MR. GOODBAR
  Judith Rossner .... 73575/$5.95
- ____ MAYBE THIS TIME
  Kathleen Giles Seidel .... 66216/$4.95
- ____ WHILE MY PRETTY ONE SLEEPS
  Mary Higgins Clark .... 67368/$5.95

POCKET BOOKS

Simon & Schuster, Mail Order Dept. FWF
200 Old Tappan Rd., Old Tappan, N.J. 07675

Please send me the books I have checked above. I am enclosing $_____ (please add 75¢ to cover
postage and handling for each order. Please add appropriate local sales tax). Send check or money order-
no cash or C.O.D.'s please. Allow up to six weeks for delivery. For purchases over $10.00 you may use
VISA: card number, expiration date and customer signature must be included.

Name _____

Address _____

City _____ State/Zip _____

VISA Card No. _____ Exp. Date _____

Signature _____ 288-15

Outstanding Bestsellers!

____ 62461 **LONESOME DOVE** Larry McMurtry $5.95
____ 73517 **TEXASVILLE** Larry McMurtry $5.95
____ 70960 **FLIGHT OF THE INTRUDER** Stephen Coonts $5.95
____ 73341 **WOMEN WHO LOVE TOO MUCH** Robin Norwood $5.95
____ 72451 **HOLLYWOOD HUSBANDS** Jackie Collins $5.95
____ 70679 **THE AWAKENING** Jude Deveraux $4.95
____ 72779 **THE COLOR PURPLE** Alice Walker $5.95
____ 72940 **FALLEN HEARTS** V. C. Andrews $5.95
____ 70464 **CYCLOPS** Clive Cussler $5.95
____ 73966 **A MATTER OF HONOR** Jeffrey Archer $5.95
____ 69374 **FIRST AMONG EQUALS** Jeffrey Archer $5.50
____ 70945 **DEEP SIX** Clive Cussler $5.95
____ 69383 **POSSESSIONS** Judith Michael $5.95
____ 69382 **DECEPTIONS** Judith Michael $5.95
____ 73212 **WHEN ALL YOU EVER WANTED**
____   **ISN'T ENOUGH** Harold S. Kushner $5.95
____ 69533 **PRIVATE AFFAIRS** Judith Michael $5.95
____ 70465 **TREASURE** Clive Cussler $5.95
____ 72754 **PRINCESS** Jude Deveraux $4.95
____ 68885 **INHERITANCE** Judith Michaels $5.95
____ 62412 **STINGER** Robert R. McCammon $4.95
____ 69267 **DIRK GENTLY'S HOLISTIC DECTECTIVE AGENCY**
____   Douglas Adams $4.95
____ 70418 **WEAVEWORLD** Clive Barker $5.95
____ 70880 **ROCK STAR** Jackie Collins $5.95
____ 72764 **A KINGDOM OF DREAMS** Judith McNaught $4.95
____ 73712 **SWORD POINT** Harold Coyle $5.95
____ 68938 **PILLARS OF FIRE** Steve Shagan $5.95
____ 67091 **ANYTHING FOR BILLY** Larry McMurtry $5.50
____ 70509 **A KNIGHT IN SHINING ARMOR**
____   Jude Deveraux $4.95
____ 67368 **WHILE MY PRETTY ONE SLEEPS**
____   Mary Higgins Clark $5.95
____ 67068 **DAWN** V.C. Andrews $5.95

POCKET BOOKS

Simon & Schuster, Mail Order Dept. OBB
200 Old Tappan Rd., Old Tappan, N.J. 07675

Please send me the books I have checked above. I am enclosing $_____ (please add 75¢ to cover postage and handling for each order. Please add appropriate local sales tax). Send check or money order—no cash or C.O.D.'s please. Allow up to six weeks for delivery. For purchases over $10.00 you may use VISA: card number, expiration date and customer signature must be included.

Name _____

Address _____

City _____ State/Zip _____

VISA Card No. _____ Exp. Date _____

Signature _____ 296-19